C000279407

OFF-PLANET

Also available by
Clifford D. Simak
in Methuen Paperbacks

Clifford D. Simak

OFF-PLANET

*Collected and edited
by Francis Lyall*

METHUEN

World first edition published in Great Britain 1988
by Methuen London Ltd
11 New Fetter Lane, London EC4P 4EE

Introduction copyright © 1988 by Francis Lyall

'Construction Shack' Copyright © 1972 by Galaxy Publishing
   Corporation. First published in WORLDS OF IF, vol. 21, no. 9,
   Feb., 1973.
'Ogre' Copyright © 1943 by Street & Smith Publications, Inc.
   Copyright renewed 1971 by Clifford D. Simak. First published in
   ASTOUNDING, vol. 32, no. 5, Jan., 1944.
'Junkyard' Copyright © 1953 by Galaxy Publishing Corporation.
   Copyright renewed 1981 by Clifford D. Simak. First published in
   GALAXY, vol. 6, no. 2, May, 1953.
'The Observer' Copyright © 1972 by the Conde Nast Publications,
   Inc. First published in ANALOG, vol. 89, no. 4, May, 1972.
'The World That Couldn't Be' Copyright © 1957 by Galaxy
   Publishing Corporation. Copyright renewed 1985 by Clifford D.
   Simak. First published in GALAXY, vol. 15, no. 3, Jan., 1958.
'Shadow World' Copyright © 1957 by Galaxy Publishing
   Corporation. Copyright renewed 1985 by Clifford D. Simak. First
   published in GALAXY, vol. 14, No. 5, Sept., 1957.
'Mirage' Copyright © 1956 by Clifford D. Simak. Copyright renewed
   1984 by Clifford D. Simak. First published in STRANGERS IN THE
   UNIVERSE, Simon & Schuster, 1956.

British Library Cataloguing in Publication Data

Simak, Clifford D.
   Off-planet.
   I. Title
   813'.54[F]   PS3537.I54

   ISBN 0-413-18500-1

Printed and bound in Great Britain by
Redwood Burn Ltd, Trowbridge, Wilts

Contents

INTRODUCTION

Clifford D. Simak is a master teller of tales, a craftsman story-smith. You may have picked up this book because you know Simak as a guarantee of quality. If you are experimenting, then you will know him for the future, and in a way I envy you, for CDS has written many wonderful stories. The memory of first coming to his work remains with me.

A good story is a satisfying thing. Plot and pace, theme and character, setting and language, are woven to produce what the reader recognizes as characteristic of a particular author. Using that perception, a reader seeks out (or avoids) further offerings by the author. Happy is the author who has a following (and happy is his publisher).

The trade of the Teller of Tales is old. Its origins are lost in time, but its craftsmen are as acceptable now as they have ever been. For long story-telling was oral. Then came books. In recent times new forms have become possible. Radio, film and television permit the use of sound and vision, and 'special effects' have brought an audience which would be impatient with reading. But the staple of story-telling remains words, prompting and leading the imagination. Mastery of the art is something to be prized, and the work of such as CDS is eagerly awaited, for his tales refresh and entertain, standing out among the welter of sf.

Science fiction is often thought of as a modern phenomenon, but many of the earliest stories we know of contain wonders and marvels and would today be classed as science fiction. To select only from Greek, the tales of Jason, Ulysses,

7

Daedelus and the like, are lineally part of sf tradition. Education has made a broader market available to story-tellers, but there remains a demand for tales of the marvellous. Amid the varied products of the fiction end of publishing science fiction is an accepted category, important for the profits of most companies, although what precisely *is* science fiction remains a matter of argument.

Among the modern writers my friend Clifford D. Simak has made a major and distinctive contribution. His published stories begin in 1931, and he hit stride in 1938. Muriel Becker in her *Clifford D. Simak: A Primary and Secondary Bibliography* (Boston: G. K. Hall, 1980) notes in the following forty years only 1945 and 1966 as years in which CDS published no new fiction, and he has carried on into the 1980s. His tally of published work is more than respectable for a full-time author, and an extraordinary feat by a part-timer, albeit a professional part-timer. The high quality of that work, much of it accomplished in evenings after a normal day's work as a newspaperman, is also remarkable. In the 1950s the novels began to be published. *City* (1952) won the International Fantasy Award of 1953 (four years before J. R. R. Tolkien), the first of CDS's many awards. 'The Big Front Yard' won the Hugo novelette award in 1959. *Way Station* won in the Hugo novel category in 1964, and in 1980 the short story 'The Grotto of the Dancing Deer' made history by winning the Hugo, Nebula and Locus awards for its author, at the age of 77. ('The Grotto' is in *The Marathon Photograph* (Methuen, 1987).) In 1977 the Science Fiction Writers of America made him their Nebula Grand Master Award for life-time achievement. These awards, and the many other 'runner-up's' he has collected, show the high regard that CDS commands both among readers and among his fellow authors.

But apart from awards, CDS holds a special place within science fiction. He is famous for the warmth of his tales, and for the extent to which ordinary individuals and traditional moral values are the key to what happens. 'Science Fiction' conjures notions of galaxies, and of exotic civilizations, heroic deeds and intellectual adventure. By contrast, much of CDS's fiction is set right here on Earth, couching the strange amid the ordinary and the familiar. Many of CDS'S short stories are set in 'Simak Country', the north-west corner of Grant

County, Wisconsin, where he was born and raised. A goodly proportion of his novels are also founded in the memories of the farms on the bluffs immediately to the south of the Wisconsin river as it flows on its last ten or so miles to the Mississippi. The collections, *The Marathon Photograph* (London: Severn House, 1986, Methuen, 1987) and *Brother* (London: Severn House, 1987, Methuen, 1988) contain notable examples of Simak Country. But not all CDS stories are so identifiably set. Nor are all on Earth.

As the title indicates, the stories in this collection are located 'off-planet': only 'Construction Shack' and 'Mirage' are set within the confines of the Solar System. But all of them are distinctively 'Simak' stories, sharing that individuality of touch and feel which hallmark his skills as a story-smith. In the 'on-Earth' stories, Millville, Woodman, Wyalusing, Patch Grove, Platteville limestone and bluff country, meadows, winding paths and the shouting tree colours of autumn often provide CDS with the literary equivalent of counterpoint and polyphony. Though 'The World that Couldn't Be' has some echoes of Simak Country, the settings of the stories in this collection do not generally have the help of drawing on such common knowledge. That they work shows that there is more to his appeal than his great skills with rural locations and country life. CDS can well carry a story on imagination alone, an imagination blended with his own special trace elements. Here you will encounter humour, kindliness and the strength of traditional virtues, allied to a quirky individuality and an ability to ask unthought questions. Does intelligence bring discontent? Why do we forget? What is it to say, 'I am human' in the contexts either of 'Ogre' or of 'The Observer'? There are also glorious inventions of aliens and of character which stick in the mind, to think on later – sometimes much later, when something triggers memory. Of the aliens, you will find yourself considering the life blankets and the singing trees of 'Ogre', and the Encyclopedia. There are the information gatherers of the 'Junkyard', the Venerables of 'Mirage', the Cytha of its 'World', and the Shadows of theirs.

The basic notions of each of these stories are themselves intriguing, and some reappear elsewhere in CDS's output. But in the work of any word-smith, certain stories carry the seeds of many others. 'Ogre' is one such seminal story, many elements in it being taken up again elsewhere. Thus the idea of vegetable life and civilization found in 'Ogre' is one which has fascinated CDS, and it recurs in several stories, for example in 'Green Thumb' (1954) and more mysteriously in the novels *All Flesh is Grass* (1965) and *The Visitors* (1980). Again, singing trees are a marvellous invention in 'Ogre' which gloriously reappear in *A Choice of Gods* (1972). (I have found the idea used with a similar magic in Alan Dean Foster's 'Ye Who Would Sing' of 1976, which is well worth seeking out.) The eavesdropper of 'Junkyard' may also be a vegetable based system, and that connects with yet other CDS creations. Listeners to the galaxies and eavesdroppers on the universe appear in a number of Simak stories. The great arrays of Listener Trees of *Destiny Doll* (1971), encoding their intercepted knowledge on their seeds, owe a great deal to the trapper of 'Junkyard'. Their abilities to bombard intruders similarly owe a lot to the rifle trees of 'Ogre'.

It may surprise some readers, who remember CDS's magnificent robots (Jenkins of *City* (1952), Hezekiah and the monastery of *A Choice of Gods* (1972), and Theodosius and his fellows of *Project Pope* (1981) to name but a few), that there is only one robot character in these tales. Yet what a robot, and again it is found in 'Ogre'. Nellie, the cantankerous bookkeeper and quoter of 'The Manual', is a paradigm of the CDS robot. This is no passionless machine controlled by the Three Laws of Robotics (now the Four Laws of Robotics – see Isaac Asimov's *Robots and Empire* 1985). In 'Ogre', a story first published just before the start of what became the *City* series, where Jenkins is so important, we find another CDS robot which is clearly a personality, and which one can only with difficulty write of as 'it'. Yet it is a robot, less than a human being in some ways and more than human in others. It is that element which allows Nellie first to repel and then to mislead the Encyclopedia's prying at her thoughts. It is the element which allows her all those rather endearing quirks. I say no more.

Typical CDS is also the musing running through several of the stories which can only be catalogued as theological. If there is a 'Construction Shack' away out there (and perhaps a Voyager spacecraft will in due course give a clue), then . . . ? While Man might send out an 'Observer', might not Man be

10

an Observer for . . . ? The Cytha on its 'World' echoes many other CDS creations which have a tutelary function on their planets. And there is the city of the 'Mirage' to which the Venerables lead (induct, even) the hapless Webb. But that story also contains other elements often found in CDS stories. Webb gains the city by his following through on traditional values, when many might have faltered and sought the easy pickings. His companions, who take the lesser path lose everything. Gavin Duncan also nearly mis-chooses in 'The World that Couldn't Be', but does not, and so his life is saved, and his future bright. Even in 'Ogre', which is an early ta'e, Mackenzie works to the best he knows, and it turns out that that was for the best as well.

There is also a related cry, that pang which occasionally surfaces in CDS stories. It is more clear elsewhere among his work, but there is a loneliness in 'Construction Shack', and more clear in the heart of 'The Observer', which resonates within the modern psyche. It is even found in 'Shadow World' when Blake uses the peeper, and finds himself in the meadow of his boyhood. That magic place, I can tell you, comes from Simak Country, and yet is it not within each of us? That sense of a real home to which we really belong, or will attain? The 'Mirage' lingers long.

But it is the comfort, the fittingness, the fulfilment which one carries from these stories, and that is enhanced by the humour with which they are presented. The situation in 'Ogre' is retrieved because that cantankerous robot, Nellie, loses her temper, and proves to have been a baseball pitcher back on Earth! The brain-drain of the 'Junkyard' can be obviated by alcohol! Sometimes the comfort is spiced by a humorous sting in the tail. Will the colony on 'Shadow World' get on better with two Macks bossing the operation? Will Duncan be pleased with the Cytha's intended present of 'The World that Couldn't Be'? (Would you?) It is almost a quarter of a century since I first read that story, and the thought has stuck all these years.

As I said, I am almost envious of those who come to these stories for the first time. May you find as much enjoyment in them as I did, and pleasure in the knowledge that CDS is still writing, his most recent novel *Highway of Eternity* being published by Del Rey in 1986 (U.K., Severn House, 1987,

Methuen, 1989). For someone first published in 1931, that is quite a record, and a great achievement. Yet we hope for more.

Aberdeen, Scotland.   F. Lyall
January 1988

CONSTRUCTION
SHACK

In that same year when men first walked on Mars the probe was launched from the moon for Pluto. Five years later the first pictures were transmitted as the orbiting probe trained its cameras on the planet's surface. The transmission quality was poor; but even so, certain features of the photographs were productive of great anguish as old theories fell to shards and were replaced by puzzlement, questions with no hint of answers. The pictures seemed to say that the planet had a smooth, almost polished surface, without a single geographic feature to break the smoothness of it. Except that at certain places, equidistant from one another along the equator, were tiny dots that would have been taken for transmission noise if they had not appeared consistently. Too, the dots still persisted when some of the noise was eliminated. So it seemed they must be small geographic features or shadows cast by geographic features, although at Pluto's distance from the sun shadows would be suspect. The other data did nothing to lessen the anguish. The planet was smaller than supposed, less than a thousand miles in diameter, and its density worked out to 3.5 grams per cubic centimetre rather than the unrealistic figure of 60 grams, previously supposed.

This meant several things. It meant that somewhere out there, perhaps something more than seven billion miles from the sun, a tenth planet of the solar system swung in orbit, for no planet the size and mass of Pluto could explain the eccentricities in the orbits of Uranus and Neptune. The calculation of Pluto's mass, now proved inaccurate, had been based on the measurement of those eccentricities and it must be admitted now that something else must account for them.

Beyond that, Pluto was most strange – a smooth planet, featureless except for the evenly spaced dots. The smoothness certainly could not be explained by a non-turbulent atmosphere, for surely Pluto had to be too small and cold to hold an atmosphere. A surface of ice, men wondered, the frozen remnants of a one-time, momentary atmosphere? But for a number of reasons that didn't seem right, either. Metal, perhaps, but if the planet were of solid metal the density should be far greater.

The men on Earth consoled themselves. In five more years the probe would come back to Earth, carrying with it the films that it had taken and from them, the actual films and not the low-quality transmissions, perhaps much that was hazy now might become understandable. The probe swung in its measured orbits and sent back more pictures, although they were little help, for the quality still was poor. Then it fired the automatic sequence that would head it back to Earth, and its beeping signals from far out in space said it was headed home on a true and steady course.

Something happened. The beeping stopped and there was a silence. Moon Base waited. It might start up again. The silence might indicate only a momentary malfunction and the signals might start again. But they never did. Somewhere, some three billion miles from the sun, some mishap had befallen the homing probe. It was never heard again – it was lost forever.

There was no sense in sending out another probe until a day when technical advances could assure better pictures. The technical advances would have to be significant – small refinements would do little good.

The second and third manned expeditions went to Mars and came back home again, bringing back, among many other things, evidence that primitive forms of life existed there, which settled once and for all the old, dark suspicion that life might be an aberration to be found only on the Earth. For with life on two planets in the same solar system there could no longer be any doubt that life was a common factor in the universe. The fourth expedition went out, landed and did not come back again and now there was on Mars a piece of ground that was forever Earth. The fifth expedition was sent out even

14

while the Earth still paid tribute to those four men who had died so far from home.

Now that life had been found on another world, now that it was apparent that another planet at one time had held seas and rivers and an atmosphere that had been an approximation of Earth's own atmosphere, now that we knew we no longer were alone in the universe, the public interest and support of space travel revived. Scientists, remembering (never having, in fact, forgotten, for it had gnawed steadily at their minds) the puzzlement of the Pluto probe, began to plan a manned Pluto expedition, as there was still no sense in sending an instrumented probe.

When the day came to lift from the Moon Base, I was a member of the expedition. I went along as a geologist – the last thing a Pluto expedition needed.

There were three of us and any psychologist will tell you that three is a number that is most unfortunate. Two gang up on one or ignore one and there is always competition to be one of the gang of two. No one wants to stand alone with the other two against him. But it didn't work that way with us. We got along all right, although there were times when it was rough going. The five years that the probe took to arrive at Pluto was cut by more than half, not only because of improved rocket capability, but because a manned craft could pile on velocity that couldn't be programmed – or at least safely programmed – into a probe. But a bit more than two years is a long time to be cooped up in a tin can rocketing along in emptiness. Maybe it wouldn't be so bad if you had some sense of speed, of really getting somewhere – but you haven't. You just hang there in space.

The three of us? Well, I am Howard Lunt and the other two men were Orson Gates, a chemist, and Tyler Hampton, an engineer.

As I say, we got along fine. We played chess tournaments – yeah, three men in a tournament and it was all right because none of us knew chess. If we had been any good I suppose we would have been at one another's throats. We dreamed up dirty ditties and were so pleased with our accomplishments that we'd spend hours singing them and none of us could sing. We did a lot of other futile things – by now you should be getting the idea. There were some rather serious scientific experiments and observations we were supposed to make, but all of us figured that our first and biggest job was to manage to stay sane.

When we neared Pluto we dropped the fooling around and spent much time peering through the scope, arguing and speculating about what we saw. Not that there was much to see. The planet resembled nothing quite as much as a billiard ball. It was smooth. There were no mountains, no valleys, no craters – nothing marred the smoothness of the surface. The dots were there, of course. We could make out seven groups of them, all positioned along the equatorial belt. And in close up they were not simply dots. They were structures of some kind.

We landed finally, near a group of them. The landing was a little harder than we had figured it would be. The planetary surface was hard – there was no give to it. But we stayed right-side up and we didn't break a thing.

People at times ask me to describe Pluto and it's a hard thing to put into words. You can say that it is smooth and that it's dark – it's dark even in broad daylight. The sun, at that distance, is not much more than a slightly brighter star. You don't have daylight on Pluto – you have starlight and it doesn't make much difference whether you're facing the sun or not. The planet is airless, of course, and waterless and cold. But cold, as far as human sensation is concerned, is a relative thing. Once the temperature gets down to a hundred Kelvin it doesn't much matter how much colder it becomes. Especially when you're wearing life support. Without a suit containing life support, you'd last only a few seconds, if that long, on a place like Pluto. I've never figured out which would kill you first – cold or internal pressure. Would you freeze, or explode before you froze?

So Pluto is dark, airless, cold and smooth. Those are the externals only. You stand there and look at the sun and realize how far away you are. You know you are standing at the edge of the solar system, that just out there, a little way beyond, you'd be clear outside the system. Which doesn't really have to be true, of course. You know about the tenth planet. Even if it's theory, it's supposed to be out there. You know about

16

the millions of circling comets that technically are a part of the solar system, although they're so far out no one ever thinks of them. You could say to yourself this really is not the edge – the hypothetical tenth planet and the comets are still out there. But this is intellectualization; you're telling yourself something that your mind says may be true, but your gut denies. For hundreds of years Pluto has been the last outpost and this, by God, is Pluto and you're farther away from home than man has ever been before and you feel it. You don't belong to anything any more. You're in the back alley, and the bright and happy streets are so far away that you know you'll never find them.

It isn't homesickness that you feel. It's more like never having had a home. Of never having belonged anywhere. You get over it, of course – or come to live with it.

So we came down out of the ship after we had landed and stood upon the surface. The first thing that struck us – other than the sense of lostness that at once grabbed all of us – was that the horizon was too near, much nearer than on the Moon. We felt at once that we stood on a small world. We noticed that horizon's nearness even before we noticed the buildings that the probe had photographed as dots and that we had dropped down to investigate. Perhaps buildings is not the right word – structures probably would be better. Buildings are enclosures and these were not enclosures. They were domes someone had set out to build and hadn't had time to finish. The basic underlying framework had been erected and then the work had stopped. Riblike arcs curved up from the surface and met overhead. Struts and braces held the frames solid, but that was as far as the construction had gone. There were three of them, one larger than the other two. The frames were not quite as simple as I may have made them seem. Tied into the ribs and struts and braces were a number of other structural units that seemed to have no purpose and make no sense at all.

We tried to make sense out of them and out of the scooped-out hollows that had been gouged out of the planetary surface within the confines of each construct – they had no floors and seemed fastened to the surface of the planet. The hollows were circular, some six feet across and three feet deep, and to

17

me they looked like nothing quite as much as indentations made in a container of ice cream by a scoop.

About this time Tyler began to have some thoughts about the surface. Tyler is an engineer and should have had his thoughts immediately – and so should the rest of us – but the first hour or so outside the ship had been considerably confusing. We had worn our suits in training, of course, and had done some walking around in them, but Pluto seemed to have even less gravity than had been calculated and we had to get used to it before we could be reasonably comfortable. Nor had anything else been exactly as we had anticipated.

'This surface,' Tyler said to me. 'There is something wrong with it.'

'We knew it was smooth,' said Orson. 'The pictures showed that. Coming in, we could see it for ourselves.'

'This smooth?' Tyler asked. 'This even?' He turned to me. 'It isn't geologically possible. Would you say it is?'

'I would think not,' I said. 'If there had been any upheaval at all this floor would be rugged. There can't have been any erosion – anything to level it down. Micrometeorite impacts, maybe, but not too many of them. We're too far out for meteorites of any size. And while micrometeorites might pit the surface there would be no levelling process.'

Tyler let himself down on his knees rather awkwardly. He brushed a hand across the surface. The seeing was not too good, but you could see that there was dust, a thin layer of dust, a powdering.

'Shine a light down here,' said Tyler.

Orson aimed his light at the spot. Some of the grey dust still clung where Tyler had wiped his hand, but there were streaks where the darker surface showed through.

'Space dust,' said Tyler.

Orson said, 'There should be damn little of it.'

'True,' said Tyler. 'But over four billion years or more, it would accumulate. It couldn't be erosion dust, could it?'

'Nothing to cause erosion,' I said. 'This must be as close to a dead planet as you ever get. Not enough gravity to hold any of the gases – if there ever were gases. At one time there must have been, but they've all gone – they went early. No atmosphere, no water. I doubt there ever was any accumulation. A molecule wouldn't hang around for long.'

18

'But space dust would?'

'Maybe. Some sort of electrostatic attraction, maybe.'

Tyler scrubbed the little patch of surface again with his gloved hand, removing more of the dust, with more of the darker surface showing through.

'Have we got a drill?' he asked. 'A specimen drill.'

'I have one in my kit,' said Orson. He took it out and handed it to Tyler. Tyler positioned the bit against the surface, pressed the button. In the light of the torch you could see the bit spinning. Tyler put more weight on the drill.

'It's harder than a bitch,' he said.

The bit began to bite. A small pile of fragments built up around the hole. The surface was hard, no doubt of that. The pit didn't go too deep and the pile of fragments was small.

Tyler gave up. He lifted out the bit and snubbed off the motor.

'Enough for analysis?' he asked.

'Should be,' said Orson. He took the bit from Tyler and handed him a small specimen bag. Tyler laid the open mouth of the bag on the surface and brushed the fragments into it.

'Now we'll know,' he said. 'Now we will know something.'

A couple of hours later, back in the ship, we knew.

'I have it,' Orson said, 'but I don't believe it.'

'Metal?' asked Tyler.

'Sure, metal. But not the kind you have in mind. It's steel.'

'Steel?' I said, horrified. 'It can't be. Steel's no natural metal. It's manufactured.'

'Iron,' said Orson. 'Nickel. Molybdenum, vanadium, chromium. That works out to steel. I don't know as much about steel as I should. But it's steel – a good steel. Corrosion resistant, tough, strong.'

'Maybe just the platform for the structures,' I said. 'Maybe a pad of steel to support them. We took the specimen close to one of them.'

'Let's find out,' said Tyler.

We opened up the garage and ran down the ramp and got out the buggy. Before we left we turned off the television camera. By this time Moon Base would have seen all they needed to see and if they wanted more they could ask for it. We had given them a report on everything we had found – all except the steel surface and the three of us agreed that until we knew more about that we would not say anything. It

19

would be a while in any case until we got an answer from them. The time lag to Earth was about sixty hours each way.

We went out ten miles and took a boring sample and came back, following the thin tracks the buggy made in the dust, taking samples every mile. We got the answer that I think all of us expected we would get, but couldn't bring ourselves to talk about. The samples were all steel.

It didn't seem possible, of course, and it took us a while to digest the fact, but finally we admitted that on the basis of best evidence Pluto was no planet, but a fabricated metal ball, small-planet size. But God-awful big for anyone to build.

Anyone?

That was the question that now haunted us. Who had built it? Perhaps more important – why had they built it? For some purpose, surely, but why, once that purpose had been fulfilled (if, in fact, it had been fulfilled) had Pluto been left out here at the solar system's rim?

'No one from the system,' Tyler said. 'There's no one but us. Mars has life, of course, but primitive life. It got a start there and hung on and that was all. Venus is too hot. Mercury is too close to the sun. The big gas planets? Maybe, but not the kind of life that would build a thing like this. It had to be something from outside.'

'How about the fifth planet?' suggested Orson.

'There probably never was a fifth planet,' I said. 'The material for it may have been there, but the planet never formed. By all the rules of celestial mechanics there should have been a planet between Mars and Jupiter, but something went haywire.'

'The tenth planet, then,' said Orson.

'No one is really positive there is a tenth,' said Tyler.

'Yeah, you're right,' said Orson. 'Even if there were it would be a poor bet for life, let alone intelligence.'

'So that leaves us with outsiders,' said Tyler.

'And a long time ago,' said Orson.

'Why do you say that?'

'The dust. There isn't much dust in the universe.'

'And no one knows what it is. There is the dirty ice theory.'

'I see what you're getting at. But it needn't be ice. Nor graphite, nor any of the other things that have been – '

'You mean it's that stuff out there.'

20

'It could be. What do you think, Howard?'

'I can't be sure,' I said. 'The only thing I know is that it couldn't be erosive.'

Before we went to sleep we tried to fix up a report to beam back to Moon Base, but anything we put together sounded too silly and unbelievable. So we gave up. We'd have to tell them some time, but we could wait.

When we awoke we had a bite to eat, then got into our suits and went out to look over the structures. They still didn't make much sense, especially all the crazy contraptions that were fastened on the ribs and struts and braces. Nor did the scooped-out hollows.

'If they were only up on legs,' said Orson, 'they could be used as chairs.'

'But not very comfortable,' said Tyler.

'If you tilted them a bit,' said Orson. But that didn't figure either. They would still be uncomfortable. I wondered why he thought of them as chairs. They didn't look like any chairs to me.

We pottered around a lot, not getting anywhere. We looked the structures over inch by inch, wondering all the while if there was something we had missed. But there didn't seem to be.

Now comes the funny part of it. I don't know why we did it – out of sheer desperation, maybe. But failing to find any clues, we got down on our hands and knees, dusting at the surface with our hands. What we hoped to find, I don't know. It was slow going and it was a dirty business, with the dust tending to stick to us.

'If we'd only brought some brooms along,' said Orson.

But we had no brooms. Who in his right mind would have thought we would want to sweep a planet?

So there we were. We had what appeared to be a manufactured planet and we had some stupid structures for which we could deduce not a single reason. We had come a long way and we had been expected to make some tremendous discovery once we landed. We had made a discovery, all right, but it didn't mean a thing.

We finally gave up with the sweeping business and stood there, scuffing our feet and wondering what to do next when

Tyler suddenly let out a yell and pointed at a place on the surface where his boots had kicked away the dust.

We all bent to look at what he had found. We saw three holes in the surface, each an inch or so across and some three inches deep, placed in a triangle and close together. Tyler got down on his hands and knees and shone his light down into the holes, each one of them in turn.

Finally he stood up. 'I don't know,' he said. 'They could maybe be a lock of some sort. Like a combination. There are little notches on the sides, down at the bottom of them. If you moved those notches just right something might happen.'

'Might blow ourselves up, maybe,' said Orson. 'Do it wrong and bang!'

'I don't think so,' said Tyler. 'I don't think it's anything like that. I don't say it's a lock, either. But I don't think it's a bomb. Why should they booby-trap a thing like this?'

'You can't tell what they might have done,' I said. 'We don't know what kind of things they were or why they were here.'

Tyler didn't answer. He got down again and began carefully dusting the surface, shining his light on it while he dusted. We didn't have anything else to do, so we helped him.

It was Orson who found it this time — a hairline crack you had to hold your face down close to the surface to see. Having found it, we did some more dusting and worried it out. The hairline described a circle and the three holes were set inside and to one edge of it. The circle was three feet or so in diameter.

'Either of you guys good at picking locks?' said Tyler.

Neither of us were.

'It's got to be a hatch of some sort,' Orson said. 'This metal ball we're standing on has to be a hollow ball. If it weren't its mass would be greater than it is.'

'And no one,' I said, 'would be insane enough to build a solid ball. It would take too much metal and too much energy to move.'

'You're sure that it was moved?' asked Orson.

'It had to be,' I told him. 'It wasn't built in this system. No one here could have built it.'

Tyler had pulled a screwdriver out of his tool kit and was poking into the hole with it.

'Wait a minute,' said Orson. 'I just thought of something.'

22

He nudged Tyler to one side, reached down and inserted three fingers into the holes and pulled. The circular section rose smoothly on its hinges.

Wedged into the area beneath the door were objects that looked like the rolls of paper you buy to wrap up Christmas presents. Bigger than rolls of paper, though. Six inches or so across.

I got hold of one of them and that first one was not easy to grip, for they were packed in tightly. But I managed with much puffing and grunting to pull it out. It was heavy and a good four feet in length.

Once we got one out, the other rolls were easier to lift. We pulled out three more and headed for the ship.

But before we left I held the remaining rolls over to one side, to keep them from tilting, while Orson shone his light down into the hole. We had half expected to find a screen or something under the rolls, with the hole extending on down into a cavity that might have been used as living quarters or a workroom. But the hole ended in machined metal. We could see the grooves left by the drill or die that had bored the hole. That hole had just one purpose, to store the rolls we had found inside it.

Back in the ship we had to wait a while for the rolls to pick up some heat before we could handle them. Even so we had to wear gloves when we began to unroll them. Now, seeing them in good light, we realized that they were made up of many sheets rolled up together. The sheets seemed to be made of some sort of extremely thin metal or tough plastic. They were stiff from the cold and we spread them out on our lone table and weighted them down to hold them flat.

On the first sheet were diagrams of some sort, drawings and what might have been specifications written into the diagrams and along the margins. The specifications, of course, meant nothing to us (although later some were puzzled out and mathematicians and chemists were able to figure out some of the formulas and equations).

'Blueprints,' said Tyler. 'This whole business was an engineering job.'

'If that's the case,' said Orson, 'those strange things fastened to the structural frames could be mounts to hold engineering instruments.'

'Could be,' said Tyler.

'Maybe the instruments are stored in some other holes like the one where we found the blueprints,' I suggested.

'I don't think so,' said Tyler. 'They would have taken the instruments with them when they left.'

'Why didn't they take the blueprints, too?'

'The instruments would have been worthwhile to take. They could be used on another job. But the blueprints couldn't. And there may have been many sets of prints and spec sheets. These we have may be only one of many sets of duplicates. There would have been a set of master prints and those they might have taken with them when they left.'

'What I don't understand,' I said, 'is what they could have been building out here. What kind of construction? And why here? I suppose we could think of Pluto as a massive construction shack, but why exactly here? With all the galaxy to pick from, why this particular spot?'

'You ask too many questions all at once,' Orson told me.

'Let's look,' said Tyler. 'Maybe we'll find out.'

He peeled the first sheet off the top and let it drop to the floor. It snapped back to the rolled-up position.

The second sheet told us nothing, nor did the third or fourth. Then came the fifth sheet.

'Now, here is something,' said Tyler.

We leaned close to look.

'It's the solar system,' Orson said.

I counted rapidly. 'Nine planets.'

'Where's the tenth?' asked Orson. 'There should be a tenth.'

'Something's wrong,' said Tyler. 'I don't know what it is.'

I spotted it. 'There's a planet between Mars and Jupiter.'

'That means there is no Pluto shown,' said Orson.

'Of course not,' said Tyler. 'Pluto never was a planet.'

'Then this means there once actually was a planet between Mars and Jupiter,' said Orson.

'Not necessarily,' Tyler told him. 'It may only mean there was supposed to be.'

'What do you mean?'

'They bungled the job,' said Tyler. 'They did a sloppy piece of engineering.'

24

'You're insane!' I shouted at him.

'Your blind spot is showing, Howard. According to what we think, perhaps it is insane. According to the theories our physicists have worked out. There is a cloud of dust and gas and the cloud contracts to form a protostar. Our scientists have invoked a pretty set of physical laws to calculate what happens. Physical laws that were automatic – since no one would be mad enough to postulate a gang of cosmic engineers who went about the universe building solar systems.'

'But the tenth planet,' persisted Orson. 'There has to be a tenth planet. A big, massive – '

'They messed up the projected fifth planet,' Tyler said. 'God knows what else they messed up. Venus, maybe. Venus shouldn't be the kind of planet it is. It should be another Earth, perhaps a slightly warmer Earth, but not the hell hole it is. And Mars. They loused that up, too. Life started there, but it never had a chance. It hung on and that was all. And Jupiter, Jupiter is a monstrosity – '

'You think the only reason for a planet's existence is its capability of supporting life?'

'I don't know, of course. But it should be in the specs. Three planets that could have been life-bearing and of these only one was successful.'

'Then,' said Orson, 'there could be a tenth planet. One that wasn't even planned.'

Tyler rapped his fist against the sheet. 'With a gang of clowns like this anything could happen.'

He jerked away the sheet and tossed it to the floor.

'There!' he cried. 'Look here.'

We crowded in and looked.

It was a cross section, or appeared to be a cross section, of a planet.

'A central core,' said Tyler. 'An atmosphere – '

'Earth?'

'Could be. Could be Mars or Venus.'

The sheet was covered with what could have been spec notations.

'It doesn't look quite right,' I protested.

'It wouldn't if it were Mars or Venus. And how sure are you of Earth?'

'Not sure at all,' I said.

25

He jerked away the sheet to reveal another one.

We puzzled over it.

'Atmospheric profile,' I guessed half-heartedly.

'These are just general specs,' said Tyler. 'The details will be in some of the other rolls. We have a lot of them out there.'

I tried to envision it. A construction shack set down in a cloud of dust and gas. Engineers who may have worked for millennia to put together stars and planets; to key into them certain factors that still would be at work, billions of years later.

Tyler said they had bungled and perhaps they had. But maybe not with Venus. Maybe Venus had been built to different specifications. Maybe it had been designed to be the way it was. Perhaps, a billion years from now, when humanity might well be gone from Earth, a new life and a new intelligence would rise on Venus.

Maybe not with Venus, maybe with none of the others, either. We could not pretend to know.

Tyler was still going through the sheets.

'Look here,' he was yelling. 'Look here – the bunglers – '

OGRE

The moss brought the news. Hundreds of miles the word had gossiped its way along, through many devious ways. For the moss did not grow everywhere. It grew only where the soil was sparse and niggardly, where the larger, lustier, more vicious plant things could not grow to rob it of light or uproot it, or crowd it out, or do it other harm.

The moss told the story of Nicodemus, life blanket of Don Mackenzie, and it all came about because Mackenzie took a bath.

Mackenzie took his time in the bathroom, wallowing around in the tub and braying out a song, while Nicodemus, feeling only half a thing, moped outside the door. Without Mackenzie, Nicodemus was, in fact, even less than half a thing. Accepted as intelligent life, Nicodemus and others of his tribe were intelligent only when they were wrapped about their humans. Their intelligence and emotions were borrowed from the things that wore them.

For the aeons before the human beings came to this twilight world, the life blankets had dragged out a humdrum existence. Occasionally one of them allied itself with a high form of plant life, but not often. After all, such an arrangement was very little better than staying as they were.

When the humans came, however, the blankets finally clicked. Between them and the men of Earth grew up a perfect mutual agreement, a highly profitable and agreeable instance of symbiosis. Overnight, the blankets became one of the greatest single factors in galactic exploration.

27

For the man who wore one of them, like a cloak around his shoulders, need never worry where a meal was coming from; knew, furthermore, that he would be fed correctly, with a scientific precision that automatically counterbalanced any upset of metabolism that might be brought by alien conditions. For the curious plants had the ability to gather energy and convert it into food for the human body, extending, to a limited extent, to certain basic medical requirements.

But if the life blankets gave men food and warmth, served as a family doctor, man lent them something that was even more precious – the consciousness of life. The moment one of the plants wrapped itself around a man it became, in a sense, the double of that man. It shared his intelligence and emotions, was whisked from the dreary round of its own existence into a more exalted pseudo-life.

Nicodemus, at first moping outside the bathroom door, gradually grew peeved. He felt his thin veneer of human life slowly ebbing from him and he was filled with a baffling resentment.

Finally, feeling very put upon, he waddled out of the trading post upon his own high lonesome, flapping awkwardly along, like a sheet billowing in the breeze.

The dull brick-red sun that was Sigma Draco shone down upon a world that even at high noon appeared to be in twilight and Nicodemus' bobbling shape cast squirming, unsubstantial purple shadows upon the green and crimson ground. A rifle tree took a shot at Nicodemus but missed him by a yard at least. That tree had been off the beam for weeks. It had missed everything it shot at. Its best effort had been scaring the life out of Nellie, the bookkeeping robot that never told a lie, when it banked one of its bulletlike seeds against the steel-sheeted post.

But no one had felt very badly about that, for no one cared for Nellie. With Nellie around, no one could chisel a red cent off the company. That, incidentally, was the reason she was at the post.

But for a couple of weeks now, Nellie hadn't bothered anybody. She had taken to chumming around with Encyclopedia, who more than likely was slowly going insane trying to figure out her thoughts.

Nicodemus told the rifle tree what he thought of it, shooting
28

at its own flesh and blood, as it were, and kept shuffling along. The tree, knowing Nicodemus for a traitor to his own, a vegetable renegade, took another shot at him, missed by two yards and gave up in disgust.

That is how he heard that Alder, a minor musician out in Melody Bowl, finally had achieved a masterpiece. Nicodemus knew it might have happened weeks before, for Melody Bowl was half a world away and the news sometimes had to travel the long way around, but just the same he scampered as fast as he could hump back towards the post.

For this was news that couldn't wait. This was news Mackenzie had to know at once. He managed to kick up quite a cloud of dust coming down the home stretch and flapped triumphantly through the door, above which hung the crudely lettered sign:

GALACTIC TRADING CO.

Just what good the sign did, no one yet had figured out. The humans were the only living things on the planet that could read it.

Before the bathroom door, Nicodemus reared up and beat his fluttering self against it with tempetuous urgency.

'All right,' yelled Mackenzie. 'All right. I know I took too long again. Just calm yourself. I'll be right out.'

Nicodemus settled down but, still wriggling with the news he had to tell, heard Mackenzie swabbing out the tub.

With Nicodemus wrapped happily about him, Mackenzie strode into the office and found Nelson Harper, the factor, with his feet up on the desk, smoking his pipe and studying the ceiling.

'Howdy, lad,' said the factor. He pointed at a bottle with his pipestem. 'Grab yourself a snort.'

Mackenzie grabbed one.

'Nicodemus has been out chewing fat with the moss,' he said. 'Tells me a conductor by the name Alder has composed a symphony. Moss says it's a masterpiece.'

Harper took his feet off the desk. 'Never heard of this chap, Alder,' he said.

'Never heard of Kadmar, either,' Mackenzie reminded him,

29

'until he produced the Red Sun symphony. Now everyone is batty over him.'

'If Alder has anything at all, we ought to get it down. Even a mediocre piece pays out. People back on Earth are plain wacky over this tree music of ours. Like that one fellow . . . that composer – '

'Wade,' Harper filled in. 'J. Edgerton Wade. One of the greatest composers Earth had ever known. Quit in mortification after he heard the Red Sun piece. Later disappeared. No one knows where he went.'

The factor nursed his pipe between his palms. 'Funny thing. Came out here figuring our best-grading bet would be new drugs or maybe some new kind of food. Something for the high-class restaurants to feature, charge ten bucks a plate for. Maybe even a new mineral. Like out on Eta Cassiop. But it wasn't any of those things. It was music. Symphony stuff. High-brow racket.'

Mackenzie took another shot at the bottle, put it back and wiped his mouth. 'I'm not so sure I like this music angle,' he declared. 'I don't know much about music. But it sounds funny to me, what I've heard of it. Brain-twisting stuff.'

Harper grunted. 'You're OK as long as you have plenty of serum along. If you can't take the music, just keep yourself shot full of serum. That way it can't touch you.'

Mackenzie nodded. 'It almost got Alexander that time, remember? Ran short on serum while he was down in the Bowl trying to dicker with the trees. Music seemed to have a hold on him. He didn't want to leave. He fought and screeched and yelled around . . . I felt like a heel, taking him away. He never has been quite the same since then. Doctors back on Earth finally were able to get him straightened out, but warned him never to come back.'

'Alexander's back again,' said Harper, quietly. 'Grant spotted him over at the Groombridge post. Throwing in with the Groomies, I guess. Just a yellow-bellied renegade. Going against his own race. You boys shouldn't have saved him that time. Should have let the music get him.'

'What are you going to do about it?' demanded Mackenzie.

Harper shrugged his shoulders. 'What can I do about it? Unless I want to declare war on the Groombridge post. And that is out. Haven't you heard it's all sweetness and light

30

between Earth and Groombridge 34? That's the reason the two posts are stuck away from Melody Bowl. So each one of us will have a fair shot at the music. All according to some pact the two companies rigged up. Galactic's got so pure they wouldn't even like it if they knew we had a spy planted on the Groomie post.'

'But they got one planted on us,' declared Mackenzie. 'We haven't been able to find him, of course, but we know there is one. He's out there in the woods somewhere, watching every move we make.'

Harper nodded his head. 'You can't trust a Groomie. The lousy little insects will stoop to anything. They don't want that music, can't use it. Probably don't even know what music is. Haven't any hearing. But they know Earth wants it, will pay any price to get it, so they are out here to beat us to it. They work through birds like Alexander. They get the stuff, Alexander peddles it.'

'What if we run across Alexander, chief?'

Harper clicked his pipestem across his teeth. 'Depends on circumstances. Try to hire him, maybe. Get him away from the Groomies. He's a good trader. The company would do right by him.'

Mackenzie shook his head. 'No soap. He hates Galactic. Something that happened years ago. He'd rather make us trouble than turn a good deal for himself.'

'Maybe he's changed,' suggested Harper. 'Maybe you boys saving him changed his mind.'

'I don't think it did,' persisted Mackenzie.

The factor reached across the desk and drew a humidor in front of him and began to refill his pipe. 'Been trying to study out something else, too,' he said. 'Wondering what to do with the Encyclopedia. He wants to go to Earth. Seems he's found out just enough from us to whet his appetite for knowledge. Says he wants to go to Earth and study our civilization.'

Mackenzie grimaced. 'That baby's gone through our minds with a fine-toothed comb. He knows some of the things we've forgotten we ever knew. I guess it's just the nature of him, but it gets my wind up when I think of it.'

'He's after Nellie now,' said Harper. 'Trying to untangle what she knows.'

'It would serve him right if he found out.'

'I've been trying to figure it out,' said Harper. 'I don't like this brain-picking of his any more than you do, but if we took him to Earth, away from his own stamping grounds, we might be able to soften him up. He certainly knows a lot about this planet that would be of value to us. He's told me a little – '

'Don't fool yourself,' said Mackenzie. 'He hasn't told you a thing more than he's had to tell to make you believe it wasn't a one-way deal. Whatever he has told you has no vital significance. Don't kid yourself, he'll exchange information for information. That cookie's out to get everything he can get for nothing.'

The factor regarded Mackenzie narrowly. 'I'm not sure but I should put you in for an Earth vacation,' he declared. 'You're letting things upset you. You're losing your perspective. Alien planets aren't Earth, you know. You have to expect wacky things, get along with them, accept them on the basis of the logic that makes them the way they are.'

'I know all that,' agreed Mackenzie, 'but honest, chief, this place gets in my hair at times. Trees that shoot at you, moss that talks, vines that heave thunderbolts at you – and now, the Encyclopedia.'

'The Encyclopedia is logical,' insisted Harper. 'He's a repository for knowledge. We have parallels on Earth. Men who study merely for the sake of learning never expect to use the knowledge they amass. They derive a strange, smug satisfaction from being well informed. Combine that yearning for knowledge with a phenomenal ability to memorize and co-ordinate that knowledge and you have the Encyclopedia.'

'But there must be a purpose to him,' insisted Mackenzie. 'There must be some reason at the back of this thirst for knowledge. Just soaking up facts doesn't add up to anything unless you use those facts.'

Harper puffed stolidly at his pipe. 'There may be a purpose in it, but a purpose so deep, so different, we could not recognize it. This planet is a vegetable world and a vegetable civilization. Back on earth the animals got the head start and plants never had a chance to learn or to evolve. But here it's a different story. The plants were the ones that evolved, became masters of the situation.'

'If there is a purpose, we should know it,' Mackenzie declared, stubbornly. 'We can't afford to go blind on a thing like this. If the Encyclopedia has a game, we should know it. Is he acting on his own, a free lance? Or is he the representation of the world, a sort of prime minister, a state department? Or is he something that was left over by another civilization, a civilization that is gone? A kind of living archive of knowledge, still working at his old trade even if the need of it is gone?'

'You worry too much,' Harper told him.

'We have to worry, chief. We can't afford to let anything get ahead of us. We have taken the attitude we're superior to this vegetable civilization, if you can call it a civilization, that has developed here. It's the logical attitude to take because nettles and dandelions and trees aren't anything to be afraid of back home. But what holds on Earth doesn't hold here. We have to ask ourselves what a vegetable civilization would be like. What would it want? What would be its aspirations and how would it go about realizing them?'

'We're getting off the subject,' said Harper, curtly. 'You came in here to tell me about some new symphony.'

Mackenzie flipped his hands. 'OK if that's the way you feel about it.'

'Maybe we better figure on grabbing up this symphony soon as we can,' said Harper. 'We haven't had a really good one since the Red Sun. And if we mess around, the Groomies will beat us to it.'

'Maybe they have already,' said Mackenzie.

Harper puffed complacently at his pipe. 'They haven't done it yet. Grant keeps me posted on every move they make. He doesn't miss a thing that happens at the Groombridge post.'

'Just the same,' declared Mackenzie, 'we can't go rushing off and tip our hand. The Groomie spy isn't asleep, either.'

'Got any ideas?' asked the factor.

'We could take the ground car,' suggested Mackenzie. 'It's slower than the flier, but if we took the flier the Groomie would know there was something up. We use the car a dozen times a day. He'd think nothing of it.'

Harper considered. 'The idea has merit, lad. Who would you take?'

'Let me have Brad Smith,' said Mackenzie. 'We'll get along all right, just the two of us. He's an old-timer out here. Knows his way around.'

Harper nodded. 'Better take Nellie, too.'

'Not on your life!' yelped Mackenzie. 'What do you want to do? Get rid of her so you can make a cleaning?'

Harper wagged his grizzled head sadly. 'Good idea, but it can't be done. One cent off and she's on your trail. Used to be a little graft a fellow could pick up here and there, but not any more. Not since they got those robot bookkeepers indoctrinated with truth and honesty.'

'I won't take her,' Mackenzie declared, flatly. 'So help me, I won't. She'll spout company law all the way there and back. With the crush she has on this Encyclopedia, she'll probably want to drag him along, too. We'll have trouble enough with rifle trees and electro vines and all the other crazy vegetables without having an educated cabbage and a tin-can lawyer underfoot.'

'You've got to take her,' insisted Harper, mildly. 'New ruling. Got to have one of the things along on every deal you make to prove you did right by the natives. Come right down to it, the ruling probably is your own fault. If you hadn't been so foxy on that Red Sun deal, the company never would have thought of it.'

'All I did was to save the company some money,' protested Mackenzie.

'You knew,' Harper reminded him crisply, 'that the standard price for a symphony is two bushels of fertilizer. Why did you have to chisel half a bushel on Kadmar?'

'Cripes,' said Mackenzie, 'Kadmar didn't know the difference. He practically kissed me for a bushel and a half.'

'That's not the point,' declared Harper. 'The company's got the idea we got to shoot square with everything we trade with, even if it's nothing but a tree.'

'I know,' said Mackenzie, drily. 'I've read the manual.'

'Just the same,' said Harper, 'Nellie goes along.' He studied Mackenzie over the bowl of his pipe. 'Just to be sure you don't forget again,' he said.

The man, who back on Earth had been known as J. Edgerton Wade, crouched on the low cliff that dropped away into Melody Bowl. The dull red sun was slipping towards the purple horizon and soon, Wade knew, the trees would play their regular evening concert. He hoped that once again it would be the wondrous new symphony Alder had composed.

Thinking about it, he shuddered in ecstasy – shuddered again when he thought about the setting sun. The evening chill would be coming soon.

Wade had no life blanket. His food, cached back in the tiny cave in the cliff, was nearly gone. His ship, smashed in his inexpert landing on the planet almost a year before, was a rusty hulk. J. Edgerton Wade was near the end of his rope – and he knew it. Strangely, he didn't care. In that year since he'd come here to the cliffs, he'd lived in a world of beauty. Evening after evening he had listened to the concerts. That was enough, he told himself. After a year of music such as that any man could afford to die.

He swept his eyes up and down the little valley that made up the Bowl, saw the trees set in orderly rows, almost as if someone had planted them. Some intelligence that may at one time, long ago, have squatted on this very cliff edge, even as he squatted now, and listened to the music.

But there was no evidence, he knew, to support such a hypothesis. No ruins of cities had been found upon this world. No evidence that any civilization, in the sense that Earth had built a civilization, ever had existed here. Nothing at all that suggested a civilized race had ever laid eyes upon this valley, had ever had a thing to do with the planning of the Bowl.

Nothing, that was, except the cryptic messages on the face of the cliff above the cave where he cached his food and slept. Scrawlings that bore no resemblance to any other writing Wade had ever seen. Perhaps, he speculated, they might have been made by other aliens who, like himself, had come to listen to the music until death had come for them.

Still crouching, Wade rocked slowly on the balls of his feet. Perhaps he should scrawl his own name there with the other scrawlings. Like one would sign a hotel register. A lonely name scratched upon the face of a lonely rock. A grave name, a brief memorial – and yet it would be the only tombstone he would ever have.

The music would be starting soon and then he would forget about the cave, about the food that was almost gone, about the rusting ship that never could carry him back to Earth again – even had he wanted to go back. And he didn't – he couldn't have gone back. The Bowl had trapped him, the music had spun a web about him. Without it, he knew, he could not live.

35

It had become a part of him. Take it from him and he would be a shell, for it was now a part of the life force that surged within his body, part of his brain and blood, a silvery thread of meaning that ran through his thoughts and purpose.

The trees stood in quiet, orderly ranks and beside each tree was a tiny mound, podia for the conductors, and beside each mound the dark mouths of burrows. The conductors, Wade knew, were in those burrows, resting for the concert. Being animals, the conductors had to get their rest.

But the trees never needed rest. They never slept. They never tired, these grey, drab music trees, the trees that sang to the empty sky, sang of forgotten days and days that had not come, of days when Sigma Draco had been a mighty sun and of the later days when it would be a cinder circling in space. And of other things an Earthman could never know, could only sense and strain towards and wish he knew. Things that stirred strange thoughts within one's brain and choked one with alien emotion an Earthman was never meant to feel. Emotion and thought that one could not even recognize, yet emotion and thought that one yearned towards and knew never could be caught.

Technically, of course, it wasn't the trees that sang. Wade knew that, but he did not think about it often. He would rather it had been the trees alone. He seldom thought of the music other than belonging to the trees and disregarded the little entities inside the trees that really made the music, using the trees for their sounding boards. Entities? That was all he knew. Insects, perhaps, a colony of insects to each tree – or maybe even nymphs or sprites or some of the other little folk that run on skipping feet through the pages of children's fairy books. Although that was foolish, he told himself – there were no sprites.

Each insect, each sprite contributing its own small part to the orchestration, compliant to the thought-vibrations of the conductors. The conductors thought the music, held it in their brains and the things in the trees responded.

It didn't sound so pretty that way, Wade told himself. Thinking it out spoiled the beauty of it. Better to simply accept it and enjoy it without explanation.

Men came at times – not often – men of his own flesh and blood, men from the trading post somewhere on the planet.

36

They came to record the music and then they went away. How anyone could go away once they had heard the music, Wade could not understand. Faintly he remembered there was a way one could immunize one's self against the music's spell, condition one's self so he could leave after he had heard it, dull his senses to a point where it could not hold him. Wade shivered at the thought. That was sacrilege. But still no worse than recording the music so Earth orchestras might play it. For what Earth orchestra could play it as he heard it here, evening after evening? If Earth music lovers only could hear it as it was played here in this ancient bowl!

When the Earthmen came, Wade always hid. It would be just like them to try to take him back with them, away from the music of the trees.

Faintly the evening breeze brought the foreign sound to him, the sound that should not have been heard there in the Bowl – the clank of steel on stone.

Rising from his squatting place, he tried to locate the origin of the sound. It came again, from the far edge of the Bowl. He shielded his eyes with a hand against the setting sun, stared across the Bowl at the moving figures.

There were three of them and one, he saw at once, was an Earthman. The other two were strange creatures that looked remotely like monster bugs, chitinous armour glinting in the last rays of Sigma Draco. Their heads, he saw, resembled grinning skulls and they wore dark harnesses, apparently for the carrying of tools or weapons.

Groombridgians! But what would Groombridgians be doing with an Earthman? The two were deadly trade rivals, were not above waging intermittent warfare when their interests collided.

Something flashed in the sun – a gleaming tool that stabbed and probed, stabbed and lifted.

J. Edgerton Wade froze in horror.

Such a thing, he told himself, simply couldn't happen!

The three across the Bowl were digging up a music tree!

The vine sneaked through the rustling sea of grass, cautious tendrils raised to keep tab on its prey, the queer, clanking thing that still rolled on unswervingly. Came on without

37

stopping to smell out the ground ahead, without zigzagging to throw off possible attack.

Its action was puzzling; that was no way for anything to travel on this planet. For a moment a sense of doubt trilled along the length of vine, doubt of the wisdom of attacking anything that seemed so sure. But the doubt was short lived, driven out by the slavering anticipation that had sent the vicious vegetable from its lair among the grove of rifle trees. The vine trembled a little – slightly drunk with the vibration that pulsed through its tendrils.

The queer thing rumbled on and the vine tensed itself, every fibre alert for struggle. Just let it get so much as one slight grip upon the thing –

The prey came closer and for one sense-shattering moment it seemed it would be out of reach. Then it lurched slightly to one side as it struck a hump in the ground and the vine's tip reached out and grasped, secured a hold, wound itself in a maddened grip and hauled, hauled with all the might of almost a quarter mile of trailing power.

Inside the ground car, Don Mackenzie felt the machine lurch sickeningly, kicked up the power and spun the tractor on its churning treads in an effort to break loose.

Back of him Bradford Smith uttered a startled whoop and dived for an energy gun that had broken from its rack and was skidding across the floor. Nellie, upset by the lurch, was flat on her back, jammed into a corner. The Encyclopedia, at the moment of shock, had whipped out its coiled-up taproot and tied up to a pipe. Now, like an anchored turtle, it swayed pendulum-wise across the floor.

Glass tinkled and metal screeched on metal as Nellie thrashed to regain her feet. The ground car reared and seemed to paw the air, slid about and ploughed great furrows in the ground.

'It's a vine!' shrieked Smith.

Mackenzie nodded, grim-lipped, fighting the wheel. As the car slewed around, he saw the arcing loops of the attacker, reaching from the grove of rifle trees. Something pinged against the vision plate, shattered into a puff of dust. The rifle trees were limbering up.

Mackenzie tramped on the power, swung the car in a wide circle, giving the vine some slack, then quartered and charged across the prairie while the vine twisted and flailed the air in looping madness. If only he could build up speed, slap into the stretched-out vine full tilt, Mackenzie was sure he could break its hold. In a straight pull, escape would have been hopeless, for the vine, once fastened on the thing, was no less than a steel cable of strength and determination.

Smith had managed to get a port open, was trying to shoot, the energy gun crackling weirdly. The car rocked from side to side, gaining speed while bulletlike seeds from the rifle trees pinged and whined against it.

Mackenzie braced himself and yelled at Smith. They must be nearing the end of their run. Any minute now would come the jolt as they rammed into the tension of the outstretched vine.

It came with terrifying suddenness, a rending thud. Instinctively, Mackenzie threw up his arms to protect himself, for one startled moment he knew he was being hurled into the vision plate. A gigantic burst of flame flared in his head and filled the universe. Then he was floating through darkness that was cool and soft and he found himself thinking that everything would be all right, everything would be . . . everything –

But everything wasn't all right. He knew that, the moment he opened his eyes and stared up into the mass of tangled wreckage that hung above him. For many seconds he did not move, did not even wonder where he was. Then he stirred and a piece of steel bit into his leg. Carefully he slid his leg upward, clearing it of the steel. Cloth ripped with an angry snarl, but his leg came free.

'Lie still, you lug,' something said, almost as if it were a voice from inside him.

Mackenzie chuckled. 'So you're all right,' he said.

'Sure. I'm all right,' said Nicodemus. 'But you got some bruises and a scratch or two and you're liable to have a headache if you – '

The voice trailed off and stopped. Nicodemus was busy. At the moment, he was the medicine cabinet, fashioning from pure energy those things that a man needed when he had a bruise or two and was scratched-up some and might have a headache later.

Mackenzie lay on his back and stared up at the mass of tangled wreckage.

'Wonder how we'll get out of here,' he said.

The wreckage above him stirred. A gadget of some sort fell away from the twisted mass and gashed his cheek. He swore – unenthusiastically.

Someone was calling his name and he answered.

The wreckage was jerked about violently, literally torn apart. Long metal arms reached down, gripped him by the shoulders and yanked him out, none too gently.

'Thanks, Nellie,' he said.

'Shut up,' said Nellie, tartly.

His knees were a bit wobbly and he sat down, staring at the ground car. It didn't look much like a ground car any more. It had smashed full tilt into a boulder and was a mess.

To his left Smith also was sitting on the ground and he was chuckling.

'What's the matter with you,' snapped Mackenzie.

'Jerked her right up by the roots,' exulted Smith. 'So help me, right smack out of the ground. That's one vine that'll never bother anyone again.'

Mackenzie stared in amazement. The vine lay coiled on the ground, stretching back towards the grove, limp and dead. Its smaller tendrils still were entwined in the tangled wreckage of the car.

'It hung on,' gasped Mackenzie. 'We didn't break its hold!'

'Nope,' agreed Smith, 'we didn't break its hold, but we sure ruined it.'

'Lucky thing it wasn't an electro,' said Mackenzie, 'or it would have fried us.'

Smith nodded glumly. 'As it is it's loused us up enough. That car will never run again. And us a couple of thousand miles from home.'

Nellie emerged from a hole in the wreckage, with the Encyclopedia under one arm and a mangled radio under the other. She dumped them both on the ground. The Encyclopedia scuttled off a few feet, drilled his taproot into the soil and was at home.

Nellie glowered at Mackenzie. 'I'll report you for this,' she declared, vengefully. 'The idea of breaking up a nice new car! Do you know what a car costs the company? No, of course, you don't. And you don't care. Just go ahead and break it up. Just like that. Nothing to it. The company's got a lot more money to buy another one. I wonder sometimes if you ever wonder where your pay is coming from. If I was the company, I'd take it out of your salary. Every cent of it, until it was paid for.'

Smith eyed Nellie speculatively. 'Some day,' he said, 'I'm going to take a sledge and play tin shinny with you.'

'Maybe you got something there,' agreed Mackenzie. 'There are times when I'm inclined to think the company went just a bit too far in making those robots cost conscious.'

'You don't need to talk like that,' shrilled Nellie. 'Like I was just a machine you didn't need to pay no attention to. I suppose next thing you will be saying it wasn't your fault, that you couldn't help it.'

'I kept a good quarter mile from all the groves,' growled Mackenzie. 'Who ever heard of a vine that could stretch that far?'

'And that ain't all, neither,' yelped Nellie. 'Smith hit some of the rifle trees.'

The two men looked towards the grove. What Nellie said was true. Pale wisps of smoke still rose above the grove and what trees were left looked the worse for wear.

Smith clucked his tongue in mock concern.

'The trees were shooting at us,' retorted Mackenzie.

'That don't make any difference,' Nellie yelled. 'The rule book says – '

Mackenzie waved her into silence. 'Yes, I know. Section 17 of the Chapter on Relations with Extraterrestrial Life: *"No employee of this company may employ weapons against or otherwise injure or attempt to injure or threaten with injury an inhabitant of any other planet except in self-defence and then only if every means of escape or settlement has failed."*'

'And now we got to go back to the post,' Nellie shrieked. 'When we were almost there, we got to turn back. News of what we did will get around. The moss probably has started already. The idea of ripping a vine up by the roots and shooting trees. If we don't start back right now, we won't get back. Every living thing along the way will be laying for us.'

'It was the vine's fault,' yelled Smith. 'It tried to trap us. It tried to steal our car, probably would have killed us, just for the few lousy ounces of radium we have in the motors. That radium was ours. Not the vine's. It belonged to your beloved company.'

'For the love of gosh, don't tell her that,' Mackenzie warned, 'or she'll go out on a one-robot expedition, yanking vines up left and right.'

'Good idea,' insisted Smith. 'She might tie into an electro. It would peel her paint.'

'How about the radio!' Mackenzie asked Nellie.

'Busted,' said Nellie, crustily.

'And the recording equipment?'

'That tape's all right and I can fix the recorder.'

'Serum jugs busted?'

'One of them ain't,' said Nellie.

'OK, then,' said Mackenzie, 'get back in there and dig out two bags of fertilizer. We're going on. Melody Bowl is only about fifty miles away.'

'We can't do that,' protested Nellie. 'Every tree will be waiting for us, every vine – '

'It's safer to go ahead than back,' said Mackenzie. 'Even if we have no radio, Harper will send someone out with the flier to look us up when we are overdue.'

He rose slowly and unholstered his pistol.

'Get in there and get that stuff,' he ordered. 'If you don't, I'll melt you down into a puddle.'

'All right,' screamed Nellie in sudden terror. 'All right. you needn't get so tough about it.'

'Any more back talk out of you,' Mackenzie warned, 'and I'll kick you so full of dents you'll walk stooped over.'

They stayed in the open, well away from the groves, keeping a close watch. Mackenzie went ahead and behind him came the Encyclopedia, humping along to keep pace with them. Back of the Encyclopedia was Nellie, loaded down with the bags of fertilizer and equipment. Smith brought up the rear.

A rifle tree took a shot at them, but the range was too far for accurate shooting. Back a way, an electro vine had come closer with a thunderbolt.

Walking was gruelling. The grass was thick and matted and one had to plough through it, as if one were walking in water.

'I'll make you sorry for this,' seethed Nellie. 'I'll make – '

'Shut up,' snapped Smith. 'For once you're doing a robot's

42

work instead of gumshoeing around to see if you can't catch a nickel out of place.'

They breasted a hill and started to climb the long grassy slope.

Suddenly a sound like the savage ripping of a piece of cloth struck across the silence.

They halted, tensed, listening. The sound came again and then again.

'Guns!' yelped Smith.

Swiftly the two men loped up the slope. Nellie galloping awkwardly behind, the bags of fertilizer bouncing on her shoulders.

From the hilltop, Mackenzie took in the situation at a glance.

On the hillside below a man was huddled behind a boulder, working a gun with fumbling desperation, while farther down the hill a ground car had toppled over. Behind the car were three figures – one man and two insect creatures.

'Groomies!' whooped Smith.

A well-directed shot from the car took the top off the boulder and the man behind it hugged the ground.

Smith was racing quarterly down the hill, heading towards another boulder that would outflank the trio at the car.

A yell of human rage came from the car and a bolt from one of the three guns snapped at Smith, ploughing a smoking furrow no more than ten feet behind him.

Another shot flared towards Mackenzie and he plunged behind a hummock. A second shot whizzed just above his head and he hunkered down trying to push himself into the ground.

From the slope below came the high-pitched, angry chittering of the Groombridgians.

The car, Mackenzie saw, was not the only vehicle on the hillside. Apparently it had been pulling a trailer to which was lashed a tree. Mackenzie squinted against the setting sun, trying to make out what it was all about. The tree, he saw, had been expertly dug, its roots balled in earth and wrapped in sacking that shone wetly. The trailer was canted at an awkward angle, the treetop sweeping the ground, the balled roots high in the air.

Smith was pouring a deadly fire into the hostile camp and

43

the three below were replying with a sheet of blasting bolts, ploughing up the soil around the boulder. In a minute or two, Mackenzie knew, they would literally cut the gound out from under Smith. Cursing under his breath, he edged around the hummock, pushing his pistol before him, wishing he had a rifle.

The third man was slinging an occasional, inexpert shot at the three below, but wasn't doing much to help the cause along. The battle, Mackenzie knew, was up to him and Smith.

He wondered abstractedly where Nellie was.

'Probably halfway back to the post by now,' he told himself, drawing a bead on the point from which came the most devastating blaze of firing.

But even as he depressed the firing button, the firing from below broke off in a chorus of sudden screams. The two Groombridgians leaped up and started to run, but before they made their second stride, something came whizzing through the air from the slope below and crumpled one of them.

The other hesitated, like a startled hare, uncertain where to go, and a second thing came whishing up from the bottom of the slope and smacking against his breastplate with a thud that could be heard from where Mackenzie lay.

Then, for the first time Mackenzie saw Nellie. She was striding up the hill, her left arm holding an armful of stones hugged tight against her metal chest, her right arm working like a piston. The ringing clang of stone against metal came as one of the stones missed its mark and struck the ground car.

The human was running wildly, twisting and ducking, while Nellie pegged rock after rock at him. Trying to get set for a shot at her, the barrage of whizzing stones kept him on the dodge. Angling down the hill, he finally lost his rifle when he tripped and fell. With a howl of terror, he bolted up the hillside, his life blanket standing out almost straight behind him. Nellie pegged her last stone at him, then set out, doggedly loping in his wake.

Mackenzie screamed hoarsely at her, but she did not stop. She passed out of sight over the hill, closely behind the fleeing man.

Smith whooped with delight. 'Look at our Nellie go for him,' he yelled. 'She'll give him a working over when she nails him.'

44

Mackenzie rubbed his eyes. 'Who was he?' he asked.

'Jack Alexander,' said Smith. 'Grant said he was around again.'

The third man got up stiffly from behind his boulder and advanced towards them. He wore no life blanket, his clothing was in tatters, his face was bearded to the eyes.

He jerked a thumb towards the hill over which Nellie had disappeared. 'A masterly military manoeuvre,' he declared. 'Your robot sneaked around and took them from behind.'

'If she lost the recording stuff and the fertilizer, I'll melt her down,' said Mackenzie, savagely.

The man stared at them. 'You are the gentlemen from the trading post?' he asked.

They nodded, returning his gaze.

'I am Wade,' he said. 'J. Edgerton Wade – '

'Wait a second,' shouted Smith. 'Not *the* J. Edgerton Wade? The lost composer?'

The man bowed, whiskers and all. 'The same,' he said. 'Although I had not been aware that I was lost. I merely came out here to spend a year, a year of music such as man has never heard before.'

He glared at them. 'I am a man of peace,' he declared, almost as if daring them to argue that he wasn't, 'but when those three dug up Delbert, I knew what I must do.'

'Delbert?' asked Mackenzie.

'The tree,' said Wade. 'One of the music trees.'

'Those lousy planet-runners,' said Smith, 'figured they'd take that tree and sell it to someone back on Earth. I can think of a lot of big shots who'd pay plenty to have one of those trees in their back yard.'

'It's a lucky thing we came along,' said Mackenzie, soberly. 'If we hadn't, if they'd got away with it, the whole planet would have gone on the warpath. We could have closed up shop. It might have been years before we dared come back again.'

Smith rubbed his hands together, smirking. 'We'll take back their precious tree,' he declared, 'and will that put us in solid! They'll give us their tunes from now on, free for nothing, just out of pure gratitude.'

'You gentlemen,' said Wade, 'are motivated by mercenary factors but you have the right idea.'

45

A heavy tread sounded behind them and when they turned they saw Nellie striding down the hill. She clutched a life blanket in her hand.

'He got away,' she said, 'but I got his blanket. Now I got a blanket, too, just like you fellows.'

'What do you need with a life blanket?' yelled Smith. 'You give that blanket to Mr Wade. Right away. You hear me.'

Nellie pouted. 'You won't let me have anything. You never act like I'm human – '

'You aren't,' said Smith.

'If you give that blanket to Mr Wade,' wheedled Mackenzie, 'I'll let you drive the car.'

'You would?' asked Nellie, eagerly.

'Really,' said Wade, shifting from one foot to the other, embarrassed.

'You take that blanket,' said Mackenzie. 'You need it. Looks like you haven't eaten for a day or two.'

'I haven't,' Wade confessed.

'Shuck into it then and get yourself a meal,' said Smith.

Nellie handed it over.

'How come you were so good pegging those rocks?' asked Smith.

Nellie's eyes gleamed with pride. 'Back on Earth I was on a baseball team,' she said. 'I was the pitcher.'

Alexander's car was undamaged except for a few dents and a smashed vision plate where Wade's first bolt had caught it, blasting the glass and startling the operator so that he swerved sharply, spinning the treads across a boulder and upsetting it.

The music tree was unharmed, its roots still well moistened in the burlap-wrapped, water-soaked ball of earth. Inside the tractor, curled in a tight ball in the darkest corner, unperturbed by the uproar that had been going on outside, they found Delbert, the two-foot high, roly-poly conductor that resembled nothing more than a poodle dog walking on its hind legs.

The Groombridgians were dead, their crushed chitinous armour proving the steam behind Nellie's delivery.

Smith and Wade were inside the tractor, settled down for the night. Nellie and the Encyclopedia were out in the night, hunting for the gun Alexander had dropped when he fled. Mackenzie, sitting on the ground, Nicodemus pulled snugly about him, leaned back against the car and smoked a last pipe before turning in.

The grass behind the tractor rustled.

'That you, Nellie?' Mackenzie called, softly.

Nellie clumped hesitantly around the corner of the car.

'You ain't sore at me?' she asked.

'No, I'm not sore at you. You can't help the way you are.'

'I didn't find the gun,' said Nellie.

'You knew where Alexander dropped it?'

'Yes,' said Nellie. 'It wasn't there.'

Mackenzie frowned in the darkness. 'That means Alexander managed to come back and get it. I don't like that. He'll be out gunning for us. He didn't like the company before. He'll really be out for blood after what we did today.'

He looked around. 'Where's the Encyclopedia?'

'I sneaked away from him. I wanted to talk to you about him.'

'OK,' said Mackenzie. 'Fire away.'

'He's been trying to read my brain,' said Nellie.

'I know. He read the rest of ours. Did a good job of it.'

'He's been having trouble,' declared Nellie.

'Trouble reading your brain? I wouldn't doubt it.'

'You don't need to talk as if my brain – ' Nellie began, but Mackenzie stopped her.

'I don't mean it that way, Nellie. Your brain is all right, far as I know. Maybe even better than ours. But the point is that it's different. Ours are natural brains, the orthodox way for things to think and reason and remember. The Encyclopedia knows about those kinds of brains and the minds that go with them. Yours isn't that kind. It's artificial. Part mechanical, part chemical, part electrical, Lord knows what else; I'm not a robot technician. He's never run up against that kind of brain before. It probably has him down. Matter of fact, our civilization probably has him down. If this planet ever had a real civilization, it wasn't a mechanical one. There's no sign of mechanization here. None of the scars machines inflict on planets.'

'I been fooling him,' said Nellie quietly. 'He's been trying to read my mind, but I been reading his.'

Mackenzie started forward. 'Well, I'll be – ' he began. Then he settled back against the car, dead pipe hanging from

47

between his teeth. 'Why didn't you ever let us know you could read minds?' he demanded. 'I suppose you been sneaking around all this time, reading our minds, making fun of us, laughing behind our backs.'

'Honest, I ain't,' said Nellie. 'Cross my heart, I ain't. I didn't even know I could. But, when I felt the Encyclopedia prying around inside my head the way he does, it kind of got my dander up. I almost hauled off and smacked him one. And then I figured maybe I better be more subtle. I figured that if he could pry around in my mind, I could pry around in his. I tried it and it worked.'

'Just like that,' said Mackenzie.

'It wasn't hard,' said Nellie. 'It come natural. I seemed to just know how to do it.'

'If the guy that made you knew what he'd let slip through his fingers, he'd cut his throat,' Mackenzie told her.

Nellie sidled closer. 'It scares me,' she said.

'What's scaring you now?'

'That Encyclopedia knows too much.'

'Alien stuff,' said Mackenzie. 'You should have expected that. Don't go messing around with an alien mentality unless you're ready for some shocks.'

'It ain't that,' said Nellie. 'I knew I'd find alien stuff. But he knows other things. Things he shouldn't know.'

'About us?'

'No, about other places. Places other than the Earth and this planet here. Places Earthmen ain't been to yet. The kind of things no Earthman could know by himself or that no Encyclopedia could know by himself, either.'

'Like what?'

'Like knowing mathematical equations that don't sound like anything we know about,' said Nellie. 'Not like he'd know about if he'd stayed here all his life. Equations you couldn't know unless you knew a lot more about space and time than even Earthmen know.

'Philosophy, too. Ideas that make sense in a funny sort of way, but make your head swim when you try to figure out the kind of people that would develop them.'

Mackenzie got out his pouch and refilled his pipe, got it going.

'Nellie, you think maybe this Encyclopedia has been at

48

other minds? Minds of other people who may have come here?'

'Could be,' agreed Nellie. 'Maybe a long time ago. He's awful old. Lets on he could be immortal if he wanted to be. Said he wouldn't die until there was nothing more in the universe to know. Said when the time came there'd be nothing more to live for.'

Mackenzie clicked his pipestem against his teeth. 'He could be, too,' he said. 'Immortal, I mean. Plants haven't got all the physiological complications animals have. Given any sort of care, they theoretically could live forever.'

Grass rustled on the hillside above them and Mackenzie settled back against the car, kept on smoking. Nellie hunkered down a few feet away.

The Encyclopedia waddled down the hill, starlight glinting from his shell-like back. Ponderously he lined up with them beside the car, pushing his taproot into the ground for an evening snack.

'Understand you may be going back to Earth with us,' said Mackenzie, conversationally.

The answer came, measured in sharp and concise thought that seemed to drill deep into Mackenzie's mind. 'I should like to. Your race is interesting.'

It was hard to talk to a thing like that, Mackenzie told himself. Hard to match one's voice against the brittle thought with which it talked.

'What do you think of us?' he asked and knew, as soon as he had asked it, that it was asinine.

'I know very little of you,' the Encyclopedia declared. 'You have created artificial lives, while we on this planet have lived natural lives. You have bent every force that you can master to your will. You have made things work for you. First impression is that, potentially, you are dangerous.'

'I guess I asked for it,' Mackenzie said.

'I do not follow you.'

'Skip it,' said Mackenzie.

'The only trouble,' said the Encyclopedia, 'is that you don't know where you're going.'

'That's what makes it so much fun,' Mackenzie told him. 'Cripes, if we knew where we were going there'd be no

49

adventure. We'd know what was coming next. As it is, every corner that we turn brings a new surprise.'

'Knowing where you're going has its advantages,' insisted the Encyclopedia.

Mackenzie knocked the pipe bowl out on his boot heel, tramped on the glowing ash.

'So you have us pegged,' he said.

'No,' said the Encyclopedia. 'Just first impressions.'

The music trees were twisted grey ghosts in the murky dawn. The conductors, except for the few who refused to let even a visit from the Earthmen rouse them from their daylight slumber, squatted like black imps on their podia.

Delbert rode on Smith's shoulder, one clawlike hand entwined in Smith's hair to keep from falling off. The Encyclopedia waddled along in the wake of the Earthman party. Wade led the way towards Alder's podium.

The Bowl buzzed with the hum of distorted thought, the thought of many little folk squatting on their mounds – an alien thing that made Mackenzie's neck hairs bristle just a little as it beat into his mind. There were no really separate thoughts, no one commanding thought, just the chitter-chatter of hundreds of little thoughts, as if the conductors might be gossiping.

The yellow cliffs stood like a sentinel wall and above the path that led to the escarpment, the tractor loomed like a straddled beetle against the early dawn.

Alder rose from the podium to greet them, a disreputable-looking gnome on gnarly legs.

The Earth delegation squatted on the ground. Delbert, from his perch on Smith's shoulder, made a face at Alder.

Silence held for a moment and then Mackenzie, dispensing with formalities, spoke to Alder. 'We rescued Delbert for you,' he told the gnome. 'We brought him back.'

Alder scowled and his thoughts were fuzzy with disgust. 'We do not want him back,' he said.

Mackenzie taken aback, stammered. 'Why, we thought . . . that is, he's one of you . . . we went to a lot of trouble to rescue him – '

'He's a nuisance,' declared Alder. 'He's a disgrace. He's a no-good. He's always trying things.'

50

'You're not so hot yourself,' piped Delbert's thought. 'Just a bunch of fuddy-duddies. A crowd of corn peddlers. You're sore at me because I want to be different. Because I dust it off – '

'You see,' said Alder to Mackenzie, 'what he is like.'

'Why, yes,' agreed Mackenzie, 'but there are times when new ideas have some values. Perhaps he may be – '

Alder levelled an accusing finger at Wade. 'He was all right until you took to hanging around,' he screamed. 'Then he picked up some of your ideas. You contaminated him. Your silly notions about music – ' Alder's thoughts gulped in sheer exasperation, then took up again. 'Why did you come? No one asked you to? Why don't you mind your own business?'

Wade, red faced behind his beard, seemed close to apoplexy.

'I've never been so insulted in all my life,' he howled. He thumped his chest with a doubled fist. 'Back on Earth I wrote great symphonies myself. I never held with frivolous music. I never – '

'Crawl back into your hole,' Delbert shrilled at Alder. 'You guys don't know what music is. You saw out the same stuff day after day. You never lay it in the groove. You never get gated up. You all got long underwear.'

Alder waved knotted fists above his head and hopped up and down in rage. 'Such language!' he shrieked. 'Never was the like heard here before.'

The whole Bowl was yammering. Yammering with clashing thoughts of rage and insult.

'Wait,' Mackenzie shouted. 'All of you, quiet down!'

Wade puffed out his breath, turned a shade less purple. Alder squatted back on his haunches, unknotted his fists, tried his best to look composed. The clamour of thought subsided to a murmur.

'You're sure about this?' Mackenzie asked Alder. 'Sure you don't want Delbert back.'

'Mister,' said Alder, 'there never was a happier day in Melody Bowl than the day we found him gone.'

A rising murmur of assent from the other conductors underscored his words.

'We have some others we'd like to get rid of, too,' said Alder.

From far across the Bowl came a yelping thought of derision.

51

'You see,' said Alder, looking owlishly at Mackenzie, 'what it is like. What we have to contend with. All because this . . . this . . . this – '

Glaring at Wade, thoughts failed him. Carefully he settled back upon his haunches, composed his face again.

'If the rest were gone,' he said, 'we could settle down. But as it is, these few keep us in an uproar all the time. We can't concentrate, we can't really work. We can't do the things we want to do.'

Mackenzie pushed back his hat and scratched his head.

'Alder,' he declared, 'you sure are in a mess.'

'I was hoping,' Alder said, 'that you might be able to take them off our hands.'

'Take them off your hands!' yelled Smith. 'I'll say we'll take them! We'll take as many – '

Mackenzie nudged Smith in the ribs with his elbow, viciously. Smith gulped into silence. Mackenzie tried to keep his face straight.

'You can't take them trees,' said Nellie, icily. 'It's against the law.'

Mackenzie gasped. 'The law?'

'Sure, the regulations. The company's got regulations. Or don't you know that? Never bothered to read them, probably. Just like you. Never pay no attention to the things you should.'

'Nellie,' said Smith savagely. 'you keep out of this. I guess if we want to do a little favour for Alder here – '

'But it's against the law!' screeched Nellie.

'I know,' said Mackenzie. 'Section 34 of the chapter on Relations with Extraterrestrial Life. "*No member of this company shall interfere in any phase of the internal affairs of another race.*" '

'That's it,' said Nellie, pleased with herself. 'And if you take some of these trees, you'll be meddling in a quarrel that you have no business having anything to do with.'

Mackenzie flipped his hands. 'You see,' he said to Alder.

'We'll give you a monopoly on our music,' tempted Alder. 'We'll let you know when we have anything. We won't let the Groomies have it and we'll keep our prices right.'

Nellie shook her head. 'No,' she said.

Alder bargained. 'Bushel and a half instead of two bushel.'

'No,' said Nellie.

52

'It's a deal,' declared Mackenzie. 'Just point out your duds and we'll haul them away.'

'But Nellie said no,' Alder pointed out. 'And you say yes. I don't understand.'

'We'll take care of Nellie,' Smith told him, soberly.

'You won't take them trees,' said Nellie. 'I won't let you take them. I'll see to that.'

'Don't pay any attention to her,' Mackenzie said. 'Just point out the ones you want to get rid of.'

Alder said primly: 'You've made us very happy.'

Mackenzie got up and looked around. 'Where's the Encyclopedia?' he asked.

'He cleared out a minute ago,' said Smith. 'Headed back for the car.'

Mackenzie saw him, scuttling swiftly up the path towards the cliff top.

It was topsy-turvy and utterly crazy, like something out of that old book for children written by a man named Carroll. There was no sense to it. It was like taking candy from a baby.

Walking up the cliff path back to the tractor, Mackenzie knew it was, felt that he should pinch himself to know it was no dream.

He had hoped – just hoped – to avert relentless, merciless war against Earthmen throughout the planet by bringing back the stolen music tree. And here he was, with other music trees for his own, and a bargain thrown in to boot.

There was something wrong, Mackenzie told himself, something utterly and nonsensically wrong. But he couldn't put his finger on it.

There was no need to worry, he told himself. The thing to do was to get those trees and get out of there before Alder and the others changed their minds.

'It's funny,' Wade said behind him.

'It is,' agreed Mackenzie. 'Everything is funny here.'

'I mean about those trees,' said Wade. 'I'd swear Delbert was all right. So were all the others. They played the same music the others played. If there had been any faulty orchestration, any digression from form, I am sure I would have noticed it.'

Mackenzie spun around and grasped Wade by the arm. 'You

53

mean they weren't lousing up the concerts? That Delbert, here, played just like the rest?'

Wade nodded.

'That ain't so,' shrilled Delbert from his perch on Smith's shoulder. 'I wouldn't play like the rest of them. I want to kick the stuff around. I always dig it up and hang it out the window. I dream it up and send it away out wide.'

'Where'd you pick up that lingo?' Mackenzie snapped. 'I never heard anything like it before.'

'I learned it from him,' declared Delbert, pointing at Wade.

Wade's face was purple and his eyes were glassy.

'It's practically prehistoric,' he gulped. 'It's terms that were used back in the twentieth century to describe a certain kind of popular rendition. I read about it in a history covering the origins of music. There was a glossary of terms. They were so fantastic they stuck in my mind.'

Smith puckered his lips, whistling soundlessly. 'So that's how he picked it up. He caught it from your thoughts. Same principle that Encyclopedia uses, although not so advanced.'

'He lacks the Encyclopedia's distinction,' explained Mackenzie. 'He didn't know the stuff he was picking up was something that had happened long ago.'

'I have a notion to wring his neck,' Wade threatened.

'You'll keep your hands off him,' grated Mackenzie. 'This deal stinks to the high heavens, but seven music trees are seven music trees. Screwy deal or not, I'm going through with it.'

'Look fellows,' said Nellie. 'I wish you wouldn't do it.'

Mackenzie puckered his brow. 'What's the matter with you, Nellie? Why did you make that uproar about the law down there? There's a rule, sure, but in a thing like this it's different. The company can afford to have a rule or two broken for seven music trees. You know what will happen, don't you, when we get those trees back home. We can charge a thousand bucks a throw to hear them and have to use a club to keep the crowds away.'

'And the best of it is,' Smith pointed out, 'that once they hear them, they'll have to come again. They'll never get tired of them. Instead of that, every time they hear them, they'll want to hear them all the more. It'll get to be an obsession, a part of the people's life. They'll steal, murder, do anything so they can hear the trees.'

'That,' said Mackenzie, soberly, 'is the one thing I'm afraid of.'

'I only tried to stop you,' Nellie said. 'I know as well as you do that the law won't hold in a thing like this. But there was something else. The way the conductors sounded. Almost as if they were jeering at us. Like a gang of boys out in the street hooting at someone they just pulled a fast one on.'

'You're batty,' Smith declared.

'We have to go through with it,' Mackenzie announced, flatly. 'If anyone ever found we'd let a chance like this slip through our fingers, they'd crucify us for it.'

'You're going to get in touch with Harper?' Smith asked.

Mackenzie nodded. 'We have to get hold of Earth, have them send out a ship right away to take back the trees.'

'I still think,' said Nellie, 'there's a nigger in the woodpile.'

Mackenzie flipped the toggle and the visiphone went dead.

Harper had been hard to convince. Mackenzie, thinking about it, couldn't blame him much. After all, it did sound incredible. But then, this whole planet was incredible.

Mackenzie reached into his pocket and hauled forth his pipe and pouch. Nellie probably would raise hell about helping to dig up those other six trees, but she'd have to get over it. They'd have to work as fast as they could. They couldn't spend more than one night up here on the rim. There wasn't enough serum for longer than that. One jug of the stuff wouldn't go too far.

Suddenly excited shouts came from outside the car, shouts of consternation.

With a single leap, Mackenzie left the chair and jumped for the door. Outside, he almost bumped into Smith, who came running around the corner of the tractor. Wade, who had been down at the cliff's edge, was racing towards them.

'It's Nellie,' shouted Smith. 'Look at that robot!'

Nellie was marching towards them, dragging in her wake a thing that bounced and struggled. A rifle-tree grove fired a volley and one of the pellets caught Nellie in the shoulder, puffing into dust, staggering her a little.

The bouncing thing was the Encyclopedia. Nellie had hold

of his taproot, was hauling him unceremoniously across the bumpy ground.

'Put him down!' Mackenzie yelled at her. 'Let him go!'

'He stole the serum,' howled Nellie. 'He stole the serum and broke it on a rock!'

She swung the Encyclopedia towards them in a looping heave. The intelligent vegetable bounced a couple of times, struggled to get right side up, then scurried off a few feet, root coiled tightly against its underside.

Smith moved towards it threateningly. 'I ought to kick the living innards out of you,' he yelled. 'We need that serum. You knew why we needed it.'

'You threaten me with force,' said the Encyclopedia. 'The most primitive method of compulsion.'

'It works,' Smith told him shortly.

The Encyclopedia's thoughts were unruffled, almost serene, as clear and concise as ever. 'You have a law that forbids your threatening or harming any alien thing.'

'Chum,' declared Smith, 'you better get wised up on laws. There are times when certain laws don't hold. And this is one of them.'

'Just a minute,' said Mackenzie. He spoke to the Encyclopedia. 'What is your understanding of a law?'

'It is a rule you live by,' the Encyclopedia said. 'It is something that is necessary. You cannot violate it.'

'He got that from Nellie,' said Smith.

'You think because there is a law against it, we won't take the trees?'

'There is a law against it,' said the Encyclopedia. 'You cannot take the trees.'

'So as soon as you found that out, you lammed up here and stole the serum, eh!'

'He's figuring on indoctrinating us,' Nellie explained. 'Maybe that word ain't so good. Maybe conditioning is better. It's sort of mixed up. I don't know if I've got it straight. He took the serum so we would hear the trees without being able to defend ourselves against them. He figured when we heard the music, we'd go ahead and take the trees.'

'Law or no law?'

'That's it,' Nellie said. 'Law or no law.'

*

Smith whirled on the robot. 'What kind of jabber is this? How do you know what he was planning?'

'I read his mind,' said Nellie. 'Hard to get at, the thing that he was planning, because he kept it deep. But some of it jarred up where I could reach it when you threatened him.'

'You can't do that!' shrieked the Encyclopedia. 'Not you! Not a machine!'

Mackenzie laughed shortly. 'Too bad, big boy, but she can. She's been doing it.'

Smith stared at Mackenzie.

'It's all right,' Mackenzie said. 'It isn't any bluff. She told me about it last night.'

'You are unduly alarmed,' the Encyclopedia said. 'You are putting a wrong interpretation – '

A quiet voice spoke, almost as if it were a voice inside Mackenzie's mind.

'Don't believe a thing he tells you, pal. Don't fall for any of his lies.'

'Nicodemus! You know something about this?'

'It's the trees,' said Nicodemus. 'The music does something to you. It changes you. Makes you different than you were before. Wade is different. He doesn't know it, but he is.'

'If you mean the music chains one to it, that is true,' said Wade. 'I may as well admit it. I could not live without the music. I could not leave the Bowl. Perhaps you gentlemen thought that I would go back with you. But I cannot go. I cannot leave. It will work the same with anyone. Alexander was here for a while when he ran short of serum. Doctors treated him and he was all right, but he came back. He had to come back. He couldn't stay away.'

'It isn't only that,' declared Nicodemus. 'It changes you, too, in other ways. It can change you any way it wants to. Change your way of thinking. Change your viewpoints.'

Wade strode forward. 'It isn't true,' he yelled. 'I'm the same as when I came here.'

'You heard things,' said Nicodemus, 'felt things in the music you couldn't understand. Things you wanted to understand, but couldn't. Strange emotions that you yearned to share, but could never reach. Strange thoughts that tantalized you for days.'

Wade sobered, stared at them with haunted eyes.

57

'That was the way it was,' he whispered. 'That was just the way it was.'

He glanced around, like a trapped animal seeking escape.

'But I don't feel any different,' he mumbled. 'I still am human. I think like a man, act like a man.'

'Of course you do,' said Nicodemus. 'Otherwise you would have been scared away. If you had known what was happening to you, you wouldn't let it happen. And you have had less than a year of it. Less than a year of this conditioning. Five years and you would be less human. Ten years and you would be beginning to be the kind of thing the trees want you to be.'

'And we were going to take some of those trees to Earth!' Smith shouted. 'Seven of them! So the people of the Earth could hear them. Listen to them, night after night. The whole world listening to them on the radio. A whole world being conditioned, being changed by seven music trees.'

'But why?' asked Wade, bewildered.

'Why did men domesticate animals?' Mackenzie asked. 'You wouldn't find out by asking the animals, for they don't know. There is just as much point asking a dog why he was domesticated as there is in asking us why the trees want to condition us. For some purpose of their own, undoubtedly, that is perfectly clear and logical to them. A purpose that undoubtedly never can be clear and logical to us.'

'Nicodemus,' said the Encycopedia and his thought was deathly cold, 'you have betrayed your own.'

Mackenzie laughed harshly. 'You're wrong there,' he told the vegetable, 'because Nicodemus isn't a plant, any more. He's a human. The same thing has happened to him as you want to have happen to us. He has become a human in everything but physical make-up. He thinks as a man does. His viewpoints are ours, not yours.'

'That is right,' said Nicodemus. 'I am a man.'

A piece of cloth ripped savagely and for an instant the group was blinded by a surge of energy that leaped from the thicket a hundred yards away. Smith gurgled once in sudden agony and the energy was gone.

Frozen momentarily by surprise, Mackenzie watched Smith stagger, face tight with pain, hand clapped to his side. Slowly the man wilted, sagged in the middle and went down.

58

Silently, Nellie leaped forward, was sprinting for the thicket. With a hoarse cry, Mackenzie bent over Smith.

Smith grinned at him, a twisted grin. His mouth worked, but no words came. His hand slid away from his side and he went limp, but his chest rose and fell with a slightly slower breath. His life blanket had shifted its position to cover the wounded side.

Mackenzie straightened up, hauling the pistol from his belt. A man had risen from the thicket, was levelling a gun at the charging Nellie. With a wild yell, Mackenzie shot from the hip. The lashing charge missed the man but half the thicket disappeared in a blinding sheet of flame.

The man with the gun ducked as the flame puffed out at him and in that instant Nellie closed in. The man yelled once, a long-drawn howl of terror as Nellie swung him above her head and dashed him down. The smoking thicket hid the rest of it. Mackenzie, pistol hanging limply by his side, watched Nellie's right fist lift and fall with brutal precision, heard the thud of life being beaten from a human body.

Sickened, he turned back to Smith. Wade was kneeling beside the wounded man. He looked up.

'He seems to be unconscious.'

Mackenzie nodded. 'The blanket put him out. Gave him an anaesthetic. It'll take care of him.'

Mackenzie glanced up sharply at a scurry in the grass. The Encyclopedia, taking advantage of the moment, was almost out of sight, scuttling towards a grove of rifle trees.

A step grated behind him.

'It was Alexander,' Nellie said. 'He won't bother us no more.'

Nelson Harper, factor at the post, was lighting up his pipe when the visiphone signal buzzed and the light flashed on.

Startled, Harper reached out and snapped on the set. Mackenzie's face came in, a face streaked with dirt and perspiration, stark with fear. He waited for no greeting. His lips were already moving even as the plate flickered and cleared.

'It's all off, chief,' he said. 'The deal is off. I can't bring in those trees.'

'You got to bring them in,' yelled Harper. 'I've already called Earth. I got them turning handsprings. They say it's the greatest thing that ever happened. They're sending out a ship within an hour.'

'Call them back and tell them not to bother,' Mackenzie snapped.

'But you told me everything was set,' yelped Harper. 'You told me nothing could happen. You said you'd bring them in if you had to crawl on hands and knees and pack them on your back.'

'I told you every word of that,' agreed Mackenzie. 'Probably even more. But I didn't know what I know now.'

Harper groaned. 'Galactic is plastering every front page in the Solar System with the news. Earth radios right now are bellowing it out from Mercury to Pluto. Before another hour is gone every man, woman and child will know those trees are coming to Earth. And once they know that, there's nothing we can do. Do you understand that, Mackenzie? We have to get them there!'

'I can't do it, chief,' Mackenzie insisted, stubbornly.

'Why can't you?' screamed Harper. 'So help me Hannah, if you don't – '

'I can't bring them in because Nellie's burning them. She's down in the Bowl right now with a flamer. When she's through, there won't be any music trees.'

'Go out and stop her!' shrieked Harper. 'What are you sitting there for! Go out and stop her! Blast her if you have to. Do anything, but stop her! That crazy robot – '

'I told her to,' snapped Mackenzie. 'I ordered her to do it. When I get through here, I'm going down to help her.'

'You're crazy, man!' yelled Harper. 'Stark, staring crazy. They'll throw the book at you for this. You'll be lucky if you just get life – '

Two darting hands loomed in the plate, hands that snapped down and closed around Mackenzie's throat, hands that dragged him away and left the screen blank, but with a certain blurring motion, as if two men might be fighting for their lives just in front of it.

'Mackenzie!' screamed Harper. 'Mackenzie!'

Something smashed into the screen and shattered it, leaving the broken glass gaping in jagged shards.

Harper clawed at the visiphone. 'Mackenzie! Mackenzie, what's happening!'

60

In answer the screen exploded in a flash of violent flame, howled like a screeching banshee and then went dead.

Harper stood frozen in the room, listening to the faint purring of the radio. His pipe fell from his hand and bounced along the floor spilling burned tobacco.

Cold, clammy fear closed down upon him, squeezing his heart. A fear that twisted him and mocked him. Galactic would break him for this, he knew. Send him out to some of the jungle planets as the rankest subordinate. He would be marked for life, a man not to be trusted, a man who had failed to uphold the prestige of the company.

Suddenly a faint spark of hope stirred deep within him. If he could get there soon enough! If he could get to Melody Bowl in time, he might stop this madness. Might at least save something, save a few of the precious trees.

The flier was in the compound, waiting. Within half an hour he could be above the Bowl.

He leaped for the door, shoved it open and even as he did a pellet whistled past his cheek and exploded into a puff of dust against the door frame. Instinctively, he ducked and another pellet brushed his hair. A third caught him in the leg with stinging force and brought him down. A fourth puffed dust into his face.

He fought his way to his knees, was staggered by another shot that slammed into his side. He raised his right arm to protect his face and a sledge-hammer blow slapped his wrist. Pain flowed along his arm and in sheer panic he turned and scrambled on hands and knees across the threshold and kicked the door shut with his foot.

Sitting flat on the floor, he held his right wrist in his left hand. He tried to make his fingers wiggle and they wouldn't. The wrist, he knew, was broken.

After weeks of being off the beam the rifle tree outside the compound suddenly had regained its aim and gone on a rampage.

Mackenzie raised himself off the floor and braced himself with one elbow, while with the other hand he fumbled at his throbbing throat. The interior of the tractor danced with wavy motion and his head thumped and pounded with pain.

Slowly, carefully, he inched himself back so he could lean

against the wall. Gradually the room stopped rocking, but the pounding in his head went on.

Someone was standing in the doorway of the tractor and he fought to focus his eyes, trying to make out who it was.

A voice screeched across his nerves.

'I'm taking your blankets. You'll get them back when you decide to leave the trees alone.'

Mackenzie tried to fashion words, but all he accomplished was a croak. He tried again.

'Wade?' he asked.

It was Wade, he saw.

The man stood within the doorway, one hand clutching a pair of blankets, the other holding a gun.

'You're crazy, Wade,' he whispered. 'We have to burn the trees. The human race never would be safe. Even if they fail this time, they'll try again. And again — and yet again. And some day they will get us. Even without going to Earth they can get us. They can twist us to their purpose with recordings alone: long distance propaganda. Take a bit longer, but it will do the job as well.'

'They are beautiful,' said Wade. 'The most beautiful things in all the universe. I can't let you destroy them. You must not destroy them.'

'But can't you see,' croaked Mackenzie, 'that's the thing that makes them so dangerous. Their beauty, the beauty of their music, is fatal. No one can resist it.'

'It was the thing I lived by,' Wade told him, soberly. 'You say it made me something that was not quite human. But what difference does that make. Must racial purity, in thought and action, be a fetish that would chain us to a drab existence when something better, something greater, is offered. And we never would have known. That is the best of it all, we never would have known. They would have changed us, yes, but so slowly, so gradually, that we would not have suspected. Our decisons and our actions and our way of thought would still have seemed to be our own. The trees never would have been anything more than something cultural.'

'They want our mechanization,' said Mackenzie. 'Plants can't develop machines. Given that, they might have taken us along a road we, in our rightful heritage, never would have taken.'

62

'How can we be sure,' asked Wade, 'that our heritage would have guided us aright?'

Mackenzie slid straighter against the wall. His head still throbbed and his throat still ached.

'You've been thinking about this?' he asked.

Wade nodded. 'At first there was the natural reaction of horror. But, logically, that reaction is erroneous. Our schools teach our children a way of life. Our press strives to formulate our adult opinion and belief. The trees were doing no more to us than we do to ourselves. And perhaps, for a purpose no more selfish.'

Mackenzie shook his head. 'We must live our own life. We must follow the path the attributes of humanity decree that we should follow. And anyway, you're wasting your time.'

'I don't understand,' said Wade.

'Nellie already is burning the trees,' Mackenzie told him. 'I sent her out before I made the call to Harper.'

'No, she's not,' said Wade.

Mackenzie sat bolt upright. 'What do you mean?'

Wade flipped the pistol as Mackenzie moved as if to regain his feet.

'It doesn't matter what I mean, ' he snapped. 'Nellie isn't burning any trees. She isn't in a position to burn any trees. And neither are you, for I've taken both your flamers. And the tractor won't run, either. I've seen to that. So the only thing that you can do is stay right here.'

Mackenzie motioned towards Smith, lying on the floor. 'You're taking his blanket, too?'

Wade nodded.

'But you can't. Smith will die. Without that blanket he doesn't have a chance. The blanket could have healed the wound, kept him fed correctly, kept him warm – '

'That,' said Wade, 'is all the more reason that you come to terms directly.'

'Your terms,' said Mackenzie, 'are that we leave the trees unharmed.'

'Those are my terms.'

Mackenzie shook his head. 'I can't take the chance,' he said.

'When you decide, just step out and shout,' Wade told him. 'I'll stay in calling distance.'

He backed slowly from the door.

*

Smith needed warmth and food. In the hour since his blanket had been taken from him he had regained consciousness, had mumbled feverishly and tossed about, his hand clawing at his wounded side.

Squatting beside him, Mackenzie had tried to quiet him, had felt a wave of slow terror as he thought of the hours ahead.

There was no food in the tractor, no means for making heat. There was no need for such provision so long as they had had their life blankets – but now the blankets were gone. There was a first-aid cabinet and with the materials that he found there, Mackenzie did his fumbling best, but there was nothing to relieve Smith's pain, nothing to control his fever. For treatment such as that they had relied upon the blankets.

The atomic motor might have been rigged up to furnish heat, but Wade had taken the firing mechanism control.

Night was falling and that meant the air would grow colder. Not too cold to live, of course, but cold enough to spell doom to a man in Smith's condition.

Mackenzie squatted on his heels and stared at Smith.

'If I could only find Nellie,' he thought.

He had tried to find her – briefly. He had raced along the rim of the Bowl for a mile or so, but had seen no sign of her. He had been afraid to go farther, afraid to stay too long from the man back in the tractor.

Smith mumbled and Mackenzie bent low to try to catch the words. But there were no words.

Slowly he rose and headed for the door. First of all, he needed heat. Then food. The heat came first. An open fire wasn't the best way to make heat, of course, but it was better than nothing.

The uprooted music tree, balled roots silhouetted against the sky, loomed before him in the dusk. He found a few dead branches and tore them off. They would do to start the fire. After that he would have to rely on green wood to keep it going. Tomorrow he could forage about for suitable fuel.

In the Bowl below, the music trees were tuning up for the evening concert.

Back in the tractor he found a knife, carefully slivered several of the branches for easy lighting, piled them ready for his pocket lighter.

64

The lighter flared and a tiny figure hopped up on the threshold of the tractor, squatting there, blinking at the light.

Startled, Mackenzie held the lighter without touching it to the wood, stared at the thing that perched in the doorway.

Delbert's squeaky thought drilled into his brain.

'What you doing?'

'Building a fire,' Mackenzie told him.

'What's a fire?'

'It's a . . . it's a . . . say, don't you know what a fire is?'

'Nope,' said Delbert.

'It's a chemical action,' Mackenzie said. 'It breaks up matter and releases energy in the form of heat.'

'What you building a fire with?' asked Delbert, blinking in the flare of the lighter.

'With branches from a tree.'

Delbert's eyes widened and his thought was jittery.

'A tree?'

'Sure, a tree. Wood. It burns. It gives off heat. I need heat.'

'What tree?'

'Why – ' And then Mackenzie stopped with sudden realization. His thumb relaxed and the flame went out.

Delbert shrieked at him in sudden terror and anger. 'It's my tree! You're building a fire with my tree!'

Mackenzie sat in silence.

'When you burn my tree, it's gone,' yelled Delbert. 'Isn't that right? When you burn my tree, it's gone?'

Mackenzie nodded.

'But why do you do it?' shrilled Delbert.

'I need heat,' said Mackenzie, doggedly. 'If I don't have heat, my friend will die. It's the only way I can get heat.'

'But my tree!'

Mackenzie shrugged. 'I need a fire, see? And I'm getting it any way I can.'

He flipped his thumb again and the lighter flared.

'But I never did anything to you,' Delbert howled, rocking on the metal door sill. 'I'm your friend, I am. I never did a thing to hurt you.'

'No?' asked Mackenzie.

'No,' yelled Delbert.

'What about that scheme of yours?' asked Mackenzie. 'Trying to trick me into taking trees to Earth?'

65

'That wasn't my idea,' yipped Delbert. 'It wasn't any of the trees' ideas. The Encyclopedia thought it up.'

A bulky form loomed outside the door. 'Someone talking about me?' it asked.

The Encyclopedia was back again.

Arrogantly, he shouldered Delbert aside, stepped into the tractor.

'I saw Wade,' he said.

Mackenzie glared at him. 'So you figured it would be safe to come.'

'Certainly,' said the Encyclopedia. 'Your formula of force counts for nothing now. You have no means to enforce it.'

Mackenzie's hand shot out and grasped the Encyclopedia with a vicious grip, hurled him into the interior of the tractor.

'Just try to get out this door,' he snarled. 'You'll soon find out if the formula of force amounts to anything.'

The Encyclopedia picked himself up, shook himself like a ruffled hen. But his thought was cool and calm.

'I can't see what this avails you.'

'It gives us soup,' Mackenzie snapped.

He sized the Encyclopedia up. 'Good vegetable soup. Something like cabbage. Never cared much for cabbage soup, myself, but – '

'Soup?'

'Yeah, soup. Stuff to eat. Food.'

'Food!' The Encyclopedia's thought held a tremor of anxiety. 'You would use me as a food.'

'Why not?' Mackenzie asked him. 'You're nothing but a vegetable. An intelligent vegetable, granted, but still a vegetable.'

He felt the Encyclopedia's groping thought-fingers prying into his mind.

'Go ahead,' he told him, 'but you won't like what you find.'

The Encyclopedia's thoughts almost gasped. 'You withheld this from me!' he charged.

'We withheld nothing from you,' Mackenzie declared. 'We never had occasion to think of it . . . to remember to what use Men at one time put plants, to what use we still put plants in certain cases. The only reason we don't use them so exten-

66

sively now is that we have advanced beyond the need of them. Let that need exist again and – '

'You ate us,' strummed the Encyclopedia. 'You used us to build your shelters! You destroyed us to create heat for your selfish purposes!'

'Pipe down,' Mackenzie told him. 'It's the way we did it that gets you. The idea that we thought we had a right to. That we went out and took, without even asking, never wondering what the plant might think about it. That hurts your racial dignity.'

He stopped, then moved closer to the doorway. From the Bowl below came the first strains of the music. The tuning up, the preliminary to the concert, was over.

'OK,' Mackenzie said, 'I'll hurt it some more. Even you are nothing but a plant to me. Just because you've learned some civilized tricks doesn't make you my equal. It never did. We humans can't slur off the experiences of the past so easily. It would take thousands of years of association with things like you before we even began to regard you as anything other than a plant, a thing that we used in the past and might use again.'

'Still cabbage soup,' said the Encyclopedia.

'Still cabbage soup,' Mackenzie told him.

The music stopped. Stopped dead still, in the middle of a note.

'See,' said Mackenzie, 'even the music fails you.'

Silence rolled at them in engulfing waves and through the stillness came another sound, the *clop*, *clop* of heavy, plodding feet.

'Nellie!' yelled Mackenzie.

A bulky shadow loomed in the darkness.

'Yeah, chief, it's me,' said Nellie. 'I brung you something.'

She dumped Wade across the doorway.

Wade rolled over and groaned. There were skittering, flapping sounds as two fluttering shapes detached themselves from Wade's shoulders.

'Nellie,' said Mackenzie, harshly, 'there was no need to beat him up. You should have brought him back just as he was and let me take care of him.'

67

'Gee, boss,' protested Nellie. 'I didn't beat him up. He was like that when I found him.'

Nicodemus was clawing his way to Mackenzie's shoulder, while Smith's life blanket scuttled for the corner where his master lay.

'It was us, boss,' piped Nicodemus. 'We laid him out.'

'You laid him out?'

'Sure, there was two of us and only one of him. We fed him poison.'

Nicodemus settled into place on Mackenzie's shoulders.

'I didn't like him,' he declared. 'He wasn't nothing like you, boss. I didn't want to change like him. I wanted to stay like you.'

'This poison?' asked Mackenzie. 'Nothing fatal, I hope.'

'Sure not, pal,' Nicodemus told him. 'We only made him sick. He didn't know what was happening until it was too late to do anything about it. We bargained with him, we did. We told him we'd quit feeding it to him if he took us back. He was on his way here, too, but he'd never have made it if it hadn't been for Nellie.'

'Chief,' pleaded Nellie, 'when he gets so he knows what it's all about, won't you let me have him for about five minutes?'

'No,' said Mackenzie.

'He strung me up,' wailed Nellie. 'He hid in the cliff and lassoed me and left me hanging there. It took me hours to get loose. Honest, I wouldn't hurt him much. I'd just kick him around a little, gentlelike.'

From the cliff top came the rustling of grass as if hundreds of little feet were advancing upon them.

'We got visitors,' said Nicodemus.

The visitors, Mackenzie saw, were the conductors, dozens of little gnomelike figures that moved up and squatted on their haunches, faintly luminous eyes blinking at them.

One of them shambled forward. As he came closer, Mackenzie saw that it was Alder.

'Well?' Mackenzie demanded.

'We came to tell you the deal is off,' Alder squeaked. 'Delbert came and told us.'

'Told you what?'

'About what you do to trees.'

'Oh, that.'

68

'Yes, that.'

'But you made the deal,' Mackenzie told him. 'You can't back out now. Why, Earth is waiting breathless – '

'Don't try to kid me,' snapped Alder. 'You don't want us any more than we want you. It was a dirty trick to start with, but it wasn't any of our doing. The Encyclopedia talked us into it. He told us we had a duty. A duty to our race. To act as missionaries to the inferior races of the Galaxy.

'We didn't take to it at first. Music, you see, is our life. We have been creating music for so long that our origin is lost in the dim antiquity of a planet that long ago has passed its zenith of existence. We will be creating music in that far day when the planet falls apart beneath our feet. You live by a code of accomplishment by action. We live by a code of accomplishment by music. Kadmar's Red Sun symphony was a greater triumph for us than the discovery of a new planetary system is for you. It pleased us when you liked our music. It will please us if you still like our music, even after what has happened. But we will not allow you to take any of us to Earth.'

'The monopoly on the music still stands?' asked Mackenzie.

'It still stands. Come whenever you want to and record my symphony. When there are others we will let you know.'

'And the propaganda in the music?'

'From now on,' Alder promised, 'the propaganda is out. If, from now on, our music changes you, it will change you through its own power. It may do that, but we will not try to shape your lives.'

'How can we depend on that?'

'Certainly,' said Alder. 'There are certain tests you could devise. Not that they will be necessary.'

'We'll devise the tests,' declared Mackenzie. 'Sorry, but we can't trust you.'

'I'm sorry that you can't,' said Alder, and he sounded as if he were.

'I was going to burn you,' Mackenzie said, snapping his words off brutally. 'Destroy you. Wipe you out. There was nothing you could have done about it. Nothing you could have done to stop me.'

'You're still barbarians,' Alder told him. 'you have conquered the distances between the stars, you have built a great

69

civilization, but your methods are still ruthless and degenerate.'

'The Encyclopedia calls it a formula of force,' Mackenzie said. 'No matter what you call it, it still works. It's the thing that took us up. I warn you. If you ever again try to trick the human race, there will be hell to pay. A human being will destroy anything to save himself. Remember that – we destroy anything that threatens us.'

Something swished out of the tractor door and Mackenzie whirled about.

'It's the Encyclopedia!' he yelled. 'He's trying to get away! Nellie!'

There was a thrashing rustle. 'Got him, boss,' said Nellie.

The robot came out of the darkness, dragging the Encyclopedia along by his leafy topknot.

Mackenzie turned back to the composers, but the composers were gone. The grass rustled eerily towards the cliff edge as dozens of tiny feet scurried through it.

'What now?' asked Nellie. 'Do we burn the trees?'

Mackenzie shook his head. 'No, Nellie. We won't burn them.'

'We got them scared,' said Nellie. 'Scared pink with purple spots.'

'Perhaps we have,' said Mackenzie. 'Let's hope so, at least. But it isn't only that they're scared. They probably loathe us and that is better yet. Like we'd loathe some form of life that bred and reared men for food – that thought of Man as nothing else than food. All the time they've thought of themselves as the greatest intellectual force in the universe. We've given them a jolt. We've scared them and hurt their pride and shook their confidence. They've run up against something that is more than a match for them. Maybe they'll think twice again before they try any more shenanigans.'

Down in the Bowl the music began again.

Mackenzie went in to look at Smith. The man was sleeping peacefully, his blanket wrapped around him. Wade sat in a corner, head held in his hands.

Outside, a rocket murmured and Nellie yelled. Mackenzie spun on his heel and dashed through the door. A ship was swinging over the Bowl, lighting up the area with floods.

Swiftly it swooped down, came to ground a hundred yards away.

Harper, right arm in a sling, tumbled out and raced towards them.

'You didn't burn them!' he was yelling. 'You didn't burn them!'

Mckenzie shook his head.

Harper pounded him on the back with his good hand. 'Knew you wouldn't. Knew you wouldn't all the time. Just kidding the chief, eh? Having a little fun.'

'Not exactly fun.'

'About them trees,' said Harper. 'We can't take them back to Earth, after all.'

'I told you that,' Mackenzie said.

'Earth just called me, half an hour ago,' said Harper. 'Seems there's a law, passed centuries ago. Against bringing alien plants to Earth. Some lunkhead once brought a bunch of stuff from Mars that just about ruined Earth, so they passed the law. Been there all the time, forgotten.'

Mackenzie nodded. 'Someone dug it up.'

'That's right,' said Harper. 'And slapped an injunction on Galactic. We can't touch those trees.'

'You wouldn't have anyhow,' said Mackenzie. 'They wouldn't go.'

'But you made the deal! They were anxious to go – '

'That,' Mackenzie told him, 'was before they found out we used plants for food – and other things.'

'But . . . but – '

'To them' said Mackenzie, 'we're just a gang of ogres. Something they'll scare the little plants with. Tell them if they don't be quiet the humans will get 'em.'

Nellie came around the corner of the tractor, still hauling the Encyclopedia by his topknot.

'Hey,' yelled Harper, 'what goes on here?'

'We'll have to build a concentration camp,' said Mackenzie. 'Big high fence.' He motioned with his thumb towards the Encyclopedia.

Harper stared. 'But he hasn't done anything!'

'Nothing but try to take over the human race,' Mackenzie said.

Harper sighed. 'That makes two fences we got to build. That rifle tree back at the post is shooting up the place.'

Mackenzie grinned. 'Maybe the one fence will do for the both of them.'

JUNKYARD

I

They had solved the mystery – with a guess, a very erudite and educated guess – but they didn't know a thing, not a single thing, for certain. That wasn't the way a planetary survey team usually did a job. Usually they nailed it down and wrung a lot of information out of it and could parade an impressive roll of facts. But here there was no actual, concrete fact beyond the one that would have been obvious to a twelve-year-old child.

Commander Ira Warren was worried about it. He said as much to Bat Ears Brady, ship's cook and slightly disreputable pal of his younger days. The two of them had been planet-checking together for more than thirty years. While they stood at opposite poles on the table of organization, they were able to say to one another things they could not have said to any other man aboard the survey ship or have allowed another man to say to them.

'Bat Ears,' said Warren, 'I'm just a little worried.'

'You're always worried,' Bat Ears retorted. 'That's part of the job you have.'

'This junkyard business . . .'

'You wanted to get ahead,' said Bat Ears, 'and I told you what would happen. I warned you you'd get yourself weighted down with worry and authority and pomp – pomp – '

'Pomposity?'

'That's the word,' said Bat Ears. 'That's the word, exactly.'

'I'm not pompous,' Warren contradicted.

'No, you're worried about this junkyard business. I got a bottle stowed away. How about a little drink?'

Warren waved away the thought. 'Someday I'll bust you wide open. Where you hide the stuff, I don't know, but every trip we make . . .'

'Now, Ira! Don't go losing your lousy temper.'

'Every trip we make, you carry enough dead weight of liquor to keep you annoyingly aglow for the entire cruise.'

'It's baggage,' Bat Ears insisted. 'A man is allowed some baggage weight. I don't have hardly nothing else. I just bring along my drinking.'

'Someday,' said Warren savagely, 'it's going to get you booted off the ship about five light-years from nowhere.'

The threat was an old one. It failed to dismay Bat Ears.

'This worrying you're doing,' Bat Ears said, 'ain't doing you no good.'

'But the survey team didn't do the job,' objected Warren. 'Don't you see what this means? For the first time in more than a hundred years of survey, we've found what appears to be evidence that some other race than Man has achieved space flight. And we don't know a thing about it. We should know. With all that junk out there, we ought to be able by this time to write a book about it.'

Bat Ears spat in contempt. 'You mean them scientists of ours.'

The way he said 'scientist' made it a dirty word.

'They're good,' said Warren. 'The very best there is.'

'Remember the old days, Ira?' asked Bat Ears. 'When you was second looey and you used to come down and we'd have a drink together and . . .'

'That has nothing to do with it.'

'We had real men in them days. We'd get ourselves a club and go hunt us up some natives and beat a little sense into them and we'd get more facts in half a day than these scientists, with all their piddling around, will get in a month of Sundays.'

'This is slightly different,' Warren said. 'There are no natives here.'

74

There wasn't, as a matter of fact, much of anything on this particular planet. It was strictly a low-grade affair and it wouldn't amount to much for another billion years. The survey, understandably, wasn't too interested in planets that wouldn't amount to much for another billion years.

Its surface was mostly rock outcroppings and tumbled boulder fields. In the last half million years or so, primal plants had gotten started and were doing well. Mosses and lichens crept into the crevices and crawled across the rocks, but aside from that there seemed to be no life. Although, strictly speaking, you couldn't be positive, for no one had been interested in the planet. They hadn't looked it over and they hadn't searched for life; everyone had been too interested in the junkyard.

They had never intended to land, but had circled the planet, making routine checks and entering routine data in the survey record.

Then someone at a telescope had seen the junkyard and they'd gone down to investigate and had been forthrightly pitchforked into a maddening puzzle.

They had called it the junkyard and that was what it was. Strewn about were what probably were engine parts, although no one was quite sure. Pollard, the mech engineer, had driven himself to the verge of frenzy trying to figure out how to put some of the parts together. He finally got three of them assembled, somehow, and they didn't mean a thing, so he tried to take them apart again to figure out how he'd done it. He couldn't get them apart. It was about that time that Pollard practically blew his top.

The engine parts, if that was what they were, were scattered all over the place, as if someone or something had tossed them away, not caring where they fell. But off to one side was a pile of other stuff, all neatly stacked, and it was apparent even to the casual glance that this stuff must be a pile of supplies.

There was what more than likely was food, though it was a rather strange kind of food (if that was what it was), and strangely fabricated bottles of plastic that held a poison liquid, and other stuff that was fabric and might have been clothing, although it gave one the shudders trying to figure out what sort of creatures would have worn that kind of clothing and

75

bundles of metallic bars, held together in the bundles by some kind of gravitational attraction instead of the wires that a human would have used to tie them in bundles. And a number of other objects for which there were no names.

'They should have found the answer,' Warren said. 'They've cracked tougher nuts than this. In the month we've been here, they should have had that engine running.'

'If it is an engine,' Bat Ears pointed out.

'What else could it be?'

'You're getting so that you sound like them. Run into something that you can't explain and think up the best guess possible and when someone questions you, you ask what else it could be. And that ain't proof, Ira.'

'You're right, Bat Ears,' Warren admitted. 'It certainly isn't proof and that's what worries me. We have no doubt the junk out there is a spaceship engine, but we have no proof of it.'

'Nobody's going to land a ship,' said Bat Ears testily, 'and rip out the engine and just throw it away. If they'd done that, the ship would still be here.'

'But if that's not the answer,' demanded Warren, 'what is all that stuff out there?'

'I wouldn't know. I'm not even curious. I ain't the one that's worrying.'

He got up from the chair and moved towards the door.

'I still got that bottle, Ira.'

'No, thanks,' Warren said.

He sat and listened to Bat Ear's feet going down the stairs.

II

Kenneth Spencer, the alien psychologist, came into the cabin and sat down in the chair across the desk from Warren.

'We're finally through,' he said.

'You aren't through,' challenged Warren. 'You haven't even started.'

'We've done all we can.'

Warren grunted at him.

'We've run all sorts of tests,' said Spencer. 'We've got a book full of analyses. We have a complete photographic record and everything is down on paper in diagrams and notes and – '

76

'Then tell me: What is that junk out there?'

'It's a spaceship engine.'

'If it's an engine,' Warren said, 'let's put it together. Let's find out how it runs. Let's figure out the kind of intelligence most likely to have built it.'

'We tried,' replied Spencer. 'All of us tried. Some of us didn't have applicable knowledge or training, but even so we worked; we helped the ones who had training.'

'I know how hard you worked.'

And they had worked hard, only snatching stolen hours to sleep, eating on the run.

'We are dealing with alien mechanics,' Spencer said.

'We've dealt with other alien concepts,' Warren reminded him. 'Alien economics and alien religions and alien psychology . . .'

'But this is different.'

'Not so different. Take Pollard, now. He is the key man in this situation. Wouldn't you have said that Pollard should have cracked it?'

'If it can be cracked, Pollard is your man. He has everything – the theory, the experience, the imagination.'

'You think we should leave?' asked Warren. 'That's what you came in to tell me? You think there is no further use of staying here?'

'That's about it,' Spencer admitted.

'All right,' Warren told him. 'If you say so, I'll take your word for it. We'll blast off right after supper. I'll tell Bat Ears to fix us up a spread. A sort of achievement dinner.'

'Don't rub it in so hard,' protested Spencer. 'We're not proud of what we've done.'

Warren heaved himself out of the chair.

'I'll go down and tell Mac to get the engines ready. On the way down, I'll stop in on Bat Ears and tell him.'

Spencer said, 'I'm worried, Warren.'

'So am I. What is worrying you?'

'Who are these things, these other people, who had the other spaceship? They're the first, you know, the first evidence we've ever run across of another race that had discovered space flight. And what happened to them here?'

'Scared?'

'Yes. Aren't you?'

'Not yet,' said Warren. 'I probably will be when I have the time to think it over.'

He went down the stairs to talk to Mac about the engines.

III

He found Mac sitting in his cubby hole, smoking his blackened pipe and reading his thumb-marked Bible.

'Good news,' Warren said to him.

Mac laid down the book and took off his glasses.

'There's but one thing you could tell me that would be good news,' he said.

'This is it. Get the engines ready. We'll be blasting off.'

'When, sir? Not that it can be too soon.'

'In a couple of hours or so,' said Warren. 'We'll eat and get settled in. I'll give you the word.'

The engineer folded the spectacles and slid them in his pocket. He tapped the pipe out in his hand and tossed away the ashes and put the dead pipe back between his teeth.

'I've never liked this place,' he said.

'You never like any place.'

'I don't like them towers.'

'You're crazy, Mac. There aren't any towers.'

'The boys and me went walking,' said the engineer. 'We found a bunch of towers.'

'Rock formations, probably.'

'Towers,' insisted the engineer doggedly.

'If you found some towers,' Warren demanded, 'why didn't you report them?'

'And have them science beagles go baying after them and have to stay another month?'

'It doesn't matter,' Warren said. 'They probably aren't towers. Who would mess around building towers on this backwash of a planet?'

'They were scary,' Mac told him. 'They had that black look about them. And the smell of death.'

'It's the Celt in you. The big, superstitious Celt you are, rocketing through space from world to world – and still believing in banshees and spooks. The medieval mind in the age of science.'

78

Mac said, 'They fair give a man the shivers.'

They stood facing one another for a long moment. Then Warren put out a hand and tapped the other gently on the shoulder.

'I won't say a word about them,' he said. 'Now get those engines rolling.'

IV

Warren sat in silence at the table's head, listening to the others talk.

'It was a jury-rigged job,' said Clyne, the physicist. 'They tore out a lot of stuff and rebuilt the engine for some reason or other and there was a lot of the stuff they tore out that they didn't use again. For some reason, they had to rebuild the engine and they rebuilt it simpler than it was before. Went back to basic principles and cut out the fancy stuff – automatics and other gadgets like that – but the one they rebuilt must have been larger and more unwieldy, less compact, than the one that they ripped down. That would explain why they left some of their supplies behind.'

'But,' asked Dyer, the chemist, 'what did they jury-rig it with? Where did they get the material?'

Briggs, the metallurgist, said, 'This place crawls with ore. If it wasn't so far out, it would be a gold mine.'

'We saw no signs of mining,' Dyer objected. 'No signs of mining or smelting and refining or of fabrication.'

'We didn't go exploring,' Clyne pointed out. 'They might have done some mining a few miles away from here and we'd have never known it.'

Spencer said, 'That's the trouble with us on this whole project. We've adopted suppositions and let them stand as fact. If they had to do some fabrication, it might be important to know a little more about it.'

'What difference does it make?' asked Clyne. 'We know the basic facts – a spaceship landed here in trouble, they finally repaired their engines, and they took off once again.'

Old Doc Spears, down at the table's end, slammed his fork on his plate.

'You don't even know,' he said, 'that it was a spaceship. I've listened to you caterwauling about this thing for weeks. I've never seen so damn much motion and so few results in all my born days.'

All of them looked a little surprised. Old Doc was normally a mild man and he usually paid little attention to what was going on, bumbling around on his regular rounds to treat a smashed thumb or sore throat or some other minor ailment. All of them had wondered, with a slight sickish feeling, how Old Doc might perform if he faced a real emergency, like major surgery, say. They didn't have much faith in him, but they liked him well enough. Probably they liked him mostly because he didn't mix into their affairs.

And here he was, mixing right into them truculently.

Lang, the communications man, said, 'We found the scratches, Doc. You remember that. Scratches on the rock. The kind of scratches that a spaceship could have made in landing.'

'*Could* have made,' said Doc derisively.

'*Must* have made!'

Old Doc snorted and went on with his eating, holding his head down over the plate, napkin tucked beneath his chin, shovelling in the food with fork and knife impartially. Doc was noted as a messy eater.

'I have a feeling,' Spencer said, 'that we may be off the beaten track in thinking of this as a simple repair job. From the amount of parts that are down there in the junkyard, I'd say that they found it necessary to do a redesigning job, to start from the beginning and build an entirely new engine to get them out of here. I have a feeling that those engine parts out there represent the whole engine, that if we knew how, we could put those parts together and we'd have an engine.'

'I tried it,' Pollard answered.

'I can't quite buy the idea that it was a complete redesigning job,' Clyne stated. 'That would mean a new approach and some new ideas that would rule out the earlier design and all the parts that had been built into the original engine as it stood. The theory would explain why there are so many parts strewn around, but it's just not possible. You don't redesign an engine when you're stranded on a barren planet. You stick to what you know.'

80

Dyer said, 'Accepting an idea like redesigning sends you back again to the problem of materials.'

'And tools,' added Lang. 'Where would they get the tools?'

'They'd probably have a machine shop right on board the ship,' said Spencer.

'For minor repairs,' Lang corrected. 'Not the kind of equipment you would need to build a complete new engine.'

'What worries me,' said Pollard, 'is our absolute inability to understand any of it. I tried to fit those parts together, tried to figure out the relationship of the various parts – and there must be some sort of relationship, because unrelated parts would make no sense at all. Finally I was able to fit three of them together and that's as far as I could get. When I got them together, they didn't spell a thing. They simply weren't going anywhere. Even with three of them together, you were no better off, no further along in understanding, than before you'd put them together. And when I tried to get them apart, I couldn't do that, either. You'd think, once a man had got a thing together, he could take it apart again, wouldn't you?'

'It was an alien ship,' Spencer offered, 'built by alien people, run by alien engines.'

'Even so,' said Pollard, 'there should have been some basic idea that we could recognize. In some way or other, their engine should have operated along at least one principle that would be basic with human mechanics. An engine is a piece of mechanism that takes raw power and controls it and directs it into useful energy. That would be its purpose, no matter what race built it.'

'The metal,' said Briggs, 'is an alien alloy, totally unlike anything we have ever run across. You can identify the components, all right, but the formula, when you get it down, reads like a metallic nightmare. It shouldn't work. By Earth standards, it *wouldn't* work. There's some secret in the combination that I can't even guess at.'

Old Doc said, from the table's end, 'You're to be congratulated, Mr Briggs, upon your fine sense of restraint.'

'Cut it out, Doc,' Warren ordered sharply, speaking for the first time.

'All right,' said Doc. 'If that's the way you want it, Ira, I will cut it out.'

V

Standing outside the ship, Warren looked across the planet. Evening was fading into night and the junkyard was no more than a grotesque blotch of deeper shadow on the hillside.

Once, not long ago, another ship had rested here, just a little way from where they rested now. Another ship – another race.

And something had happened to that ship, something that his survey party had tried to ferret out and had failed to discover.

It had not been a simple repair job; he was sure of that. No matter what any of them might say, it had been considerably more than routine repair.

There had been some sort of emergency, a situation with a strange urgency about it. They had left in such a hurry that they had abandoned some of their supplies. No commander of any spaceship, be he human or alien, would leave supplies behind except when life or death was involved in his escape.

There was what appeared to be food in the stack of supplies – at least, Dyer had said that it was food, although it didn't look edible. And there were the plastic-like bottles filled with a poison that might be, as like as not, the equivalent of an alien whisky. And no man, Warren said, leaves food and whisky behind except in the direst emergency.

He walked slowly down the trail they'd beaten between the ship's lock and the junkyard and it struck him that he walked in a silence that was as deep as the awful stillness of far space. There was nothing here to make any sound at all. There was no life except the mosses and the lichens and the other primal plants that crept among the rocks. In time there would be other life, for the planet had the air and water and the basic ingredients for soil and here, in another billion years or so, there might arise a life economy as complex as that of Earth.

But a billion years, he thought, is a long, long time.

He reached the junkyard and walked its familiar ground, dodging the larger pieces of machinery that lay all about,

82

stumbling on one or two of the smaller pieces that lay unseen in the darkness.

The second time he stumbled, he stooped and picked up the thing he had stumbled on and it was, he knew, one of the tools that the alien race had left behind them when they fled. He could picture them, dropping their tools and fleeing, but the picture was not clear. He could not decide what these aliens might have looked like or what they might have fled from.

He tossed the tool up and down, catching it in his hand. It was light and handy and undoubtedly there was some use for it, but he did not know the use nor did any of the others up there in the ship. Hand or tentacle, claw or paw — what appendage had it been that had grasped the tool? What mind lay behind the hand or tentacle, claw or paw that had grasped and used it?

He stood and threw back his head and looked at the stars that shone above the planet and they were not the familiar stars he had known when he was a child.

Far out, he thought, far out. The farthest out that Man had ever been.

A sound jerked him around, the sound of running feet coming down the trail.

'Warren!' cried a voice. 'Warren! Where are you?'

There was fright in that voice, the frantic note of panic that one hears in the screaming of a terrified child.

'Warren!'

'Here!' shouted Warren. 'Over here. I'm coming.'

He swung around and hurried to meet the man who was running in the dark.

The runner would have charged on past him if he had not put out a hand and gripped him by the shoulder and pulled him to a halt.

'Warren! Is that you?'

'What's the matter, Mac?' asked Warren.

'I can't . . . I can't . . . I . . .'

'What's wrong? Speak up! You can't what, Mac?'

He felt the engineer's fumbling hands reaching out for him, grasping at his coat lapels, hanging onto him as if the engineer were a drowning man.

'Come on, come on,' Warren urged with the impatience of alarm.

'I can't start the engines, sir,' said Mac.

'Can't start the . . .'

'I can't start them, sir, And neither can the others. None of us can start them, sir.'

'The engines!' said Warren, terror rising swiftly. 'What's the matter with the engines?'

'There's nothing the matter with the engines. It's us, sir. We can't start them.'

'Talk sense, man. Why can't you?'

'We can't remember how. We've forgotten how to start the engines!'

VI

Warren switched on the light above the desk and straightened, seeking out the book among the others on the shelf.

'It's right here, Mac,' he said. 'I knew I had it here.'

He found it and took it down and opened it beneath the light. He leafed the pages rapidly. Behind him he could hear the tense, almost terrified breathing of the engineer.

'It's all right, Mac. It's all here in the book.'

He leafed too far ahead and had to back up a page or two and reached the place and spread the book wide beneath the lamp.

'Now,' he said, 'we'll get those engines started. It tells right here . . .'

He tried to read and couldn't.

He could understand the words all right and the symbols, but the sum of the words he read made little sense and the symbols none at all.

He felt the sweat breaking out on him, running down his forehead and gathering in his eyebrows, breaking out of his armpits and trickling down his ribs.

'What's the matter, Chief?' asked Mac. 'What's the matter now?'

Warren felt his body wanting to shake, straining every nerve to tremble, but it wouldn't move. He was frozen stiff.

'This is the engine manual,' he said, his voice cold and low.

'It tells all about the engines – how they operate, how to locate trouble, how to fix them.'

'Then we're all right,' breathed Mac, enormously relieved.

Warren closed the book.

'No, we aren't, Mac. I've forgotten all the symbols and most of the terminology.'

'You what!'

'I can't read the book,' said Warren.

VII

'It just isn't possible,' argued Spencer.

'It's not only possible,' Warren told him. 'It happened. Is there any one of you who can read that book?'

They didn't answer him.

'If there's anyone who can,' invited Warren. 'Step up and show us how.'

Clyne said quietly, 'There's none of us can read it.'

'And yet,' declared Warren, 'an hour ago any one of you – any single one of you – probably would have bet his life that he not only could start the engines if he had to, but could take the manual if he couldn't and figure how to do it.'

'You're right,' Clyne agreed. 'We would have bet our lives. An hour ago we would have. It would have been a safe, sure bet.'

'That's what you think,' said Warren. 'How do you know how long it's been since you couldn't read the manual?'

'We don't, of course,' Clyne was forced to admit.

'There's something more. You didn't find the answer to the junkyard. You *guessed* an answer, but you didn't *find* one. And you should have. You know damn well you should have.'

Clyne rose to his feet. 'Now see here, Warren . . .'

'Sit down, John,' said Spencer. 'Warren's got us dead to rights. We didn't find an answer and we know we didn't. We took a guess and substituted it for the answer that we didn't find. And Warren's right about something else – we should have found the answer.'

Under any other circumstances, Warren thought, they might have hated him for those blunt truths, but now they

85

didn't. They just sat there and he could see the realization seeping into them.

Dyer finally said, 'You think we failed out there because we forgot – just like Mac forgot.'

'You lost some of your skills,' replied Warren, 'some of your skills and knowledge. You worked as hard as ever. You went through the motions. You didn't have the skill or knowledge any more, that's all.'

'And now?' asked Lang.

'I don't know.'

'This is what happened to that other ship,' said Briggs emphatically.

'Maybe,' Warren said with less conviction.

'But they got away,' Clyne pointed out.

'So will we,' promised Warren. 'Somehow.'

VIII

The crew of that other, alien ship had evidently forgotten, too. But somehow or other they had blasted off – somehow or other they had remembered, or forced themselves to remember. But if it had been the simple matter of remembering, why had they rebuilt the engines? They could have used their own.

Warren lay in his bunk, staring into the blackness, knowing that a scant two feet above his head there was a plate of steel, but he couldn't see the steel. And he knew there was a way to start the engines, a simple way once you knew it or remembered it, but he couldn't see that, either.

Man experienced incidents, gathered knowledge, knew emotion – and then, in the course of time, forgot the incident and knowledge and emotion. Life was a long series of forgettings. Memories were wiped out and old knowledge dulled and skill was lost, but it took time to wipe it out or dull it or lose it. You couldn't know a thing one day and forget it on the next.

But here on this barren world, in some impossible way, the forgetting had been speeded up. On Earth it took years to forget an incident or to lose a skill. Here it happened overnight.

He tried to sleep and couldn't. He finally got up and dressed and went down the stairs, out the lock into the alien night.

86

A low voice asked, 'That you, Ira?'

'It's me, Bat Ears. I couldn't sleep. I'm worried.'

'You're always worried,' said Bat Ears. 'It's an occu ...
occu ...'

'Occupational?'

'That's it,' said Bat Ears, hiccoughing just a little. 'That's the
word I wanted. Worry is an occupational disease with you.'

'We're in a jam, Bat Ears.'

'There's been planets,' Bat Ears said, 'I wouldn't have
minded so much being marooned on, but this ain't one of
them. This here place is the tail end of creation.'

They stood together in the darkness with the sweep of alien
stars above them and the silent planet stretching off to a vague
horizon.

'There's something here,' Bat Ears went on. 'You can smell
it in the air. Them fancy-pants in there said there wasn't
nothing here because they couldn't see nothing and the books
they'd read said nothing much could live on a planet that was
just rocks and moss. But, me, I've seen planets. Me, I was
planet-checking when most of them was in diapers and my
nose can tell me more about a planet than their brains all
lumped together, which, incidentally, ain't a bad idea.'

'I think you're right,' confessed Warren. 'I can feel it myself.
I couldn't before. Maybe it's just because we're scared that we
can feel it now.'

'I felt it before I was scared.'

'We should have looked around. That's where we made our
mistake. But there was so much work to do in the junkyard
that we never thought of it.'

'Mac took a little jaunt,' said Bat Ears. 'Says he found some
towers.'

'He told me about them, too.'

'Mac was just a little green around the gills when he was
telling me.'

'He told me he didn't like them.'

'If there was any place to run to, Mac would be running
right now.'

'In the morning,' Warren said, 'we'll go and see those
towers.'

IX

They were towers, all right, and there were eight of them in line, like watch-towers that at one time had stretched across the planet, but something had happened and all the others had been levelled except the eight that were standing there.

They were built of undressed native rock, crudely piled, without mortar and with little wedges and slabs of stone used in the interstices to make the stones set solid. They were the kind of towers that might have been built by a savage race and they had an ancient look about them. They were about six feet at the base and tapered slightly towards the top and each of them was capped by a huge flat stone with an enormous boulder placed upon the slab to hold it in its place.

Warren said to Ellis, 'This is your department. Take over.'

The little archaeologist didn't answer. He walked around the nearest tower and went up close to it and examined it. He put out his hands and acted as if he meant to shake the tower, but it didn't shake.

'Solid,' he said. 'Well built and old.'

'Type F culture, I would say,' guessed Spencer.

'Maybe less than that. No attempt at an aesthetic effect – pure utility. But good craftsmanship.'

Clyne said, 'Its purpose is the thing. What were the towers built for?'

'Storage space,' said Spencer.

'A marker,' Lang contradicted. 'A claim marker, a cache marker . . .'

'We can find the purpose,' Warren said. 'That is something we needn't argue nor speculate about. All we have to do is knock off the boulder and lift the cap and have a look inside.'

He strode up to the tower and started climbing it.

It was an easy thing to climb, for there were niches in the stones and hand and toe holds were not too hard to find.

He reached the top.

'Look out below,' he yelled, and heaved at the boulder.

It rolled and then slowly settled back. He braced himself and heaved again and this time it toppled. It went plunging off the tower, smashed to the ground, went rumbling down the slope, gathering speed, hitting other boulders in its path, zigzagging with the deflection of its course, thrown high into the air by the boulders that it hit.

Warren said, 'Throw a rope up to me. I'll fasten it to the capstone and then we can haul it off.'

'We haven't got a rope,' said Clyne.

'Someone run back to the ship and get one. I'll wait here till he returns.'

Briggs started back towards the ship.

Warren straightened up. From the tower he had a fine view of the country and he swivelled slowly, examining it.

Somewhere nearby, he thought, the men – well, not men, but the things that built these towers – must have had their dwelling. Within a mile or so there had been at one time a habitation. For the towers would have taken time in building and that meant that the ones who built them must have had at least a semi-permanent location.

But there was nothing to see – nothing but tumbled boulder fields and great outcroppings and the blankets of primal plants that ran across their surfaces.

What did they live on? Why were they here? What would have attracted them? What would have held them here?

He halted in his pivoting, scarcely believing what he saw. Carefully he traced the form of it, making sure that the light on some boulder field was not befuddling his vision.

It couldn't be, he told himself. It couldn't happen three times. He must be wrong.

He sucked in his breath and held it and waited for the illusion to go away.

It didn't go away. The thing was there.

'Spencer,' he called. 'Spencer, please come up here.'

He continued watching it. Below him, he heard Spencer scrabbling up the tower. He reached down a hand and helped him.

'Look,' Warren said, pointing. 'What is that out there?'

'A ship!' cried Spencer. 'There's another ship out there!'

The spaceship was old, incredibly old. It was red with rust; you could put your hand against its metal hide and sweep your hand across it and the flakes of rust would rain down upon the rock and your hand would come away painted with rust.

The airlock once had been closed, but someone or something had battered a hole straight through it without opening it, for the rim was still in place against the hull and the jagged hole ran to the ship's interior. For yards around the lock, the ground was red with violently scattered rust.

They clambered through the hole. Inside, the ship was bright and shining, without a trace of rust, although there was a coating of dust over everything. Through the dust upon the floor was a beaten track and many isolated footprints where the owners of the prints had stepped out of the path. They were alien tracks, with a heavy heel and three great toes, for all the world like the tracks of a mighty bird or some long-dead dinosaur.

The trail led through the ship back to the engine room and there the empty platform stood, with the engines gone.

'That's how they got away,' said Warren, 'the ones who junked their engines. They took the engines off this ship and put them in their ship and then they took off.'

'But they wouldn't know – ' argued Clyne.

'They evidently did,' Warren interrupted bluntly.

Spencer said, 'They must have been the ones. This ship has been here for a long time – the rust will tell you that. And it was closed, hermetically sealed, because there's no rust inside. That hole was punched through the lock fairly recently and the engines taken.'

'That means, then,' said Lang, 'that they did junk their engines. They ripped them out entire and heaved them in the junkpile. They tore them out and replaced them with the engines from this ship.'

'But why?' asked Clyne. 'Why did they have to do it?'

'Because,' said Spencer, 'they didn't know how to operate their own engines.'

'But if they didn't know how to operate their engines, how could they run this one?'

'He's got you there,' said Dyer. 'That's one that you can't answer.'

'No, I can't,' shrugged Warren. 'But I wish I could, because then we'd have the answer ourselves.'

'How long ago,' asked Spencer, 'would you say this ship landed here? How long would it take for a spaceship hull to rust?'

'It's hard to tell,' Clyne answered. 'It would depend on the kind of metal they used. But you can bet on this – any spaceship hull, no matter who might have built it, would be the toughest metal the race could fabricate.'

'A thousand years?' Warren suggested.

'I don't know,' said Clyne. 'Maybe a thousand years. Maybe more than that. You see this dust. That's what's left of whatever organic material there was in the ship. If the beings that landed here remained within the ship, they still are here in the form of dust.'

Warren tried to think, tried to sort out the chronology of the whole thing.

A thousand years ago, or thousands of years ago, a spaceship had landed here and had not got away.

Then another spaceship landed, a thousand or thousands of years later, and it, too, was unable to get away. But it finally escaped when the crew robbed the first ship of its engines and substituted them for the ones that had brought it here.

Then years, or months, or days later, the Earth survey ship had landed here, and it, too, couldn't get away – because the men who ran it couldn't remember how to operate its engines.

He swung around and strode from the engine room, leaving the others there, following the path in the dust back to the shattered lock.

And just inside the port, sitting on the floor, making squiggles in the dust with an awkward finger, sat Briggs, who had gone back to the ship to get a length of rope.

'Briggs,' said Warren sharply. 'Briggs, what are you doing here?'

Briggs looked up with vacant, laughing eyes.

'Go away,' he said.

Then he went back to making squiggles in the dust.

X

Doc Spears said, 'Briggs reverted to childhood. His mind is wiped as clean as a one-year-old's. He can talk, which is about the only difference between a child and him. But his vocabulary is limited and what he says makes very little sense.'

'He can be taught again?' asked Warren.

'I don't know.'

'Spencer had a look at him. What does Spencer say?'

'Spencer said a lot,' Doc told him. 'It adds up, substantially, to practically total loss of memory.'

'What can we do?'

'Watch him. See he doesn't get hurt. After a while we might try re-education. He may even pick up some things by himself. Something happened to him. Whether whatever it was that took his memory away also injured his brain is something I can't say for sure. It doesn't appear injured, but without a lot of diagnostic equipment we don't have, you can't be positive.'

'There's no sign of injury?'

'There's not a single mark anywhere,' said Doc. 'He isn't hurt. That is, not physically. It's only his mind that's been injured. Maybe not his mind, either – just his memory gone.'

'Amnesia?'

'Not amnesia. When you have that, you're confused. You are haunted by the thought that you have forgotten something. You're all tangled up. Briggs isn't confused or tangled. He seems to be happy enough.'

'You'll take care of him, Doc? Kind of keep an eye on him.'

Doc snorted and got up and left.

Warren called after him. 'If you see Bat Ears down there, tell him to come up.'

Doc clumped down the stairs.

Warren sat and stared at the blank wall opposite him.

First Mac and his crew had forgotten how to run the engines. That was the first sign of what was happening – the first recognizable sign – for it had been going on long before Mac found he'd forgotten all his engine lore.

The crew of investigators had lost some of their skills and their knowledge almost from the first. How else could one account for the terrible mess they'd made of the junkyard business? Under ordinary circumstances, they would have wrung some substantial information from the engine parts and the neatly stacked supplies. They had gotten information of a sort, of course, but it added up to nothing. Under ordinary circumstances, it should have added up to an extraordinary something.

He heard feet coming up the stairs, but the tread was too crisp for Bat Ears.

It was Spencer.

Spencer flopped into one of the chairs. He sat there opening and closing his hands, looking down at them with helpless anger.

'Well?' asked Warren. 'Anything to report?'

'Briggs got into that first tower,' said Spencer. 'Apparently he came back with the rope and found us gone, so he climbed up and threw a hitch around the capstone, then climbed down again and pulled it off. The capstone is lying on the ground, at the foot of the tower, with the rope still hitched around it.'

Warren nodded. 'He could have done that. The capstone wasn't too heavy. One man could have pulled it off.'

'There's something in that tower.'

'You took a look?'

'After what happened to Briggs? Of course not. I posted a guard to keep everyone away. We can't go monkeying around with the tower until we've thought a few things through.'

'What do you think is in there?'

'I don't know,' said Spencer. 'All I have is an idea. We know what it can do. It can strip your memory.'

'Maybe it's fright that did it,' Warren said. 'Something down in the tower so horrible . . .'

Spencer shook his head. 'There is no evidence of fright in Briggs. He's calm. Sits there happy as a clam, playing with his fingers and talking silly sentences – happy sentences. The way a kid would talk.'

'Maybe what he's saying will give us a hint. Keep someone listening all the time. Even if the words don't mean much . . .'

'It wouldn't do any good. Not only is his memory gone, but even the memory of what took it away.'

'What do you plan to do?'

'Try to get into the tower,' said Spencer. 'Try to find out what's in there. There must be a way of getting at whatever is there and coming out okay.'

'Look,' Warren stated, 'we have enough as it is.'

'I have a hunch.'

'This is the first time I've ever heard you use that word. You gents don't operate on hunches. You operate on fact.'

Spencer put up an outspread hand and wiped it across his face.

'I don't know what's the matter with me, Warren. I know I've never thought in hunches before. Perhaps because now I can't help myself, the hunch comes in and fills the place of knowledge that I've lost.'

'You admit there's been knowledge lost?'

'Of course I do,' said Spencer. 'You were right about the junkyard. We should have done a better job.'

'And now you have a hunch.'

'It's crazy,' said Spencer. 'At least, it sounds crazy. That memory, that lost knowledge and lost skill went somewhere. Maybe there's something in the tower that took it away. I have the silly feeling we might get it back again, take it back from the thing that has it.'

He looked challengingly at Warren. 'You think I'm cracked.'

Warren shook his head. 'No, not that. Just grasping at straws.'

Spencer got up heavily. 'I'll do what I can. I'll talk with the others. We'll try to think it out before we try anything.'

When he had gone, Warren buzzed the engine room communicator.

Mac's voice came reedily out of the box.

'Having any luck, Mac?'

'None at all,' Mac told him. 'We sit and look at the engines. We are going out of our heads trying to remember.'

'I guess that's all you can do, Mac.'

'We could mess around with them, but I'm afraid if we do, we'll get something out of kilter.'

'Keep your hands off everything,' commanded Warren in sudden alarm. 'Don't touch a single thing. God knows what you might do.'

94

'We're just sitting,' Mac said, 'and looking at the engines and trying to remember.'

Crazy, thought Warren.

Of course it was crazy.

Down there were men trained to operate spaceship engines, men who had lived and slept with engines for year on lonesome year. And now they sat and looked at engines and wondered how to run them.

Warren got up from his desk and went slowly down the stairs.

In the cook's quarters, he found Bat Ears.

Bat Ears had fallen off a chair and was fast asleep upon the floor, breathing heavily. The room reeked with liquor fumes. An almost empty bottle sat upon the table.

Warren reached out a foot and prodded Bat Ears gently. Bat Ears moaned a little in his sleep.

Warren picked up the bottle and held it to the light. There was one good, long drink.

He tilted the bottle and took the drink, then hurled the empty bottle against the wall. The broken plastiglass sprayed in a shower down on Bat Ears' head.

Bat Ears raised a hand and brushed it off, as if brushing away a fly. Then he slept on, smiling, with his mind comfortably drugged against memories he no longer had.

XI

They covered the tower with the capstone once again and rigged a tripod and pulley above it. Then they took the capstone off and used the pulley to lower an automatic camera into the pit and they got their pictures.

There was something in the tower, all right.

They spread the pictures out on the table in the mess room and tried to make out what they had.

It was shaped like a watermelon or an egg stood on one end with the lower end slightly mashed so that it would stand upright. It sprouted tiny hairs all over and some of the hairs were blurred in the pictures, as if they might have been vibrating. There was tubing and what seemed to be wiring, even if it didn't look exactly the way you thought of wiring, massed around the lower end of the egg.

They made other tests, lowering the instruments with the pulley, and they determined that the egg was alive and that it was the equivalent of a warm-blooded animal, although they were fairly sure that its fluids would not be identical with blood.

It was soft and unprotected by any covering shell and it pulsed and gave out some sort of vibrations. They couldn't determine what sort of vibrations. The little hairs that covered it were continually in motion.

They put the capstone back in place again, but left the tripod and the pulley standing.

Howard, the biologist, said, 'It's alive and it's an organism of some kind, but I'm not at all convinced that it's pure animal. Those wires and that piping lead straight into it, as if, you'd almost swear, the piping and the wires were a part of it. And look at these – what would you call them? – these studs, almost like connections for other wires.'

'It's not conceivable,' said Spencer, 'that an animal and a mechanism should be joined together. Take Man and his machines. Man and the machines work together, but Man maintains his individual identity and the machines maintain their own. In a lot of cases it would make more sense, economically, if not socially, that Man and machine should be one, that the two of them be joined together, become, in fact, one organism.'

Dyer said, 'I think that may be what we have here.'

'Those other towers?' asked Ellis.

'They could be connected,' Spencer suggested, 'associated in some way. All eight of them could be, as a matter of principle, one complex organism.'

'We don't know what's in those other towers,' said Ellis.

'We could find out,' Howard answered.

'No, we can't,' objected Spencer. 'We don't dare. We've fooled around with them more than was safe. Mac and his crew went for a walk and found the towers and examined them, just casually, you understand, and they came back not knowing how to operate the engines. We can't take the chance of fooling around with them a minute longer than is necessary. Already we may have lost more than we suspect.'

96

'You mean,' said Clyne, 'that the loss of memory we may have experienced will show up later? That we may not know now we've lost it, but will find later that we did?'

Spencer nodded. 'That's what happened to Mac. He or any member of his crew would have sworn, up to the minute that they tried to start the engines, that they could start them. They took it for granted, just as we take our knowledge for granted. Until we come to use the specific knowledge we have lost, we won't realize we've lost it.'

'It scares you just to think about it,' Howard said.

Lang said, 'It's some sort of communications system.'

'Naturally you'd think so. You're a communications man.'

'Those wires.'

'And what about the pipes?' asked Howard.

'I have a theory on that one,' Spencer told them. 'The pipes supply the food.'

'Attached to some food supply,' said Clyne. 'A tank of food buried in the ground.'

'More likely roots,' Howard put in. 'To talk of tanks of food would mean these are transplanted things. They could just as easily be native to this planet.'

'They couldn't have built those towers,' said Ellis. 'If they were native, they'd have had to build those towers themselves. Something or someone else built the towers, like a farmer builds a barn to protect his cattle. I'd vote for tanks of food.'

Warren spoke for the first time. 'What makes you think it's a communications set up?'

Lang shrugged. 'Nothing specific. Those wires, I guess, and the studs. It *looks* like a communications rig.'

'Communications might fill the bill,' Spencer nodded. 'But a communications machine built to take in information rather than to pass information along or disseminate it.'

'What are you getting at?' demanded Lang. 'How would that be communication?'

'I mean,' said Spencer, 'that something has been robbing us of our memory. It stole our ability to run the engines and it took enough knowledge away from us so we bungled the junkyard job.'

'It couldn't be that,' said Dyer.

97

'Why couldn't it?' asked Clyne.

'It's just too damn fantastic.'

'No more fantastic,' Spencer told him, 'than a lot of other things we've found. Say that egg is a device for gathering knowledge . . .'

'But there's no knowledge to gather here,' protested Dyer. 'Thousands of years ago, there was knowledge to gather from the rusted ship out there. And then, just a while ago, there was knowledge to gather from the junkyard ship. And now there's us. But the next shipload of knowledge won't come along for maybe uncounted thousands of years. It's too long to wait, too big a gamble. Three ships we know of have come here; it would be just as reasonable to suppose that no ship would ever come here. It doesn't make any sense.'

'Who said that the knowledge had to be collected here? Even back on Earth we forget, don't we?'

'Good Lord!' gasped Clyne, but Spencer rushed ahead.

'If you were some race setting out fish traps for knowledge and had plenty of time to gather it, where would you put your traps? On a planet that swarmed with sentient beings, where the traps might be found and destroyed or their secrets snatched away? Or would you put them on some uninhabited, out-of-the-way planet, some second-rate world that won't be worth a tinker's damn to anyone for another billion years?'

Warren said, 'I'd put them on a planet just like this.'

'Let me give you the picture,' Spencer continued. 'Some race is bent on trapping knowledge throughout the Galaxy. So they hunt up the little, insignificant, good-for-nothing planets where they can hide their traps. That way, with traps planted on strategically spaced planets, they sweep all space and there's little chance that their knowledge traps ever will be found.'

'You think that's what we've found here?' asked Clyne.

'I'm tossing you the idea,' said Spencer, 'to see what you think of it. Now let's hear your comments.'

'Well, the distance, for one thing – '

'What we have here,' said Spencer, 'is mechanical telepathy hooked up with a recording device. We know that distance has little to do with the speed of thought waves.'

98

'There's no other basis for this belief beyond speculation?' asked Warren.

'What else can there be? You certainly can't expect proof. We don't dare to get close enough to find out what this egg is. And maybe, even if we could, we haven't got enough knowledge left in us to make an intelligent decision or a correct deduction.'

'So we guess again,' said Warren.

'Have you some better method?'

Warren shook his head. 'No, I don't think I have.'

XII

Dyer put on a spacesuit, with a rope running from it to the pulley in the tripod set above the tower. He carried wires to connect to the studs. The other ends of the wires were connected to a dozen different instruments to see what might come over them – if anything.

Dyer climbed the tower and they lowered him down into the inside of the tower. Almost immediately, he quit talking to them, so they pulled him out.

When they loosened the spacesuit helmet and hinged it back, he gurgled and blew bubbles at them.

Old Doc gently led him back to sick bay.

Clyne and Pollard worked for hours designing a lead helmet with television installed instead of vision plates. Howard, the biologist, climbed inside the spacesuit and was lowered into the tower.

When they hauled him out a minute later, he was crying – like a child. Ellis hurried him after Old Doc and Dyer, with Howard clutching his hands and babbling between sobs.

After ripping the television unit out of the helmet, Pollard was all set to go in the helmet made of solid lead when Warren put a stop to it.

'You keep this up much longer,' he told them, 'and we'll have no one left.'

'This one has a chance of working,' Clyne declared. 'It might have been the television lead-ins that let them get at Howard.'

'It has a chance of not working, too.'

'But we have to try.'

'Not until I say so.'

Pollard started to put the solid helmet on his head.

'Don't put that thing on,' said Warren. 'You're not going anywhere you'll be needing it.'

'I'm going in the tower,' Pollard said flatly.

Warren took a step towards him and without warning lashed out with his fist. It caught Pollard on the jaw and crumpled him.

Warren turned to face the rest of them. 'If there's anyone else who thinks he wants to argue, I'm ready to begin the discussion – in the same way.'

None of them wanted to argue. He could see the tired disgust for him written on their faces.

Spencer said, 'You're upset, Warren. You don't know what you're doing.'

'I know damned well what I'm doing,' Warren retorted. 'I know there must be a way to get into that tower and get out again with some of your memory left. But the way you're going about it isn't the right way.'

'You know another?' asked Ellis bitterly.

'No, I don't,' said Warren. 'Not yet.'

'What do you want us to do?' demanded Ellis. 'Sit around and twiddle our thumbs?'

'I want you to behave like grown men,' said Warren, 'not like a bunch of crazy kids out to rob an orchard.'

He stood and looked at them and none of them had a word to say.

'I have three mewling babies on my hands right now,' he added. 'I don't want any more.'

He walked away, up the hill, heading for the ship.

XIII

Their memory had been stolen, probably by the egg that squatted in the tower. And although none of them had dared to say the thought aloud, the thing that all of them were thinking was that maybe there was a way to steal the knowledge back, to tap and drain all the rest of the knowledge that was stored within the egg.

Warren sat at his desk and held his head in his hands, trying to think.

Maybe he should have let them go ahead with what they had been doing. But if he had, they'd have kept right on, using variations of the same approach – and when the approach had failed twice, they should have figured out that approach was wrong and tried another.

Spencer had said that they'd lost knowledge and not known they had lost it, and that was the insidious part of the whole situation. They still thought of themselves as men of science, and they were, of course, but not as skilled, not as knowledgable as they once had been.

That was the hell of it – they still thought they were.

They despised him now and that was all right with him. Anything was all right with him if it would help them discover a way to escape.

Forgetfulness, he thought. All through the Galaxy, there was forgetfulness. There were explanations for that forgetfulness, very learned and astute theories on why a being should forget something it had learned. But might not all these explanations be wrong? Might it not be that forgetfulness could be traced, not to some kink within the brain, not to some psychic cause, but to thousands upon thousands of memory tapes planted through the Galaxy, traps that tapped and drained and nibbled away at the mass memory of all the sentient beings which lived among the stars?

On Earth a man would forget slowly over the span of many years and that might be because the memory traps that held Earth in their orbit were very far away. But here a man forgot completely and suddenly. Might that not be because he was within the very shadow of the memory traps?

He tried to imagine Operation Mind Trap and it was a shocking concept too big for the brain to grasp. Someone came to the backwoods planets, the good-for-nothing planets, the sure-to-be-passed-by planets and set out the memory traps.

They hooked them up in series and built towers to protect them from weather or from accident, and set them operating and connected them to tanks of nutrients buried deep within the soil. Then they went away.

And years later – how many years later, a thousand, ten thousand? – they came back again and emptied the traps of

101

the knowledge they had gathered. As a trapper sets out traps to catch animals for fur, or a fisherman should set the pots for lobsters or drag the seine for fish.

A harvest, Warren thought – a continual, never-ending harvest of the knowledge of the Galaxy.

If this were true, what kind of race would it be that set the traps? What kind of trapper would be plodding the starways, gathering his catch?

Warren's reason shrank away from the kind of race that it would be.

The creatures undoubtedly came back again, after many years, and emptied the traps of the knowledge they had snared. That must be what they'd do, for why otherwise would they bother to set out the traps? And if they could empty the traps of the knowledge they had caught, that meant there was some way to empty them. And if the trappers themselves could drain off the knowledge, so could another race.

If you could get inside the tower and have a chance to figure out the way, you could do the job, for probably it was a simple thing, once you had a chance to see it. But you couldn't get inside. If you did, you were robbed of all memory and came out a squalling child. The moment you got inside, the egg grabbed onto your mind and wiped it clean and you didn't even know why you were there or how you'd got there or where you were.

The trick was to get inside and still keep your memory, to get inside and still know what there was to do.

Spencer and the others had tried shielding the brain and shielding didn't work. Maybe there was a way to make it work, but you'd have had to use trial and error methods and that meant too many men coming out with their memories gone before you had the answer. It meant that maybe in just a little while you'd have no men at all.

There must be another way.

When you couldn't shield a thing, what did you do?

A communications problem, Lang had said. Perhaps Lang was right – the egg was a communications set up. And what did you do to protect communications? When you couldn't shield a communication, what did you do with it?

102

There was an answer to that one, of course – you scrambled it.

But there was no solution there, nor any hint of a solution. He sat and listened and there was no sound. No one had stopped by to see him; no one had dropped in to pass the time of day.

They're sore, he thought. They're off sulking in a corner. They're giving me the silent treatment.

To hell with them, he said.

He sat alone and tried to think and there were no thoughts, just a mad merry-go-round of questions revolving in his skull.

Finally there were footsteps on the stair and from their unsteadiness, he knew whose they were.

It was Bat Ears coming up to comfort him and Bat Ears had a skin full.

He waited, listening to the stumbling feet tramping up the stairs, and Bat Ears finally appeared. He stood manfully in the doorway, putting out both hands and bracing them against the jambs on either side of him to keep the place from swaying.

Bat Ears nerved himself and plunged across the space from doorway to chair and grabbed the chair and hung onto it and wrestled himself into it and looked up at Warren with a smirk of triumph.

'Made it,' Bat Ears said.

'You're drunk,' snapped Warren disgustedly.

'Sure, I'm drunk. It's lonesome being drunk all by yourself. Here . . .'

He found his pocket and hauled the bottle out and set it gingerly on the desk.

'There you are,' he said. 'Let's you and me go and hang one on.'

Warren stared at the bottle and listened to the little imp of thought that jigged within his brain.

'No, it wouldn't work.'

'Cut out the talking and start working on that jug. When you get through with that one, I got another hid out.'

'Bat Ears,' said Warren.

'What do you want?' asked Bat Ears. 'I never saw a man that wanted – '

'How much more have you got?'

'How much more what, Ira?'

'Liquor. How much more do you have stashed away?'

'Lots of it. I always bring along a marg . . . a marg . . .'

'A margin?'

'That's right,' said Bat Ears. 'That is what I meant. I always figure what I need and then bring along a margin just in case we get marooned or something.'

Warren reached out and took the bottle. He uncorked it and threw the cork away.

'Bat Ears,' he said, 'go and get another bottle.'

Bat Ears blinked at him. 'Right away, Ira? You mean right away?'

'Immediately,' said Warren. 'And on your way, would you stop and tell Spencer that I want to see him soon as possible?'

Bat Ears wobbled to his feet.

He regarded Warren with forthright admiration.

'What you planning on doing, Ira?' he demanded.

'I'm going to get drunk,' said Warren. 'I'm going to hang one on that will make history in the survey fleet.'

XIV

'You can't do it, man,' protested Spencer. 'You haven't got a chance.'

Warren put out a hand against the tower and tried to hold himself a little steadier, for the whole planet was gyrating at a fearful pace.

'Bat Ears,' Warren called out.

'Yes, Ira.'

'Shoot the – *hic* – man who tries to shtop me.'

'I'll do that, Ira,' Bat Ears assured him.

'But you're going in there unprotected,' Spencer said anxiously. 'Without even a spacesuit.'

'I'm trying out a new appro . . . appro . . .'

'Approach?' supplied Bat Ears.

'Thash it,' said Warren. 'I thank you, Bat Ears. Thash exactly what I'm doing.'

Lang said, 'It's got a chance. We tried to shield ourselves

104

and it didn't work. He's trying a new approach. He's scrambled up his mind with liquor. I think he might have a chance.'

'The shape he's in,' said Spencer, 'he'll never get the wires connected.'

Warren wobbled a little. 'The hell you shay.'

He stood and blurredly watched them. Where there had been three of each of them before, there now, in certain cases, were only two of them.

'Bat Ears.'

'Yes, Ira.'

'I need another drink. It's wearing off a little.'

Bat Ears took the bottle from his pocket and handed it across. It was not quite half full. Warren tipped it up and drank, his Adam's apple bobbing. He did not quit drinking until the last of it was gone. He let the bottle drop and looked at them again. This time there were three of each of them and it was all right.

He turned to face the tower.

'Now,' he said, 'if you gen'men will jush – '

Ellis and Clyne hauled on the rope and Warren sailed into the air.

'Hey, there!' he shouted. 'Wha' you trying to do?'

He had forgotten about the pulley rigged on the tripod above the tower.

He dangled in the air, kicking and trying to get his balance, with the blackness of the tower's mouth looming under him and a funny, shining glow at the bottom of it.

Above him the pulley creaked and he shot down and was inside the tower.

He could see the thing at the bottom now. He hiccoughed politely and told it to move over, he was coming down. It didn't move an inch. Something tried to take his head off and it didn't come off.

The earphones said, 'Warren, you all right? You all right? Talk to us.'

'Sure,' he said. 'Sure, all right. Wha' matter wish you?'

They let him down and he stood beside the funny thing that pulsated in the pit. He felt something digging at his brain and laughed aloud, a gurgling, drunken laugh.

'Get your handsh out my hair,' he said. 'You tickle.'

'Warren,' said the earphones. 'The wires. The wires. You remember, we talked about the wires.'

'Sure,' he said. 'The wires.'

There were little studs on the pulsating thing and they'd be fine things to attach a wire to.

Wires? What the hell were wires?

'Hooked on your belt,' said the earphones. 'The wires are hooked on your belt.'

His hand moved to his belt and he found the wires. He fumbled with them and they slipped out of his fingers and he got down and scrabbled around and grabbed hold of them again. They were all tangled up and he couldn't make head or tail of them and what was he messing around with wires for, anyhow?

What he wanted was another drink – another little drink.

He sang: *'I'm a ramblin' wreck from Georgia Tech and a hell of an engineer!'*

He said to the egg: 'Friend, I'd be mosh pleashed if you'd join me in a drink.'

The earphones said, 'Your friend can't drink until you get those wires hooked up. He can't hear without the wires hooked up. He can't tell what you're saying until you get those wires hooked up.

'You understand, Warren? Hook up the wires. He can't hear till you do.'

'Now, thash too bad,' said Warren. 'Thash an awful thing.'

He did the best he could to get the wires hooked up and he told his new friend just to be patient and hold still, he was doing the best he could. He yelled for Bat Ears to hurry with the bottle and he sang a ditty which was quite obscene. And finally he got the wires hooked up, but the man in the earphones said that wasn't right, to try it once again. He changed the wires around some more and they still weren't right, and so he changed them around again, until the man in the earphones said, 'That's fine! We're getting something now!'

And then someone hauled him out of there before he even had a drink with his pal.

XV

He stumbled up the stairs and negotiated his way around the desk and plopped into the chair. Someone had fastened a steel bowl securely over the top half of his head and two men or possibly three, were banging it with a hammer, and his mouth had a wool blanket wadded up in it, and he could have sworn that at any moment he'd drop dead of thirst.

He heard footsteps on the stairs and hoped that it was Bat Ears, for Bat Ears would know what to do.

But it was Spencer.

'How're you feeling?' Spencer asked.

'Awful,' Warren groaned.

'You turned the trick!'

'That tower business?'

'You hooked up the wires,' said Spencer, 'and the stuff is rolling out. Lang has a recorder hooked up and we're taking turns listening in and the stuff we're getting is enough to set your teeth on edge.'

'Stuff?'

'Certainly. The knowledge that mind trap has been collecting. It'll take us years to sort out all the knowledge and try to correlate it. Some of it is just in snatches and some of it is fragmentary, but we're getting lots of it in hunks.'

'Some of our own stuff being fed back to us?'

'A little. But mostly alien.'

'Anything on the engines?'

Spencer hesitated. 'No, not on *our* engines. That is – '

'Well?'

'We got the dope on the junkyard engine. Pollard's already at work. Mac and the boy are helping him get it assembled.'

'It'll work?'

'Better than what we have. We'll have to modify our tubes and make some other changes.'

'And you're going to – '

Spencer nodded. 'We're ripping out our engines.'

Warren couldn't help it. He couldn't have helped it if he'd been paid a million dollars. He put his arms down on the desk

107

and hid his face in them and shouted raucously with incoherent laughter.

After a time he looked up again and mopped at laughter-watered eyes.

'I fail to see – ' Spencer began stiffly.

'Another junkyard,' Warren said. 'Oh, God, another junkyard!'

'It's not so funny, Warren. It's brain-shaking – a mass of knowledge such as no one ever dreamed of. Knowledge that had been accumulating for years, maybe a thousand years. Ever since that other race came and emptied the trap and then went away again.'

'Look,' said Warren, 'couldn't we wait until we came across the knowledge of our engines? Surely it will come out soon. It went in, was fed in, whatever you want to call it, later than any of the rest of this stuff you are getting. If we'd just wait, we'd have the knowledge that we lost. We wouldn't have to go to all the work of ripping out the engines and replacing them.'

Spencer shook his head.

'Lang figured it out. There seems to be no order or sequence in the way we get the information. The chances are that we might have to wait for a long, long time. We have no way of knowing how long the information will keep pouring out. Lang thinks for maybe years. But there's something else. We've got to get away as soon as possible.'

'What's the matter with you, Spencer?'

'I don't know.'

'You're afraid of something. Something's got you scared.'

Spencer bent over and grasped the desk edge with his hands, hanging on.

'Warren, it's not only knowledge in that thing. We're monitoring it and we know. There's also – '

'I'll take a guess,' said Warren. 'There's personality.'

He saw the stricken look on Spencer's face.

'Quit monitoring it,' ordered Warren sharply. 'Turn the whole thing off. Let's get out of here.'

'We can't. Don't you understand? We can't! There are certain points. We are – '

108

'Yes, I know,' said Warren. 'You are men of science. Also downright fools.'

'But there are things coming out of that tower that – '

'Shut it off!'

'No,' said Spencer obstinately. 'I can't. I won't.'

'I warn you,' Warren said grimly, 'if any of you turn alien, I'll shoot you without hesitation.'

'Don't be a fool.' Spencer turned sharply about and went out the door.

Warren sat, sober now, listening to Spencer's feet go down the steps.

It was all very clear to Warren now.

Now he knew why there had been evidence of haste in that other ship's departure, why supplies had been left behind and tools still lying where they had been dropped as the crew had fled.

After a while Bat Ears came up the stairs, lugging a huge pot of coffee and a couple of cups.

He set the cups down on the desk and filled them, then banged down the pot.

'Ira,' he said, 'it was a black day when you gave up your drinking.'

'How is that?' asked Warren.

'Because there ain't no one, nowhere, who can hang one on like you.'

They sat silently, gulping the hot, black coffee.

Then Bat Ears said, 'I still don't like it.'

'Neither do I,' admitted Warren.

'The cruise is only half over,' said Bat Ears.

'The cruise is completely over,' Warren told him bluntly. 'When we lift out of here, we're heading straight for Earth.'

They drank more coffee.

Warren asked: 'How many on our side, Bat Ears?'

'There's you and me,' said Bat Ears, 'and Mac and the four engineers. That's seven.'

'Eight,' corrected Warren. 'Don't forget Doc. He hasn't been doing any monitoring.'

'Doc don't count for nothing one way or the other.'

'In a pinch, he still can handle a gun.'

After Bat Ears had gone, Warren sat and listened to the sound of Mac's crew ripping out the engines and he thought of the long way home. Then he got up and strapped on a gun and went out to see how things were shaping up.

THE
OBSERVER

It existed. Whether it has slept and wakened, or been turned on, or if this might be the first instant of its creation, it had no way of knowing. There was no memory of other time, or place.

Words came to fit where it found itself. Words emerging out of nowhere, symbols quite unbidden – awakened or turned on or first appearing, as it had itself.

It was in a place of red and yellow. The land was red. The sky was yellow. A brightness stood straight above the red land in the yellow sky. Liquid ran gurgling down a channel in the land.

In a little time it knew more, had a better understanding. It knew the brightness was a sun. It knew the running liquid was a brook. It thought of the liquid as a compound, but it wasn't water. Life forms sprang from the redness of the soil. Their stems were green. They had purple fruits at the top of them.

It had the names now, identifying symbols it could use – life, liquid, land, sky, red, yellow, purple, green, sun, bright, water. Each instant it had more words, more names, more terms. And it could see, although seeing might not be the proper term, for it had no eyes. Nor legs. Nor arms. Not body.

It had no eyes and seemed to have no body, either. It had no idea of position – standing up or lying down or sitting. It could look anywhere it wished without turning its head, since it hadn't any head. Although, strangely, it did seem to occupy a specific position in relation to the landscape.

111

It looked straight up into the sky at the brightness of the sun and could look directly at the brightness since it was seeing without eyes, without frail organic structures that might be harmed by brilliance.

The sun was a B8 star, five times more massive than the Sun, and it lay 3.76 A.U. distant from this planet.

Sun, capitalized? A.U.? Five? 3.76? Planet?

Sometime in the past — when past, where past, what past — it had known the terms, a sun that was capitalized, water that ran in brooks, the idea of a body and of eyes. Or had it known them? Had it ever had a past in which it could have known them? Or were they simply terms that were being fed into it from another source, to be utilized as the need arose, tools — and there was yet another term — to be used in interpreting this place where it found itself? Interpreting this place for what? For itself? That was ridiculous, for it did not need to know, did not even care to know.

Knowing, how did it know? How did it know the sun was a B8 star, and what was a B8 star? How did it know its distance, its diameter, its mass just by looking at it? How did it know a star, for it had never seen a star before?

Then, even thinking this, it knew it had. It had known many suns, a long string of suns across the galaxy and it had looked at each of them and known its spectral type, its distance and diameter, its mass, its very composition, its age and probable length of remaining life, stable or variable, its spectral lines, any small peculiarities that might set it apart from other stars. Red giants, supergiants, white dwarfs, even one black dwarf. But mostly main sequence stars and the planets that went with them, for it made few stops at stars that had no planets.

Perhaps nothing had even seen more suns than it. Or knew more of suns than it.

And the purpose of all this? It tried to think of purpose, but there seemed no purpose. The purpose utterly escaped it. If there were, in fact, a purpose.

It stopped looking at the sun and looked at the rest of it, at all of it at once, at all the planetary surface in its sight — as if, it thought, it had eyes all around its nonexistent head. Why did it, it wondered, keep dwelling on this idea of a head and eyes?

Had it, at one time perhaps, had a head and eyes? Was the ideal of head and eyes an old residual, perhaps a primitive, memory that persistently refused to go away, but that for some reason must linger and thrust itself forward at the slightest opportunity?

It tried to think it out, to reach back and grasp the idea or the memory and drag it squalling from its hole. And failed.

It concentrated on the surface. It was located – if located was the word – on a steep hillside with massive rock outcroppings. The hill shut off the view of one portion of the surface, but the rest lay bare before it to the horizon line.

The rest of the surface was level, except for one place, far distant, where what appeared to be a circular prominence arose. The top of the prominence was jagged and the sides were furrowed and it looked very like an ancient crater.

But the rest was level and through it ran several little streams of something that was liquid but was not water. The sparse vegetation stood up on its dark green stems, surmounted by its purple fruit and now it was apparent that there were several kinds of vegetation. The purple fruit vegetation at first had seemed to be the only vegetation because it was more abundant, and certainly more spectacular.

The soil seemed to be little more than sand. It put out a hand – no, not a hand, for it had no hand – but it thought of its action as putting out a hand. It put out a hand and thrust the fingers deep into the soil and the data on the soil came flowing into it. Sand. Almost pure sand. Silicon, some iron, some aluminium, traces of oxygen, hydrogen, potassium, magnesium. Almost no acidity. There were figures, percentages, but it hardly noticed. They simply passed along.

The atmosphere was deadly. Deadly to what? The radiation lancing in from the B-type star was deadly and again, deadly to what?

What do I have to know, it wondered. And there was another word it had not used before. I. Me. Myself. An entity. A self. A single thing, standing all alone, no part of another. A personality.

What am I? it asked. Where am I? And why? Why must I go on collecting all this data? What care I for soil, or radiation, or the atmosphere? Why should I have to know what kind of star is standing overhead? I have no body that can be affected

113

by any of it. I seem to have no form, I only have a being. A disembodied entity. A nebulous I.

It desisted for a time, unmoving, doing nothing, collecting no more data, only looking at the red and yellow of the planet, the purple of the flowers.

Then, after a time, it took up its work again. It touched the rocky outcrops on the hillside, found the planes that lay between the layers, seeped into the rock, following the cleavages.

Limestone. Massive, hard limestone. Put down millenia ago at the bottom of the sea.·

It paused for a moment, vaguely disturbed, then recognized the cause of its disturbance. Fossils!

Why should fossils disturb it, it asked itself and then suddenly it knew with something that amounted to excitement, or as close as it could come to what might be excitement. These were not the fossils of plants, primordial ancestors to those purple plants growing on the present surface. These were animals – well-organized forms of life, sophisticated in their structure, well up the evolutionary ladder.

So few of the other planets had any life at all, the few that did more often than not had only the simplest of vegetable life or, perhaps, tiny organisms on the borderline, things that might be slightly more than vegetable, but not yet animal. I should have known, it thought. The purple plants should have alerted me. For they are highly organized; they are not simple plants. On this planet, despite its deadly atmosphere and its deadly radiation and its liquid that is not water, evolutionary forces still had been at work.

It traced one particular fossil. Not large. A chitin covering, apparently, but still it had a skeleton of sorts. It had a head, a body, legs. It had a flattened tail for swimming in whatever evil chemical brew the ocean might have been. It had jaws for seizing and for holding. It had eyes, a great many more eyes, perhaps, than it had any need of. There were faint tracings of an alimentary canal, fragments of nerves here and there that were still preserved, or at least the canals in which they ran had been preserved.

And it thought of that faint, misty time when he –

He? First an I. And then a he.

114

Two identities – or rather two terms of identity.
No longer an it, but an I and he.

He lay thin and spread out along the tight seams of the limestone and knew the fossils and pondered on the he. Especially that one particular fossil and that other misty time in which the first fossil had been found, the first time he had ever known there was such a thing as fossil. He recalled the finding of it and recalled its name as well. It had been called a trilobite. Someone had told him the name, but he could not remember who it might have been. A place so faint in time, so far in space, that all he had left of it was a fossil called a trilobite.

But there had been another time and another place and he was not new – he had not in that first instant of awareness been turned on, or newly hatched, or born. He had a history. There had been times of other awareness and he had held identity in those other times. Not new, he thought, but old. A creature with a past.

The thought of eyes, of body, or arms and legs – could all of them be memories from that other time or times? Could there have been a time when he did have a head and eyes, a body?

Or could he be mistaken? Could all of this be a phantom memory fashioned out of some happening, or event, or some combination of happenings and events that had occurred to some other being? Was it, perhaps, a misplaced memory, not of himself, but of something else? If the memory should prove to be his own, what had happened to him – what changes had been made?

He forgot the limestone and the fossils. He lay spread out in the fissures of the rock and stayed quiet and limp, hoping that out of the limpness and the quietness he might devise an answer. A partial answer came, an infuriating answer, unspecific and tantalizing. Not one place, but many; not one time, but many times. Not on one planet, but on many planets spaced over many light-years.

If all of this were true, he thought, there must be purpose in it. Otherwise, why the many planets and the data on those planets? And this was a new, unbidden thought – the data on the planets. Why the data? For what purpose was it gathered? Certainly not for himself, for he did not need the data, had no use for it. Could it be that he was only the gatherer, the harvester, the storer and communicator of the data that he gathered?

If not for himself, for whom? He waited for the answer to come welling up, for the memory to reassert itself and in time he realized that he had gone groping back as far as he could go.

Slowly he withdrew from the rock, once more was upon the hillside above the red land beneath the yellow sky.

A portion of the nearby surface moved and as it moved, he saw that it was not a portion of the surface, but a creature that had a coloration which made it seem to be a part of the planet's surface. It moved quickly, as if a shadow had brushed along and blurred the surface. It moved in short and flowing motions and when it stopped its motion it became a part of the surface, blending into it.

It was watching him, he knew, looking him over, although what there was to see of him he could not imagine. Sensitive, perhaps, to another personality, to another thing that shared with it that strange and undefinable quality which made up life. A force field, he wondered – was that what he was, a disembodied intelligence carried in a force field?

He stayed still so the thing could look him over. It moved in its short, flowing dashes, all around him. It left a furrowed track behind it, it kicked up little spurts of sand as it made its dashes. It moved in closer.

And he had it. He held it motionless, wrapped up as if he held it in many hands. He examined it, not closely, not analytically, but only enough so he could tell what kind of thing it was. Protoplasmic and heavily shielded against the radiations, even designed, perhaps – although he could not be sure – to take advantage of the energy contained in the radiation. An organism, more than likely, that could not exist without the radiations, that needed them as other creatures might need warmth, or food, or oxygen. Intelligent and laced with a multitude of emotions – not, perhaps, the kind of intelligence that could build a complex culture, but a high level of animal intelligence. Perhaps still evolving in its intelligence. Give it a few more million years and it might contrive a culture.

He turned it loose. It flowed away, moving rapidly, straight

116

away from him. He lost sight of it, but still could follow its movement for a time by its unreeling track and the spurts of sand it kicked into the air.

There was much work to do. An atmospheric profile, an analysis of the soil and of the micro-organisms that it might contain, a determination of the liquid in the brook, an examination of the plant life, a geological survey, measurement of the magnetic field, the intensity of the radiation. But first there should be a general survey of the planet to determine what sort of place it was, a pin-pointing of those areas that might be of economic interest.

And there it was again, another word he had not had before. Economic.

He searched inside himself, inside the theoretical intelligence enclosed within the hypothetical force field, for the purpose that was hinted in that single word. When he found it, it stood out sharp and clear – the one thing he had found that was sharp and clear. What was here that could be used and what would be the cost of obtaining it? A treasure hunt, he thought. That was the purpose of him. It was clear immediately that he, himself, had no use for treasure of any kind at all. There must be someone else who would have a use for it. Although when he thought of treasure a pleasurable thrill went through him.

What might there be in it for him, he wondered, this location of a treasure? What had been the profit to him in the finding of all those other treasures on all those other planets – although, come to think of it, there had not been treasure on every one of them. And on some of the others where there'd been, it had been meaningless, for planetary conditions had been such that it could not be got at. Many of the planets, he recalled, far too many of them, were such that only a thing such as himself would dare even to approach them.

There had been attempts, he remembered now, to recall him from some of the planets when it had become apparent they had no economic worth and that to further explore them would be a waste of time. He had resisted those attempts; he had ignored the summons to return to wherever it was he went when he did return. Because, in his simplistic ethic, when there was a job to do he did it and he did not quit until

117

the job was done. Having started something, he was incapable of leaving off until it had been finished. It was a part of him, this single-minded stubbornness; it was a characteristic that was necessary to do the work he did.

If they had it one way, they could not have it two. He either was, or wasn't. He did the job, or didn't. He was so made that he had an interest in each problem that was presented him and would not leave off until he'd wrung the problem dry. They had to go along with that and they knew it now; they no longer bothered trying to recall him from a non-productive planet.

They? he asked himself and remembered faintly other creatures such as he had been. They had indoctrinated him, they had made him what he was and they used him as they used the priceless planets he had found, but he did not mind the using, for it was a life and the only life he had. It either had been this life, or no life at all. He tried to recall circumstances, but something moved to block the recall. Exactly as he never could recall in all entirety, but only in fragments, the other planets he had visited. That, he thought at the time, might be a great mistake, for experience he had gathered on the other planets might have been valuable as guide lines on the one to which he currently had been sent. But for some reason, they did not allow it, but did their imperfect best to wipe from his memory all past experiences before he was sent out again. To keep him clear, they said; to guard him from confusion; to send a bright new mind, freed of all encumbrances, out to each new planet. That was why, he knew, he always arrived upon each planet groping for a meaning and purpose, with the feeling of being newly born to this particular planet and to nowhere else.

He did not mind. It still was a life and he saw a lot of places – very different places – and saw them, no matter what conditons might obtain, in perfect safety. For there was nothing that could touch him – tooth, or claw, or poison, no matter what the atmosphere, no matter what the radiation, there was nothing that could touch him. There was nothing of him to be touched. He walked – no, not walked, but moved – in utter nonchalance through all the hells the galaxy could muster.

*

118

A second sun was rising, a great swollen, brick-red star pushing its way above the horizon, with the first one just beginning to slide towards the west – as a matter of convenience, he thought of the big red one as rising in the east.

K2, he read it, thirty times, or so, the diameter of the Sun with a surface temperature that was possibly no more than 4,000°. A binary system and maybe more than that; there might be other suns that he still had yet to see. He tried to calculate the distance, but that would not be possible with any accuracy until the giant had moved higher in the sky, until it had moved above the horizon that now bisected it.

But the second sun could wait, all the rest of it could wait. There was one thing he must see. He had not realized it before, but now he knew there was one thing about the landscape that had been nagging him. The crater did not fit. It had all the appearances of a crater, but it had no right to be there. It could not be volcanic, for it sat in the middle of a sandy terrain and the limestone thrusting from the hillside was sedimentary rock. There was no trace of igneous rock, no ancient lava flows. And the same objections still would hold if the crater had been formed by meteoric impact, for any meteorite that threw up a crater of that size would have turned tons of material into a molten mass and would have thrown out a sheet of magma, of which there was no sign.

He began drifting slowly in the direction of the crater. Beneath him the terrain remained unchanged – the red soil, the purple fruit and little else.

He came to rest – if that is what his action could be called – on the crater's rim and for a moment failed to understand what he was seeing.

Some sort of shining substance extended all around the rim and sloped inward to the centre to form what appeared to be a concave mirror. But it was not a mirror, for it was nonreflective.

Then, quite suddenly, an image formed upon it and if he could have caught his breath he would have.

Two creatures, one large, the other smaller, stood on a ledge above a deep cut in the earth, with a striated sandstone bluff rising up above them. The smaller one was digging in the bluff with a hand tool of some sort – a hand tool that was grasped in what must be a hand, which was attached to an arm and the arm hooked up to a body, which had a head and eyes.

Myself, he thought – the smaller one, myself.

He felt a weakness and a haziness and the image in the mirror seemed to be trying to pull him down to join and coalesce with this image of himself. The gates of memory opened and the old, restricted data came pouring in upon him – the terms and relationships – and he cried out against it and tried to push it back, but it would not push back. It was as if someone were holding him so he could not get away and, with a mouth close against his ear, was telling him things he did not wish to know.

Humans, father, son, a railroad cut, the Earth, the finding of that first trilobite. Relentlessly the information came pouring into him, into the intellectual force field that he had become, that he had evolved into, or been engineered into, and that had been a comfort and a refuge until this very moment.

His father wore an old sweater, with holes in the elbows of the sleeves, and an old pair of black trousers that were baggy at the knees. He smoked an ancient pipe with a fire-charred bowl and a stem half-bitten through, and he watched with deep paternal interest as the boy, working carefully, dug out the tiny slab of stone that bore the imprint of an ancient form of life.

Then the image flickered and went out and he sat (?) upon the crater's rim, with the dead mirror sweeping downward to its centre, showing nothing but the red and blue reflections of the suns.

Now he knew, he thought. He knew, not what he was, but what he once had been – a creature that had walked upon two legs, that had a body and two arms, a head and eyes and a mouth that cried out in excited triumph at the finding of a trilobite. A creature that walked proudly and with misplaced confidence, for it had none of the immunity against its environment such as he now possessed.

From that feeble, vulnerable creature, how had he evolved?

Could it be death, he wondered, and was aghast at death, which was a new concept. Death, an ending, and there was no end, never would be one; a thing that was an intellect trapped within a force field could exist forever. But some-

120

where along the way, somewhere in the course of evolution, or of engineering, could death have played a part? Must a man come to death before he came to this?

He sat upon the crater's rim and knew the surface of the planet all about him – the red of land, the yellow of the sky, the green and purple of the flowers, the gurgle of the liquid running in its courses, the red and blue of suns and the shadows that they cast, the running thing that threw up spurts of sand, the limestone and the fossils.

And something else as well and with the sensing of that something else a fear and panic he had never known before. Had never had the need to know, for he had been protected and immune, untouchable, secure, perhaps even in the centre of a sun. There had been nothing that could get at him, no way he could be reached.

But that was true no longer, for now he could be reached. Something had torn from him an ancient memory and had shown it to him. Here, on this planet, there was a factor that could get at him, that could reach into him and tear from him something even he had not suspected.

He screamed a question and phantom echoes ran across the land, bouncing back to mock him. Who are you? Who are you? Who are you? Fainter and fainter and the only answers were the echoes.

It could afford not to answer him, he knew. It need not answer him. It could sit smug and silent while he screamed the question, waiting until it wished to strip other memories from him, memories for its own strange use, or to further mock him.

He was safe no longer. He was vulnerable. Naked to this thing that used a mirror to convince him of his own vulnerability.

He screamed again and this time the scream was directed to those others of his kind who had sent him out.

Take me back! I am naked! Save me!

Silence.

I have worked for you – I have dug out the data for you – I have done my job – You owe me something now!

Silence.

Please!

Silence.

Silence – and something more than silence. Not only silence, but an absence, a not being there, a vacuum.

The realization came thudding hard into his understanding. He had been abandoned, all ties with him had been cut – in the depth of unguessed space, he had been set adrift. They had washed their hands of him and he was not only naked, but alone.

They knew what had happened. They knew everything that ever happened to him, they monitored him continuously and would know everything he knew. And they had sensed the danger, perhaps even before he, himself, had sensed it. Had recognized the danger, not only to himself, but to themselves as well. If something could get to him, it could trace back the linkage and get to them as well. So the linkage had been cut and would not be restored. They weren't taking any chances. It had been something that had been emphasized time and time again. You must remain not only unrecognized, but entirely unsuspected. You must do nothing that will make you known. You must never point a finger at us.

Cold, callous, indifferent. And frightened. More frightened, perhaps, than he was. For now they knew there was something in the galaxy that could become aware of the disembodied observer they had been sending out. They could never send another, if indeed they had another, for the old fear would be there. And perhaps an even greater fear – based upon the overriding suspicion that the linkage had been cut not quite soon enough, that this factor which had spotted their observer had already traced it back to them.

Fear for their bodies and their profits . . .

Not for their bodies, a voice said inside him. Not their biologic bodies. There are no longer any of your kind who have biologic bodies . . .

Then what? he asked.

An extension of their bodies, carrying on the purpose those with bodies gave them in a time when the bodies still existed. Carried on mindlessly ever since, but without a purpose, only with a memory of a purpose . . .

Who are you? he asked. How do you know all this? What will you do with me?

122

In a very different way, it said, I am one like you. You can be like me. You have your freedom now.

I have nothing, he said.

You have yourself, it said. Is that not enough?

But is self enough? he asked.

And did not need an answer.

For self was the basis of all life, all sentience. The institutions, the cultures, the economics were no more than structures for the enhancement of the self. Self now was all he had and self belonged to him. It was all he needed.

Thank you, sir, said he, the last human in the universe.

THE WORLD THAT
COULDN'T BE

I

The tracks went up one row and down another, and in those rows the *vua* plants had been sheared off an inch or two above the ground. The raider had been methodical; it had not wandered about haphazardly, but had done an efficient job of harvesting the first ten rows on the west side of the field. Then, having eaten its fill, it had angled off into the bush – and that had not been long ago, for the soil still trickled down into the great pug marks, sunk deep into the finely cultivated loam.

Somewhere a sawmill bird was whirring through a log, and down in one of the thorn-choked ravines, a choir of chatterers was clicking through a ghastly morning song. It was going to be a scorcher of a day. Already the smell of desiccated dust was rising from the ground and the glare of the newly risen sun was dancing off the bright leaves of the hula-trees, making it appear as if the bush were filled with a million flashing mirrors.

Gavin Duncan hauled a red bandanna from his pocket and mopped his face.

'No, mister,' pleaded Zikkara, the native foreman of the farm. 'You cannot do it, mister. You do not hunt a Cytha.'

'The hell I don't,' said Duncan, but he spoke in English and not the native tongue.

He stared out across the bush, a flat expanse of sun-cured grass interspersed with thickets of hula-scrub and thorn and

124

occasional groves of trees, crisscrossed by treacherous ravines and spotted with infrequent water holes.

It would be murderous out there, he told himself, but it shouldn't take too long. The beast probably would lay up shortly after its pre-dawn feeding and he'd overhaul it in an hour or two. But if he failed to overhaul it, then he must keep on.

'Dangerous,' Zikkara pointed out. 'No one hunts the Cytha.'

'I do,' Duncan said, speaking now in the native language. 'I hunt anything that damages my crop. A few nights more of this and there would be nothing left.'

Jamming the bandanna back into his pocket, he tilted his hat lower across his eyes against the sun.

'It might be a long chase, mister. It is the *skun* season now. If you were caught out there . . .'

'Now listen,' Duncan told it sharply. 'Before I came, you'd feast one day, then starve for days on end; but now you eat each day. And you like the doctoring. Before, when you got sick, you died. Now you get sick, I doctor you, and you live. You like staying in one place, instead of wandering all around.'

'Mister, we like all this,' said Zikkara, 'but we do not hunt the Cytha.'

'If we do not hunt the Cytha, we lose all this,' Duncan pointed out. 'If I don't make a crop, I'm licked. I'll have to go away. Then what happens to you?'

'We will grow the corn ourselves.'

'That's a laugh,' said Duncan, 'and you know it is. If I didn't kick your backsides all day long, you wouldn't do a lick of work. If I leave, you go back to the bush. Now let's go get that Cytha.'

'But it is such a little one, mister! It is such a young one! It is scarcely worth the trouble. It would be a shame to kill it.'

Probably just slightly smaller than a horse, thought Duncan, watching the native closely.

It's scared, he told himself. It's scared dry and spitless.

'Besides, it must have been most hungry. Surely, mister, even a Cytha has the right to eat.'

'Not from my crop,' said Duncan savagely. 'You know why we grow the *vua*, don't you? You know it is great medicine. The berries that it grows cures those who are sick inside their heads. My people need that medicine — need it very badly.

125

And what is more, out there' – he swept his arm towards the sky – 'out there they pay very much for it.'

'But, mister . . .'

'I tell you this,' said Duncan gently, 'you either dig me up a bush-runner to do the tracking for me or you can all get out, the kit and caboodle of you. I can get other tribes to work the farm.'

'No, mister!' Zikkara screamed in desperation.

'You have your choice,' Duncan told it coldly.

He plodded back across the field towards the house. Not much of a house as yet. Not a great deal better than a native shack. But someday it would be, he told himself. Let him sell a crop or two and he'd build a house that would really be a house. It would have a bar and swimming pool and a garden filled with flowers, and at last, after years of wandering, he'd have a home and broad acres and everyone, not just one lousy tribe, would call him mister.

Gavin Duncan, planter, he said to himself, and liked the sound of it. Planter on the planet Layard. But not if the Cytha came back night after night and ate the *vua* plants.

He glanced over his shoulder and saw that Zikkara was racing for the native village.

Called their bluff, Duncan informed himself with satisfaction.

He came out of the field and walked across the yard, heading for the house. One of Shotwell's shirts was hanging on the clothesline, limp in the breathless morning.

Damn the man, thought Duncan. Out here mucking around with those stupid natives, always asking questions, always underfoot. Although, to be fair about it, that was Shotwell's job. That was what the Sociology people had sent him out to do.

Duncan came up to the shack, pushed the door open and entered. Shotwell, stripped to the waist, was at the wash bench.

Breakfast was cooking on the stove, with an elderly native acting as cook.

Duncan strode across the room and took down the heavy rifle from its peg. He slapped the action open, slapped it shut again.

Shotwell reached for a towel.

126

'What's going on?' he asked.

'Cytha got into the field.'

'Cytha?'

'A kind of animal,' said Duncan. 'It ate ten rows of *vua*.'

'Big? Little? What are its characteristics?'

The native began putting breakfast on the table. Duncan walked to the table, laid the rifle across one corner of it and sat down. He poured a brackish liquid out of a big stew pan into their cups.

God, he thought, what I would give for a cup of coffee.

Shotwell pulled up his chair. 'You didn't answer me. What is a Cytha like?'

'I wouldn't know,' said Duncan.

'Don't know. But you're going after it, looks like, and how can you hunt it if you don't know – '

'Track it. The thing tied to the other end of the trail is sure to be the Cytha. We'll find out what it's like once we catch up to it.'

'We?'

'The natives will send up someone to do the tracking for me. Some of them are better than a dog.'

'Look, Gavin. I've put you to a lot of trouble and you've been decent with me. If I can be any help, I would like to go.'

'Two make better time than three. And we have to catch this Cytha fast or it might settle down to an endurance contest.'

'All right, then. Tell me about the Cytha.'

Duncan poured porridge gruel into his bowl, handed the pan to Shotwell. 'It's a sort of special thing. The natives are scared to death of it. You hear a lot of stories about it. Said to be unkillable. It's always capitalized, always a proper noun. It has been reported at different times from widely scattered places.'

'No one's ever bagged one?'

'Not that I ever heard of.' Duncan patted the rifle. 'Let me get a bead on it.'

He started eating, spooning the porridge into his mouth, munching on the stale corn bread left from the night before. He drank some of the brackish beverage and shuddered.

'Someday,' he said, 'I'm going to scrape together enough money to buy a pound of coffee. You'd think – '

'It's the freight rates,' Shotwell said. 'I'll send you a pound when I go back.'

'Not at the price they'd charge to ship it out,' said Duncan. 'I wouldn't hear of it.'

They ate in silence for a time. Finally Shotwell said: 'I'm getting nowhere, Gavin. The natives are willing to talk, but it all adds up to nothing.'

'I tried to tell you that. You could have saved your time.'

Shotwell shook his head stubbornly. 'There's an answer, a logical explanation. It's easy enough to say you cannot rule out the sexual factor, but that's exactly what has happened here on Layard. It's easy to exclaim that a sexless animal, a sexless race, a sexless planet is impossible, but that is what we have. Somewhere there is an answer and I have to find it.'

'Now hold up a minute,' Duncan protested. 'There's no use blowing a gasket. I haven't got the time this morning to listen to your lecture.'

'But it's not the lack of sex that worries me entirely,' Shotwell said, 'although it's the central factor. There are subsidiary situations deriving from that central fact which are most intriguing.'

'I have no doubt of it,' said Duncan, 'but if you please – '

'Without sex, there is no basis for the family, and without the family there is no basis for a tribe, and yet the natives have an elaborate tribal setup, with taboos by way of regulation. Somewhere there must exist some underlying, basic unifying factor, some common loyalty, some strange relationship which spells out to brotherhood.'

'Not brotherhood,' said Duncan, chuckling. 'Not even sisterhood. You must watch your terminology. The word you want is ithood.'

The door pushed open and a native walked in timidly.

'Zikkara said that mister want me,' the native told them. 'I am Sipar. I can track anything but screamers, stilt-birds, longhorns, and donovans. Those are my taboos.'

'I am glad to hear that,' Duncan replied. 'You have no Cytha taboo, then?'

'Cytha!' yipped the native. 'Zikkara did not tell me Cytha!'

Duncan paid no attention. He got up from the table and went to the heavy chest that stood against one wall. He rummaged in it and came out with a pair of binoculars, a hunting knife, and an extra drum of ammuniton. At the kitchen cupboard, he rummaged once again, filling a small leather sack with a gritty powder from a can he found.

'Rockahominy,' he explained to Shotwell. 'Emergency rations thought up by the primitive North American Indians. Parched corn, ground fine. It's no feast exactly, but it keeps a man going.'

'You figure you'll be gone that long?'

'Maybe overnight. I don't know. Won't stop until I get it. Can't afford to. It could wipe me out in a few days.'

'Good hunting,' Shotwell said. 'I'll hold the fort.'

Duncan said to Sipar: 'Quit snivelling and come on.'

He picked up the rifle, settled it in the crook of his arm. He kicked open the door and strode out.

Sipar followed meekly.

II

Duncan got his first shot late in the afternoon of that first day.

In the middle of the morning, two hours after they had left the farm, they had flushed the Cytha out of its bed in a thick ravine. But there had been no chance for a shot. Duncan saw no more than a huge black blur fade into the bush.

Through the bake-oven afternoon, they had followed its trail, Sipar tracking and Duncan bringing up the rear, scanning every piece of cover, with the sun-hot rifle always held at ready.

Once they had been held up for fifteen minutes while a massive donovan tramped back and forth, screaming, trying to work up its courage for attack. But after a quarter hour of showing off, it decided to behave itself and went off at a shuffling gallop.

Duncan watched it go with a lot of thankfulness. It could soak up a lot of lead, and for all its awkwardness, it was handy with its feet once it set itself in motion. Donovans had killed a lot of men in the twenty years since Earthmen had come to Layard.

With the beast gone, Duncan looked around for Sipar. He found it fast asleep beneath a hula-shrub. He kicked the native

129

awake with something less than gentleness and they went on again.

The bush swarmed with other animals, but they had no trouble with them.

Sipar, despite its initial reluctance, had worked well at the trailing. A misplaced bunch of grass, a twig bent to one side, a displaced stone, the faintest pug mark were Sipar's stock in trade. It worked like a lithe, well-trained hound. This bush country was its special province; here it was at home.

With the sun dropping towards the west, they had climbed a long, steep hill and as they neared the top of it. Duncan hissed at Sipar. The native looked back over its shoulder in surprise. Duncan made motions for it to stop tracking.

The native crouched and as Duncan went past it, he saw that a look of agony was twisting its face. And in the look of agony he thought he saw as well a touch of pleading and a trace of hatred. It's scared, just like the rest of them, Duncan told himself. But what the native thought or felt had no significance; what counted was the beast ahead.

Duncan went the last few yards on his belly, pushing the gun ahead of him, the binoculars bumping on his back. Swift, vicious insects ran out of the grass and swarmed across his hands and arms and one got on his face and bit him.

He made it to the hilltop and lay there, looking at the sweep of land beyond. It was more of the same, more of the blistering, dusty slogging, more of thorn and tangled ravine and awful emptiness.

He lay motionless, watching for a hint of motion, for the fitful shadow, for any wrongness in the terrain that might be the Cytha.

But there was nothing. The land lay quiet under the declining sun. Far on the horizon, a herd of some sort of animals was grazing, but there was nothing else.

Then he saw the motion, just a flicker, on the knoll ahead – about halfway up.

He laid the rifle carefully on the ground and hitched the binoculars around. He raised them to his eyes and moved them slowly back and forth. The animal was there where he had seen the motion.

It was resting, looking back along the way that it had come, watching for the first sign of its trailers. Duncan tried to make

130

out the size and shape, but it blended with the grass and the dun soil and he could not be sure exactly what it looked like.

He let the glasses down and now that he had located it, he could distinguish its outline with the naked eye.

His hand reached out and slid the rifle to him. He fitted it to his shoulder and wriggled his body for closer contact with the ground. The cross-hairs centred on the faint outline on the knoll and then the beast stood up.

It was not as large as he had thought it might be – perhaps a little larger than Earth lion-size, but it certainly was no lion. It was a square-set thing and black and inclined to lumpiness and it had an awkward look about it, but there were strength and ferociousness as well.

Duncan tilted the muzzle of the rifle so that the cross-hairs centred on the massive neck. He drew in a breath and held it and began the trigger squeeze.

The rifle bucked hard against his shoulder and the report hammered in his head and the beast went down. It did not lurch or fall; it simply melted down and disappeared, hidden in the grass.

'Dead centre,' Duncan assured himself.

He worked the mechanism and the spent cartridge case flew out. The feeding mechanism snicked and the fresh shell clicked as it slid into the breech.

He lay for a moment, watching. And on the knoll where the thing had fallen, the grass was twitching as if the wind were blowing, only there was no wind. But despite the twitching of the grass, there was no sign of the Cytha. It did not struggle up again. It stayed where it had fallen.

Duncan got to his feet, dug out the bandanna and mopped at his face. He heard the soft thud of the step behind him and turned his head. It was the tracker.

'It's all right, Sipar,' he said. 'You can quit worrying. I got it. We can go home now.'

It had been a long, hard chase. Longer than he had thought it might be. But it had been successful and that was the thing that counted. For the moment, the *vua* crop was safe.

He tucked the bandanna back into his pocket, went down the slope and started up the knoll. He reached the place where the Cytha had fallen. There were three small gouts of torn,

131

mangled fur and flesh lying on the ground and there was nothing else.

He spun around and jerked his rifle up. Every nerve was screamingly alert. He swung his head, searching for the slightest movement, for some shape or colour that was not the shape or colour of the bush or grass or ground. But there was nothing. The heat droned in the hush of afternoon. There was not a breath of moving air. But there was danger — a saw-toothed sense of danger close behind his neck.

'Sipar!' he called in a tense whisper. 'Watch out!'

The native stood motionless, unheeding, its eyeballs rolling up until there was only white, while the muscles stood out along its throat like straining ropes of steel.

Duncan slowly swivelled, rifle held almost at arm's length, elbows crooked a little, ready to bring the weapon into play in a fraction of a second.

Nothing stirred. There was no more than emptiness — the emptiness of sun and molten sky, of grass and scraggy bush, of a brown-and-yellow land stretching into foreverness.

Step by step, Duncan covered the hillside and finally came back to the place where the native squatted on its heels and moaned, rocking back and forth, arms locked tightly across its chest, as if it tried to cradle itself in a sort of illusory comfort.

The Earthman walked to the place where the Cytha had fallen and picked up, one by one, the bits of bleeding flesh. They had been mangled by his bullet. They were limp and had no shape. And it was queer, he thought. In all his years of hunting, over many planets, he had never known a bullet to rip out hunks of flesh.

He dropped the bloody pieces back into the grass and wiped his hands upon his thighs. He got up a little stiffly.

He'd found no trail of blood leading through the grass, and surely an animal with a hole of that size would leave a trail.

And as he stood there upon the hillside, with the bloody fingerprints still wet and glistening upon the fabric of his trousers, he felt the first cold touch of fear, as if the fingertips of fear might momentarily, almost casually, have trailed across his heart.

He turned around and walked back to the native, reached down, and shook it.

'Snap out of it,' he ordered.

132

He expected pleading, cowering, terror, but there was none.

Sipar got swiftly to its feet and stood looking at him and there was, he thought, an odd glitter in its eyes.

'Get going,' Duncan said. 'We still have a little time. Start circling and pick up the trail. I will cover you.'

He glanced at the sun. An hour and a half still left – maybe as much as two. There might still be time to get this buttoned up before the fall of night.

A half mile beyond the knoll, Sipar picked up the trail again and they went ahead, but now they travelled more cautiously, for any bush, any rock, any clump of grass might conceal the wounded beast.

Duncan found himself on edge and cursed himself savagely for it. He'd been in tight spots before. This was nothing new to him. There was no reason to get himself tensed up. It was a deadly business, sure, but he had faced others calmly and walked away from them. It was those frontier tales he'd heard about the Cytha – the kind of superstitious chatter that one always heard on the edge of unknown land.

He gripped the rifle tighter and went on.

No animal, he told himself, was unkillable.

Half an hour before sunset, he called a halt when they reached a brackish water hole. The light soon would be getting bad for shooting. In the morning, they'd take up the trail again, and by that time the Cytha would be at an even greater disadvantage. It would be stiff and slow and weak. It might be even dead.

Duncan gathered wood and built a fire in the lee of a thorn-bush thicket. Sipar waded out with the canteens and thrust them at arm's length beneath the surface to fill them. The water still was warm and evil-tasting, but it was fairly free of scum and a thirsty man could drink it.

The sun went down and darkness fell quickly. They dragged more wood out of the thicket and piled it carefully close at hand.

Duncan reached into his pocket and brought out the little bag of rockahominy.

'Here,' he said to Sipar. 'Supper.'

The native held one hand cupped and Duncan poured a little mound into its palm.

'Thank you, mister,' Sipar said. 'Food-giver.'

133

'Huh?' asked Duncan, then caught what the native meant. 'Dive into it,' he said, almost kindly. 'It isn't much, but it gives you strength. We'll need strength tomorrow.'

Food-giver, eh? Trying to butter him up, perhaps. In a little while, Sipar would start whining for him to knock off the hunt and head back for the farm.

Although, come to think of it, he really was the food-giver to this bunch of sexless wonders. Corn, thank God, grew well on the red and stubborn soil of Layard – good old corn from North America. Fed to hogs, made into corn pone for breakfast back on Earth, and here, on Layard, the staple food crop for a gang of shiftless varmints who still regarded, with some good solid scepticism and round-eyed wonder, this unorthodox idea that one should take the trouble to grow plants to eat rather than go out and scrounge for them.

Corn from North America, he thought, growing side by side with the *vua* of Layard. And that was the way it went. Something from one planet and something from another and still something further from a third and so was built up through the wide social confederacy of space a truly cosmic culture which in the end, in another ten thousand years or so, might spell out some way of life with more sanity and understanding than was evident today.

He poured a mound of rockahominy into his own hand and put the bag back into his pocket.

'Sipar.'

'Yes, mister?'

'You were not scared today when the donovan threatened to attack us.'

'No, mister. The donovan would not hurt me.'

'I see. You said the donovan was taboo to you. Could it be that you, likewise, are taboo to the donovan?'

'Yes, mister. The donovan and I grew up together.'

'Oh, so that's it,' said Duncan.

He put a pinch of the parched and powdered corn into his mouth and took a sip of brackish water. He chewed reflectively on the resultant mash.

He might go ahead, he knew, and ask why and how and where Sipar and the donovan had grown up together, but there was no point to it. This was exactly the kind of tangle that Shotwell was forever getting into.

134

Half the time, he told himself, I'm convinced the little stinkers are doing no more than pulling our legs.

What a fantastic bunch of jerks! Not men, not women, just things. And while there were never babies, there were children, although never less than eight or nine years old. And if there were no babies, where did the eight- and nine-year-olds come from?

'I suppose,' he said, 'that these other things that are your taboos, the stilt-bird and the screamers and the like, also grew up with you.'

'That is right, mister.'

'Some playground that must have been,' said Duncan.

He went on chewing, staring out into the darkness beyond the ring of firelight.

'There's something in the thorn bush, mister.'

'I didn't hear a thing.'

'Little pattering. Something is running there.'

Duncan listened closely. What Sipar said was true. A lot of little things were running in the thicket.

'More than likely mice,' he said.

He finished his rockahominy and took an extra swig of water, gagging on it slightly.

'Get your rest,' he told Sipar. 'I'll wake you later so I can catch a wink or two.'

'Mister,' Sipar said, 'I'll stay with you to the end.'

'Well,' said Duncan, somewhat startled, 'that is decent of you.'

'I will stay to the death,' Sipar promised earnestly.

'Don't strain yourself,' said Duncan.

He picked up the rifle and walked down to the water hole.

The night was quiet and the land continued to have that empty feeling. Empty except for the fire and the water hole and the little micelike animals running in the thicket.

And Sipar — Sipar lying by the fire, curled up and sound asleep already. Naked, with not a weapon to its hand — just the naked animal, the basic humanoid, and yet with underlying purpose that at times was baffling. Scared and shivering this morning at mere mention of the Cytha, yet never faltering on the trail; in pure funk back there on the knoll where they had lost the Cytha, but now ready to go on to the death.

135

Duncan went back to the fire and prodded Sipar with his toe. The native came straight up out of sleep.

'Whose death?' asked Duncan. 'Whose death were you talking of?'

'Why, ours, of course,' said Sipar, and went back to sleep.

III

Duncan did not see the arrow coming. He heard the swishing whistle and felt the wind of it on the right side of his throat and then it thunked into a tree behind him.

He leaped aside and dived for the cover of a tumbled mound of boulders and almost instinctively his thumb pushed the fire control of the rifle up to automatic.

He crouched behind the jumbled rocks and peered ahead. There was not a thing to see. The hula-trees shimmered in the blaze of sun and the thorn bush was grey and lifeless and the only things astir were three stilt-birds walking gravely a quarter of a mile away.

'Sipar!' he whispered.

'Here, mister.'

'Keep low. It's still out there.'

Whatever it might be. Still out there and waiting for another shot. Duncan shivered, remembering the feel of the arrow flying past his throat. A hell of a way for a man to die – out at the tail end of nowhere with an arrow in his throat and a scared-stiff native heading back for home as fast as it could go.

He flicked the control on the rifle back to single fire, crawled around the rock pile, and sprinted for a grove of trees that stood on higher ground. He reached them and there he flanked the spot from which the arrow must have come.

He unlimbered the binoculars and glassed the area. He still saw no sign. Whatever had taken the pot shot at them had made its getaway.

He walked back to the tree where the arrow still stood out, its point driven deep into the bark. He grasped the shaft and wrenched the arrow free.

'You can come out now,' he called to Sipar. 'There's no one around.'

The arrow was unbelievably crude. The unfeathered shaft
136

looked as if it had been battered off to the proper length with a jagged stone. The arrowhead was unflaked flint picked up from some outcropping or dry creek bed, and it was awkwardly bound to the shaft with the tough but pliant inner bark of the hula-tree.

'You recognize this?' he asked Sipar.

The native took the arrow and examined it. 'Not my tribe.'

'Of course not your tribe. Yours wouldn't take a shot at us. Some other tribe, perhaps?'

'Very poor arrow.'

'I know that. But it could kill you just as dead as if it were a good one. Do you recognize it?'

'No tribe made this arrow,' Sipar declared.

'Child, maybe?'

'What would child do way out here?'

'That's what I thought, too,' said Duncan.

He took the arrow back, held it between his thumbs and forefingers and twirled it slowly, with a terrifying thought nibbling at his brain. It couldn't be. It was too fantastic. He wondered if the sun was finally getting him that he had thought of it at all.

He squatted down and dug at the ground with the makeshift arrow point. 'Sipar, what do you actually know about the Cytha?'

'Nothing, mister. Scared of it is all.'

'We aren't turning back. If there's something that you know – something that would help us . . .'

It was as close as he could come to begging aid. It was further than he had meant to go. He should not have asked at all, he thought angrily.

'I do not know,' the native said.

Duncan cast the arrow to one side and rose to his feet. He cradled the rifle in his arm. 'Let's go.'

He watched Sipar trot ahead. Crafty little stinker, he told himself. It knows more than it's telling.

They toiled into the afternoon. It was, if possible, hotter and drier than the day before. There was a sense of tension in the air – no, that was rot. And even if there were, a man must act as if it were not there. If he let himself fall prey to every mood out in this empty land, he only had himself to blame for whatever happened to him.

The tracking was harder now. The day before, the Cytha had only run away, straight-line fleeing to keep ahead of them, to stay out of their reach. Now it was becoming tricky. It backtracked often in an attempt to throw them off. Twice in the afternoon, the trail blanked out entirely and it was only after long searching that Sipar picked it up again – in one instance, a mile away from where it had vanished in thin air.

That vanishing bothered Duncan more than he would admit. Trails do not disappear entirely, not when the terrain remains the same, not when the weather is unchanged. Something was going on, something, perhaps, that Sipar knew far more about than it was willing to divulge.

He watched the native closely and there seemed nothing suspicious. It continued at its work. It was, for all to see, the good and faithful hound.

Late in the afternoon, the plain on which they had been travelling suddenly dropped away. They stood poised on the brink of a great escarpment and looked far out to great tangled forests and a flowing river.

It was like suddenly coming into another and beautiful room that one had not expected.

This was new land, never seen before by any Earthman. For no one had ever mentioned that somewhere to the west a forest lay beyond the bush. Men coming in from space had seen it, probably, but only as a different colour-marking on the planet. To them, it made no difference.

But to the men who lived on Layard, to the planter and the trader, the prospector and the hunter, it was important. And I, thought Duncan with a sense of triumph, am the man who found it.

'Mister!'

'Now what?'

'Out there. *Skun!*'

'I don't – '

'Out there, mister. Across the river.'

Duncan saw it then – a haze in the blueness of the rift – a puff of copper moving away fast, and as he watched, he heard the far-off keening of the storm, a shiver in the air rather than a sound.

He watched in fascination as it moved along the river and saw the boiling fury it made out of the forest. It struck and

138

crossed the river, and the river for a moment seemed to stand on end, with a sheet of silvery water splashed towards the sky.

Then it was gone as quickly as it had happened, but there was a tumbled slash across the forest where the churning winds had travelled.

Back at the farm, Zikkara had warned him of the *skun*. This was the season for them, it had said, and a man caught in one wouldn't have a chance.

Duncan let his breath out slowly.

'Bad,' said Sipar.

'Yes, very bad.'

'Hit fast. No warning.'

'What about the trail?' asked Duncan. 'Did the Cytha – '

Sipar nodded downward.

'Can we make it before nightfall?'

'I think so,' Sipar answered.

It was rougher than they had thought. Twice they went down blind trails that pinched off, with sheer rock faces opening out into drops of hundreds of feet, and were forced to climb again and find another way.

They reached the bottom of the escarpment as the brief twilight closed in and they hurried to gather firewood. There was no water, but a little was still left in their canteens and they made do with that.

After their scant meal of rockahominy, Sipar rolled himself into a ball and went to sleep immediately.

Duncan sat with his back against a boulder which one day, long ago, had fallen from the slope above them, but was now half buried in the soil that through the ages had kept sifting down.

Two days gone, he told himself.

Was there, after all, some truth in the whispered tales that made the rounds back at the settlements – that no one should waste his time in tracking down a Cytha, since a Cytha was unkillable?

Nonsense, he told himself. And yet the hunt had toughened, the trail become more difficult, the Cytha a much more cunning and elusive quarry. Where it had run from them the day before, now it fought to shake them off. And if it did that the second day, why had it not tried to throw them off the first? And what about the third day – tomorrow?

He shook his head. It seemed incredible that an animal would become more formidable as the hunt progressed. But that seemed to be exactly what had happened. More spooked, perhaps, more frightened – only the Cytha did not act like a frightened beast. It was acting like an animal that was gaining savvy and determination, and that was somehow frightening.

From far off to the west, towards the forest and the river, came the laughter and the howling of a pack of screamers. Duncan leaned his rifle against the boulder and got up to pile more wood on the fire. He stared out into the western darkness, listening to the racket. He made a wry face and pushed a hand absent-mindedly through his hair. He put out a silent hope that the screamers would decide to keep their distance. They were something a man could do without.

Behind him, a pebble came bumping down the slope. It thudded to a rest just short of the fire.

Duncan spun around. Foolish thing to do, he thought, to camp so near the slope. If something big should start to move, they'd be out of luck.

He stood and listened. The night was quiet. Even the screamers had shut up for the moment. Just one rolling rock and he had his hackles up. He'd have to get himself in hand.

He went back to the boulder, and as he stooped to pick up the rifle, he heard the faint beginning of a rumble. He straightened swiftly to face the scarp that blotted out the star-strewn sky – and the rumble grew!

In one leap, he was at Sipar's side. He reached down and grasped the native by an arm, jerked it erect, held it on its feet. Sipar's eyes snapped open, blinking in the firelight.

The rumble had grown to a roar and there were thumping noises, as of heavy boulders bouncing, and beneath the roar the silky, ominous rustle of sliding soil and rock.

Sipar jerked its arm free of Duncan's grip and plunged into the darkness. Duncan whirled and followed.

They ran, stumbling in the dark, and behind them the roar of the sliding, bouncing rock became a throaty roll of thunder that filled the night from brim to brim. As he ran, Duncan could feel, in dread anticipation, the gusty breath of hurtling debris blowing on his neck, the crushing impact of a boulder smashing into him, the engulfing flood of tumbling talus snatching at his legs.

140

A puff of billowing dust came out and caught them and they ran choking as well as stumbling. Off to the left of them, a mighty chunk of rock chugged along the ground in jerky, almost reluctant fashion.

Then the thunder stopped and all one could hear was the small slitherings of the lesser debris as it trickled down the slope.

Duncan stopped running and slowly turned around. The campfire was gone, buried, no doubt, beneath tons of overlay, and the stars had paled because of the great cloud of dust which still billowed up into the sky.

He heard Sipar moving near him and reached out a hand, searching for the tracker, not knowing exactly where it was. He found the native, grasped it by the shoulder, and pulled it up beside him.

Sipar was shivering.

'It's all right,' said Duncan.

And it *was* all right, he reassured himself. He still had the rifle. The extra drum of ammunition and the knife were on his belt, the bag of rockahominy in his pocket. The canteens were all they had lost – the canteens and the fire.

'We'll have to hole up somewhere for the night,' Duncan said. 'There are screamers on the loose.'

He didn't like what he was thinking, nor the sharp edge of fear that was beginning to crowd in upon him. He tried to shrug it off, but it still stayed with him, just out of reach.

Sipar plucked at his elbow.

'Thorn thicket, mister. Over there. We could crawl inside. We would be safe from screamers.'

It was torture, but they made it. 'Screamers and you are taboo,' said Duncan, suddenly remembering. 'How come you are afraid of them?'

'Afraid for you, mister, mostly. Afraid for myself just a little. Screamers could forget. They might not recognize me until too late. Safer here.'

'I agree with you,' said Duncan.

The screamers came and padded all about the thicket. The beasts sniffed and clawed at the thorns to reach them, but finally went away.

When morning came, Duncan and Sipar climbed the scarp, clambering over the boulders and the tons of soil and rock

141

that covered their camping place. Following the gash cut by the slide, they clambered up the slope and finally reached the point of the slide's beginning.

There they found the depression in which the poised slab of rock had rested and where the supporting soil had been dug away so that it could be started, with a push, down the slope above the campfire.

And all about were the deeply sunken pug marks of the Cytha!

IV

Now it was more than just a hunt. It was a knife against the throat, kill or be killed. Now there was no stopping, when before there might have been. It was no longer sport and there was no mercy.

'And that's the way I like it,' Duncan told himself.

He rubbed his hand along the rifle barrel and saw the metallic glints shine in the noonday sun. One more shot, he prayed. Just give me one more shot at it. This time there will be no slip up. This time there will be more than three sodden hunks of flesh and fur lying in the grass to mock me.

He squinted his eyes against the heat shimmer rising from the river, watching Sipar hunkered beside the water's edge.

The native rose to its feet and trotted back to him.

'It crossed,' said Sipar. 'It walked out as far as it could go and it must have swum.'

'Are you sure? It might have waded out to make us think it crossed, then doubled back again.'

He stared at the purple-green of the trees across the river. Inside that forest, it would be hellish going.

'We can look,' said Sipar.

'Good. You go downstream. I'll go up.'

An hour later, they were back. They had found no tracks. There seemed little doubt the Cytha had really crossed the river.

They stood side by side, looking at the forest.

'Mister, we have come far. You are brave to hunt the Cytha. You have no fear of death.'

142

'The fear of death,' Duncan said, 'is entirely infantile. And it's beside the point as well. I do not intend to die.'

They waded out into the stream. The bottom shelved gradually and they had to swim no more than a hundred yards or so.

They reached the forest bank and threw themselves flat to rest.

Duncan looked back the way that they had come. To the east, the escarpment was a dark blue smudge against the pale blue burnished sky. And two days back of that lay the farm and the *vua* field, but they seemed much farther off than that. They were lost in time and distance; they belonged to another existence and another world.

All his life, it seemed to him, had faded and become inconsequential and forgotten, as if this moment in his life were the only one that counted; as if all the minutes and the hours, all the breaths and heartbeats, wake and sleep, had pointed towards this certain hour upon this certain stream, with the rifle moulded to his hand and the cool, calculated bloodlust of a killer riding in his brain.

Sipar finally got up and began to range along the stream. Duncan sat up and watched.

Scared to death, he thought, and yet it stayed with me. At the campfire that first night, it had said it would stick to the death and apparently it had meant exactly what it said. It's hard, he thought, to figure out these jokers, hard to know what kind of mental operation, what seethings of emotion, what brand of ethics and what variety of belief and faith go to make them and their way of life.

It would have been so easy for Sipar to have missed the trail and swear it could not find it. Even from the start, it could have refused to go. Yet fearing, it had gone. Reluctant, it had trailed. Without any need for faithfulness and loyalty, it had been loyal and faithful. But loyal to what, Duncan wondered, to him, the outlander and intruder? Loyal to itself? Or perhaps, although that seemed impossible, faithful to the Cytha?

What does Sipar think of me, he asked himself, and maybe more to the point, what do I think of Sipar? Is there a common meeting ground? Or are we, despite our humanoid forms, condemned forever to be alien and apart?

143

He held the rifle across his knees and stroked it, polishing it, petting it, making it even more closely a part of him, an instrument of his deadliness, an expression of his determination to track and kill the Cytha.

Just another chance, he begged. Just one second, or even less, to draw a steady bead. That is all I want, all I need, all I'll ask.

Then he could go back across the days that he had left behind him, back to the farm and field, back into that misty other life from which he had been so mysteriously divorced, but which in time undoubtedly would become real and meaningful again.

Sipar came back. 'I found the trail.'

Duncan heaved himself to his feet. 'Good.'

They left the river and plunged into the forest and there the heat closed in more mercilessly than ever – humid, stifling heat that felt like a soggy blanket wrapped tightly round the body.

The trail lay plain and clear. The Cytha now, it seemed, was intent upon piling up a lead without recourse to evasive tactics. Perhaps it had reasoned that its pursuers would lose some time at the river and it may have been trying to stretch out that margin even further. Perhaps it needed that extra time, he speculated, to set up the necessary machinery for another dirty trick.

Sipar stopped and waited for Duncan to catch up. 'Your knife, mister?'

Duncan hesitated. 'What for?'

'I have a thorn in my foot,' the native said. 'I have to get it out.'

Duncan pulled the knife from his belt and tossed it. Sipar caught it deftly.

Looking straight at Duncan, with the flicker of a smile upon its lips, the native cut its throat.

V

He should go back, he knew. Without the tracker, he didn't have a chance. The odds were now with the Cytha – if, indeed, they had not been with it from the very start.

Unkillable? Unkillable because it grew in intelligence to meet emergencies? Unkillable because, pressed, it could fashion a bow and arrow, however crude? Unkillable because it had a sense of tactics, like rolling rocks at night upon its enemy? Unkillable because a native tracker would cheerfully kill itself to protect the Cytha?

A sort of crisis-beast, perhaps? One able to develop intelligence and abilities to meet each new situation and then lapsing back to the level of non-intelligent contentment? That, thought Duncan, would be a sensible way for anything to live. It would do away with the inconvenience and the irritability and the discontentment of intelligence when intelligence was unneeded. But the intelligence, and the abilities which went with it, would be there, safely tucked away where one could reach in and get them, like a necklace or a gun – something to be used or to be put away as the case might be.

Duncan hunched forward and with a stick of wood pushed the fire together. The flames blazed up anew and sent sparks flying up into the whispering darkness of the trees. The night had cooled off a little, but the humidity still hung on and a man felt uncomfortable – a little frightened, too.

Duncan lifted his head and stared up into the fire-flecked darkness. There were no stars because the heavy foliage shut them out. He missed the stars. He'd feel better if he could look up and see them.

When morning came, he should go back. He should quit this hunt which now had become impossible and even slightly foolish.

But he knew he wouldn't. Somewhere along the three-day trail, he had become committed to a purpose and a challenge, and he knew that when morning came, he would go on again. It was not hatred that drove him, nor vengeance, nor even the trophy-urge – the hunter-lust that prodded men to kill something strange or harder to kill or bigger than any man had ever killed before. It was something more than that, some weird entangling of the Cytha's meaning with his own.

He reached out and picked up the rifle and laid it in his lap. Its barrel gleamed dully in the flickering campfire light and he rubbed his hand along the stock as another man might stroke a woman's throat.

'Mister,' said a voice.

145

It did not startle him, for the word was softly spoken and for a moment he had forgotten that Sipar was dead – dead with a half-smile fixed upon its face and with its throat laid wide open.

'Mister?'

Duncan stiffened.

Sipar was dead and there was no one else – and yet someone had spoken to him, and there could be only one thing in all this wilderness that might speak to him.

'Yes,' he said.

He did not move. He simply sat there, with the rifle in his lap.

'You know who I am?'

'I suppose you are the Cytha.'

'You have done well,' the Cytha said. 'You've made a splendid hunt. There is no dishonour if you should decide to quit. Why don't you go back? I promise you no harm.'

It was over there, somewhere in front of him, somewhere in the brush beyond the fire, almost straight across the fire from him, Duncan told himself. If he could keep it talking, perhaps even lure it out –

'Why should I?' he asked. 'The hunt is never done until one gets the thing one is after.'

'I can kill you,' the Cytha told him. 'But I do not want to kill. It hurts to kill.'

'That's right,' said Duncan. 'You are most perceptive.'

For he had it pegged now. He knew exactly where it was. He could afford a little mockery.

His thumb slid up the metal and nudged the fire control to automatic and he flexed his legs beneath him so that he could rise and fire in one single motion.

'Why did you hunt me?' the Cytha asked. 'You are a stranger on my world and you had no right to hunt me. Not that I mind, of course. In fact, I found it stimulating. We must do it again. When I am ready to be hunted, I shall come and tell you and we can spend a day or two at it.'

'Sure we can,' said Duncan, rising. And as he rose into his crouch, he held the trigger down and the gun danced in insane fury, the muzzle flare a flicking tongue of hatred and the hail of death hissing spitefully in the underbrush.

'Anytime you want to,' yelled Duncan gleefully, 'I'll come

146

and hunt you! You just say the word and I'll be on your tail. I might even kill you. Now do you like it, chump!'

And he held the trigger tight and kept his crouch so the slugs would not fly high, but would cut their swath just above the ground, and he moved the muzzle back and forth a lot so that he covered extra ground to compensate for any miscalculations he might have made.

The magazine ran out and the gun clicked empty and the vicious chatter stopped. Powder smoke drifted softly in the campfire light and the smell of it was perfume in the nostrils and in the underbrush many little feet were running, as if a thousand frightened mice were scurrying from catastrophe.

Duncan unhooked the extra magazine from where it hung upon his belt and replaced the empty one. Then he snatched a burning length of wood from the fire and waved it frantically until it burst into a blaze and became a torch. Rifle grasped in one hand and the torch in the other, he plunged into the underbrush. Little chittering things fled to escape him.

He did not find the Cytha. He found chewed-up bushes and soil churned by flying metal, and he found five lumps of flesh and fur, and these he brought back to the fire.

Now the fear that had been stalking him, keeping just beyond his reach, walked out from the shadows and hunkered by the campfire with him.

He placed the rifle within easy reach and arranged the five bloody chunks on the ground close to the fire and he tried with trembling fingers to restore them to the shape they'd been before the bullets struck them. And that was a good one, he thought with grim irony, because they had no shape. They had been part of the Cytha and you killed a Cytha inch by inch, not with a single shot. You knocked a pound of meat off it the first time, and the next time you shot off another pound or two, and if you got enough shots at it, you finally carved it down to size and maybe you could kill it then, although he wasn't sure.

He was afraid. He admitted that he was and he squatted there and watched his fingers shake and he kept his jaws clamped tight to stop the chatter of his teeth.

The fear had been getting closer all the time; he knew it had moved in by a step or two when Sipar cut its throat, and why in the name of God had the damn fool done it? It made no

147

sense at all. He had wondered about Sipar's loyalties, and the very loyalties that he had dismissed as a sheer impossibility had been the answer, after all. In the end, for some obscure reason – obscure to humans, that is – Sipar's loyalty had been to the Cytha.

But then what was the use of searching for any reason in it? Nothing that had happened made any sense. It made no sense that a beast one was pursuing should up and talk to one – although it did fit in with the theory of the crisis-beast he had fashioned in his mind.

Progressive adaptation, he told himself. Carry adaptation far enough, and you'd reach communication. But might not the Cytha's power of adaptation be running down? Had the Cytha gone about as far as it could force itself to go? Maybe so, he thought. It might be worth a gamble. Sipar's suicide, for all its casualness, bore the overtones of last-notch desperation. And the Cytha's speaking to Duncan, its attempt to parley with him, contained a note of weakness.

The arrow had failed and the rockslide had failed and so had Sipar's death. What next would the Cytha try? Had it anything to try?

Tomorrow he'd find out. Tomorrow he'd go on. He couldn't turn back now.

He was too deeply involved. He'd always wonder, if he turned back now, whether another hour or two might not have seen the end of it. There were too many questions, too much mystery – there was now far more at stake than ten rows of *vua*.

Another day might make some sense of it, might banish the dread walker that trod upon his heels, might bring some peace of mind.

As it stood right at the moment, none of it made sense.

But even as he thought it, suddenly one of the bits of bloody flesh and mangled fur made sense.

Beneath the punching and prodding of his fingers, it had assumed a shape.

Breathlessly, Duncan bent above it, not believing, not even wanting to believe, hoping frantically that it should prove completely wrong.

But there was nothing wrong with it. The shape was there and could not be denied. It had somehow fitted back into its

148

natural shape and it was a baby screamer – well, maybe not a baby, but at least a tiny screamer.

Duncan sat back on his heels and sweated. He wiped his bloody hands upon the ground. He wondered what other shapes he'd find if he put back into proper place the other hunks of limpness that lay beside the fire.

He tried and failed. They were too smashed and torn.

He picked them up and tossed them in the fire. He took up his rifle and walked around the fire, sat down with his back against a tree, cradling the gun across his knees.

Those little scurrying feet, he wondered – like the scampering of a thousand busy mice. He had heard them twice, that first night in the thicket by the water hole and again tonight.

And what could the Cytha be? Certainly not the simple, uncomplicated, marauding animal he had thought to start with.

A hive-beast? A host animal? A thing masquerading in many different forms?

Shotwell, trained in such deductions, might make a fairly accurate guess, but Shotwell was not here. He was at the farm, fretting, more than likely, over Duncan's failure to return.

Finally the first light of morning began to filter through the forest and it was not the glaring, clean white light of the open plain and bush, but a softened, diluted, fuzzy green light to match the smothering vegetation.

The night noises died away and the noises of the day took up – the sawings of unseen insects, the screechings of hidden birds, and something far away began to make a noise that sounded like an empty barrel falling slowly down a stairway.

What little coolness the night had brought dissipated swiftly and the heat clamped down, a breathless, relentless heat that quivered in the air.

Circling, Duncan picked up the Cytha trail not more than a hundred yards from camp.

The beast had been travelling fast. The pug marks were deeply sunk and widely spaced. Duncan followed as rapidly as he dared. It was a temptation to follow at a run, to match the Cytha's speed, for the trail was plain and fresh and it fairly beckoned.

And that was wrong, Duncan told himself. It was too fresh,

149

too plain – almost as if the animal had gone to endless trouble so that the human could not miss the trail.

He stopped his trailing and crouched beside a tree and studied the tracks ahead. His hands were too tense upon the gun, his body keyed too high and fine. He forced himself to take slow, deep breaths. He had to calm himself. He had to loosen up.

He studied the tracks ahead – four bunched pug marks, then a long leap interval, then four more bunched tracks, and between the sets of marks the forest floor was innocent and smooth.

Too smooth, perhaps. Especially the third one from him. Too smooth and somehow artificial, as if someone had patted it with gentle hands to make it unsuspicious.

Duncan sucked his breath in slowly.

Trap?

Or was his imagination playing tricks on him?

And if it were a trap, he would have fallen into it if he had kept on following as he had started out.

Now there was something else, a strange uneasiness, and he stirred uncomfortably, casting frantically for some clue to what it was.

He rose and stepped out from the tree, with the gun at ready. What a perfect place to set a trap, he thought. One would be looking at the pug marks, never at the space between them, for the space between would be neutral ground, safe to stride out upon.

Oh, clever Cytha, he said to himself. Oh, clever, clever Cytha!

And now he knew what the other trouble was – the great uneasiness. It was the sense of being watched.

Somewhere up ahead, the Cytha was crouched, watching and waiting – anxious or exultant, maybe even with laughter rumbling in its throat.

He walked slowly forward until he reached the third set of tracks and he saw that he had been right. The little area ahead was smoother than it should be.

'Cytha!' he called.

His voice was far louder than he had meant it to be and he stood astonished and a bit abashed.

Then he realized why it was so loud.

It was the only sound there was!

The forest suddenly had fallen silent. The insects and birds were quiet and the thing in the distance had quit falling down the stairs. Even the leaves were silent. There was no rustle in them and they hung limp upon their stems.

There was a feeling of doom and the green light had changed to a copper light and everything was still.

And the light was *copper!*

Duncan spun around in panic. There was no place for him to hide.

Before he could take another step, the *skun* came and the winds rushed out of nowhere. The air was clogged with flying leaves and debris. Trees snapped and popped and tumbled in the air.

The wind hurled Duncan to his knees, and as he fought to regain his feet, he remembered, in a blinking flash of total recall, how it had looked from atop the escarpment – the boiling fury of the winds and the mad swirling of the coppery mist and how the trees had whipped in whirlpool fashion.

He came half erect and stumbled, clawing at the ground in an attempt to get up again, while inside his brain an insistent, clicking voice cried out for him to run, and somewhere another voice said to lie flat upon the ground, to dig in as best he could.

Something struck him from behind and he went down, pinned flat, with his rifle wedged beneath him. He cracked his head upon the ground and the world whirled sickeningly and plastered his face with a handful of mud and tattered leaves.

He tried to crawl and couldn't, for something had grabbed him by the ankle and was hanging on.

With a frantic hand, he clawed the mess out of his eyes, spat it from his mouth.

Across the spinning ground, something black and angular tumbled rapidly. It was coming straight towards him and he saw it was the Cytha and that in another second it would be on top of him.

He threw up an arm across his face, with the elbow crooked, to take the impact of the wind-blown Cytha and to ward it off.

But it never reached him. Less than a yard away, the ground opened up to take the Cytha and it was no longer there.

151

Suddenly the wind cut off and the leaves once more hung motionless and the heat clamped down again and that was the end of it. The *skun* had come and struck and gone.

Minutes, Duncan wondered, or perhaps no more than seconds. But in those seconds, the forest had been flattened and the trees lay in shattered heaps.

He raised himself on an elbow and looked to see what was the matter with his foot and he saw that a fallen tree had trapped his foot beneath it.

He tugged a few times experimentally. It was no use. Two close-set limbs, branching almost at right angles from the hole, had been driven deep into the ground and his foot, he saw, had been caught at the ankle in the fork of the buried branches.

The foot didn't hurt – not yet. It didn't seem to be there at all. He tried wiggling his toes and felt none.

He wiped the sweat off his face with a shirt sleeve and fought to force down the panic that was rising in him. Getting panicky was the worst thing a man could do in a spot like this. The thing to do was to take stock of the situation, figure out the best approach, then go ahead and try it.

The tree looked heavy, but perhaps he could handle it if he had to, although there was the danger that if he shifted it, the bole might settle more solidly and crush his foot beneath it. At the moment, the two heavy branches, thrust into the ground on either side of his ankle, were holding most of the tree's weight off his foot.

The best thing to do, he decided, was to dig the ground away beneath his foot until he could pull it out.

He twisted around and started digging with the fingers of one hand. Beneath the thin covering of humus, he struck a solid surface and his fingers slid along it.

With mounting alarm, he explored the ground, scratching at the humus. There was nothing but rock – some long-buried boulder, the top of which lay just beneath the ground.

His foot was trapped beneath a heavy tree and a massive boulder, held securely in place by forked branches that had forced their splintering way down along the boulder's sides.

He lay back, propped on an elbow. It was evident that he could do nothing about the buried boulder. If he was going to do anything, his problem was the tree.

152

To move the tree, he would need a lever and he had a good, stout lever in his rifle. It would be a shame, he thought a little wryly, to use a gun for such a purpose, but he had no choice.

He worked for an hour and it was no good. Even with the rifle as a pry, he could not budge the tree.

He lay back, defeated, breathing hard, wringing wet with perspiration.

He grimaced at the sky.

All right, Cytha, he thought, you won out in the end. But it took a *skun* to do it. With all your tricks, you couldn't do the job until . . .

Then he remembered.

He sat up hurriedly.

'Cytha!' he yelled.

The Cytha had fallen into a hole that had opened in the ground. The hole was less than an arm's length away from him, with a little debris around its edges still trickling into it.

Duncan stretched out his body, lying flat upon the ground, and looked into the hole. There, at the bottom of it, was the Cytha.

It was the first time he'd gotten a good look at the Cytha and it was a crazily put-together thing. It seemed to have nothing functional about it and it looked more like a heap of something, just thrown on the ground, than it did an animal.

The hole, he saw, was more than an ordinary hole. It was a pit and very cleverly constructed. The mouth was about four feet in diameter and it widened to roughly twice that at the bottom. It was, in general, bottle-shaped, with an incurving shoulder at the top so that anything that fell in could not climb out. Anything falling into that pit was to stay.

This, Duncan knew, was what had lain beneath that too-smooth interval between the two sets of Cytha tracks. The Cytha had worked all night to dig it, then had carried away the dirt dug out of the pit and had built a flimsy camouflage cover over it. Then it had gone back and made the trail that was so loud and clear, so easy to make out and follow. And having done all that, having laboured hard and stealthily, the Cytha had settled down to watch, to make sure the following human had fallen in the pit.

'Hi, pal,' said Duncan. 'How are you making out?'

The Cytha did not answer.

153

'Classy pit,' said Duncan. 'Do you always den up in luxury like this?'

But the Cytha didn't answer.

Something queer was happening to the Cytha. It was coming all apart.

Duncan watched with fascinated horror as the Cytha broke down into a thousand lumps of motion that scurried in the pit and tried to scramble up its sides, only to fall back in tiny showers of sand.

Amid the scurrying lumps, one thing remained intact, a fragile object that resembled nothing quite so much as the stripped skeleton of a Thanksgiving turkey. But it was a most extraordinary Thanksgiving skeleton, for it throbbed with pulsing life and glowed with a steady violet light.

Chitterings and squeakings came out of the pit and the soft patter of tiny running feet, and as Duncan's eyes became accustomed to the darkness of the pit, he began to make out the forms of some of the scurrying shapes. There were tiny screamers and some donovans and sawmill birds and a bevy of kill-devils and something else as well.

Duncan raised a hand and pressed it against his eyes, then took it quickly away. The little faces still were there, looking up as if beseeching him, with the white shine of their teeth and the white rolling of their eyes.

He felt horror wrenching at his stomach and the sour, bitter taste of revulsion welled into his throat, but he fought it down, harking back to that day at the farm before they had started on the hunt.

'I can track down anything but screamers, stilt-birds, long-horns and donovans,' Sipar had told him solemnly. 'These are my taboos.'

And Sipar was also their taboo, for he had not feared the donovan. Sipar had been, however, somewhat fearful of the screamers in the dead of night because, the native had told him reasonably, screamers were forgetful.

Forgetful of what!

Forgetful of the Cytha-mother? Forgetful of the motley brood in which they had spent their childhood?

For that was the only answer to what was running in the pit and the whole, unsuspected answer to the enigma against

154

which men like Shotwell had frustratedly banged their heads for years.

Strange, he told himself. All right, it might be strange, but if it worked, what difference did it make? So the planet's denizens were sexless because there was no need of sex – what was wrong with that? It might, in fact, Duncan admitted to himself, head off a lot of trouble. No family spats, no triangle trouble, no fighting over mates. While it might be unexciting, it did seem downright peaceful.

And since there was no sex, the Cytha species was the planetary mother – but more than just a mother. The Cytha, more than likely, was mother-father, incubator, nursery, teacher, and perhaps many other things besides, all rolled into one.

In many ways, he thought, it might make a lot of sense. Here natural selection would be ruled out and ecology could be controlled in considerable degree and mutation might even be a matter of deliberate choice rather than random happenstance.

And it would make for a potential planetary unity such as no other world had ever known. Everything here was kin to everything else. Here was a planet where Man, or any other alien, must learn to tread most softly. For it was not inconceivable that, in a crisis or a clash of interests, one might find himself faced suddenly with a unified and co-operating planet, with every form of life making common cause against the interloper.

The little scurrying things had given up; they'd gone back to their places, clustered around the pulsing violet of the Thanksgiving skeleton, each one fitting into place until the Cytha had taken shape again. As if, Duncan told himself, blood and nerve and muscle had come back from a brief vacation to form the beast anew.

'Mister,' asked the Cytha, 'what do we do now?'

'You should know,' Duncan told it. 'You were the one who dug the pit.'

'I split myself,' the Cytha said. 'A part of me dug the pit and the other part that stayed on the surface got me out when the job was done.'

'Convenient,' grunted Duncan.

And it *was* convenient. That was what had happened to the

Cytha when he had shot at it – it had split into all its component parts and had got away. And that night beside the water hole, it had spied on him, again in the form of all its separate parts, from the safety of the thicket.

'You are caught and so am I,' the Cytha said. 'Both of us will die here. It seems a fitting end to our association. Do you not agree with me?'

'I'll get you out,' said Duncan wearily. 'I have no quarrel with children.'

He dragged the rifle toward him and unhooked the sling from the stock. Carefully he lowered the gun by the sling, still attached to the barrel, down into the pit.

The Cytha reared up and grasped it with its forepaws.

'Easy now,' Duncan cautioned. 'You're heavy. I don't know if I can hold you.'

But he needn't have worried. The little ones were detaching themselves and scrambling up the rifle and the sling. They reached his extended arms and ran up them with scrabbling claws. Little sneering screamers and the comic stilt-birds and the mouse-size kill-devils that snarled at him as they climbed. And the little grinning natives – not babies, scarcely children, but small editions of full-grown humanoids. And the weird donovans scampering happily.

They came climbing up his arms and across his shoulders and milled about on the ground beside him, waiting for the others.

And finally the Cytha, not skinned down to the bare bones of its Thanksgiving-turkey-size, but far smaller than it had been, climbed awkwardly up the rifle and the sling to safety.

Duncan hauled the rifle up and twisted himself into a sitting position.

The Cytha, he saw, was reassembling.

He watched in fascination as the restless miniatures of the planet's life swarmed and seethed like a hive of bees, each one clicking into place to form the entire beast.

And now the Cytha was complete. Yet small – still small – no more than lion-size.

'But it is such a little one,' Zikkara had argued with him that morning at the farm. 'It is such a young one.'

Just a young brood, no more than suckling infants – if suckling was the word, or even some kind of wild approximation. And through the months and years, the Cytha would grow, with the growing of its diverse children, until it became a monstrous thing.

It stood there looking at Duncan and the tree.

'Now,' said Duncan, 'if you'll push on the tree, I think that between the two of us – '

'It is too bad,' the Cytha said, and wheeled itself about.

He watched it go loping off.

'Hey!' he yelled.

But it didn't stop.

He grabbed up the rifle and had it halfway to his shoulder before he remembered how absolutely futile it was to shoot at the Cytha.

He let the rifle down.

'The dirty, ungrateful, double-crossing – '

He stopped himself. There was no profit in rage. When you were in a jam, you did the best you could. You figured out the problem and you picked the course that seemed best and you didn't panic at the odds.

He laid the rifle in his lap and started to hook up the sling and it was not till then that he saw the barrel was packed with sand and dirt.

He sat numbly for a moment, thinking back to how close he had been to firing at the Cytha, and if that barrel was packed hard enough or deep enough, he might have had an exploding weapon in his hands.

He had used the rifle as a crowbar, which was no way to use a gun. That was one way, he told himself, that was guaranteed to ruin it.

Duncan hunted around and found a twig and dug at the clogged muzzle, but the dirt was jammed too firmly in it and he made little progress.

He dropped the twig and was hunting for another stronger one when he caught the motion in a nearby clump of brush.

He watched closely for a moment and there was nothing, so he resumed the hunt for a stronger twig. He found one and started poking at the muzzle and there was another flash of motion.

He twisted around. Not more than twenty feet away, a screamer sat easily on its haunches. Its tongue was lolling out and it had what looked like a grin upon its face.

And there was another, just at the edge of the clump of brush where he had caught the motion first.

There were others as well, he knew. He could hear them sliding through the tangle of fallen trees, could sense the soft padding of their feet.

The executioners, he thought.

The Cytha certainly had not wasted any time.

He raised the rifle and rapped the barrel smartly on the fallen tree, trying to dislodge the obstruction in the bore. But it didn't budge; the barrel still was packed with sand.

But no matter – he'd have to fire anyhow and take whatever chance there was.

He shoved the control to automatic and tilted up the muzzle.

There were six of them now, sitting in a ragged row, grinning at him, not in any hurry. They were sure of him and there was no hurry. He'd still be there when they decided to move in.

And there were others – on all sides of him.

Once it started, he wouldn't have a chance.

'It'll be expensive, gents,' he told them.

And he was astonished at how calm, how coldly objective he could be, now that the chips were down. But that was the way it was, he realized.

He'd thought, a while ago, how a man might suddenly find himself face to face with an aroused and co-operating planet. Maybe this was it in miniature.

The Cytha had obviously passed the word along: *Man back there needs killing. Go and get him.*

Just like that, for a Cytha would be the power here. A life force, the giver of life, the decider of life, the repository of all animal life on the entire planet.

There was more than one of them, of course. Probably they had home districts, spheres of influence and responsibility mapped out. And each one would be a power supreme in its own district.

Momism, he thought with a sour grin. Momism at its absolute peak.

Nevertheless, he told himself, it wasn't too bad a system if you wanted to consider it objectively.

But he was in a poor condition to be objective about that or anything else.

158

The screamers were inching closer, hitching themselves forward slowly on their bottoms.

'I'm going to set up a deadline for you critters,' Duncan called out. 'Just two feet farther, up to that rock, and I let you have it.'

He'd get all six of them, of course, but the shots would be the signals for the general rush by all those other animals slinking in the brush.

If he were free, if he were on his feet, possibly he could beat them off. But pinned as he was, he didn't have a chance. It would be all over less than a minute after he opened fire. He might, he figured, last as long as that.

The six inched closer and he raised the rifle.

But they stopped and moved no farther. Their ears lifted just a little, as if they might be listening, and the grins dropped from their faces. They squirmed uneasily and assumed a look of guilt and, like shadows, they were gone, melting away so swiftly that he scarcely saw them go.

Duncan sat quietly, listening, but he could hear no sound.

Reprieve, he thought. But for how long? Something had scared them off, but in a while they might be back. He had to get out of here and he had to make it fast.

If he could find a longer lever, he could move the tree. There was a branch slanting up from the topside of the fallen tree. It was almost four inches at the butt and it carried its diameter well.

He slid the knife from his belt and looked at it. Too small, too thin, he thought, to chisel through a four-inch branch, but it was all he had. When a man was desperate enough, though, when his very life depended on it, he would do anything.

He hitched himself along, sliding toward the point where the branch protruded from the tree. His pinned leg protested with stabs of pain as his body wrenched it around. He gritted his teeth and pushed himself closer. Pain slashed through his leg again and he was still long inches from the branch.

He tried once more, then gave up. He lay panting on the ground.

There was just one thing left.

He'd have to try to hack out a notch in the trunk just above his leg. No, that would be next to impossible, for he'd be cutting into the whorled and twisted grain at the base of the supporting fork.

Either that or cut off his foot, and that was even more impossible. A man would faint before he got the job done.

It was useless, he knew. He could do neither one. There was nothing he could do.

For the first time, he admitted to himself: He would stay here and die. Shotwell, back at the farm, in a day or two might set out hunting for him. But Shotwell would never find him. And anyhow, by nightfall, if not sooner, the screamers would be back.

He laughed gruffly in his throat – laughing at himself.

The Cytha had won the hunt hands down. It had used a human weakness to win and then had used that same human weakness to achieve a viciously poetic vengeance.

After all, what could one expect? One could not equate human ethics with the ethics of the Cytha. Might not human ethics, in certain cases, seem as weird and illogical, as infamous and ungrateful, to an alien?

He hunted for a twig and began working again to clean the rifle bore.

A crashing behind him twisted him around and he saw the Cytha. Behind the Cytha stalked a donovan.

He tossed away the twig and raised the gun.

'No,' said the Cytha sharply.

The donovan tramped purposefully forward and Duncan felt the prickling of the skin along his back. It was a frightful thing. Nothing could stand before a donovan. The screamers had turned tail and run when they had heard it a couple of miles or more away.

The donovan was named for the first known human to be killed by one. That first was only one of many. The roll of donovan-victims ran long, and no wonder, Duncan thought. It was the closest he had ever been to one of the beasts and he felt a coldness creeping over him. It was like an elephant and a tiger and a grizzly bear wrapped in the selfsame hide. It was the most vicious fighting machine that ever had been spawned.

He lowered the rifle. There would be no point in shooting. In two quick strides, the beast could be upon him.

The donovan almost stepped on him and he flinched away.

160

Then the great head lowered and gave the fallen tree a butt and the tree bounced for a yard or two. The donovan kept on walking. Its powerfully muscled stern moved into the brush and out of sight.

'Now we are even,' said the Cytha. 'I had to get some help.'

Duncan grunted. He flexed the leg that had been trapped and he could not feel the foot. Using his rifle as a cane, he pulled himself erect. He tried putting weight on the injured foot and it screamed with pain.

He braced himself with the rifle and rotated so that he faced the Cytha.

'Thanks, pal,' he said. 'I didn't think you'd do it.'

'You will not hunt me now?'

Duncan shook his head. 'I'm in no shape for hunting. I am heading home.'

'It was the *vua*, wasn't it? That was why you hunted me?'

'The *vua* is my livelihood,' said Duncan. 'I cannot let you eat it.'

The Cytha stood silently and Duncan watched it for a moment. Then he wheeled. Using the rifle for a crutch, he started hobbling away.

The Cytha hurried to catch up with him.

'Let us make a bargain, mister. I will not eat the *vua* and you will not hunt me. Is that fair enough?'

'That is fine with me,' said Duncan. 'Let us shake on it.'

He put down a hand and the Cytha lifted up a paw. They shook, somewhat awkwardly, but very solemnly.

'Now,' the Cytha said, 'I will see you home. The screamers would have you before you got out of the woods.'

VI

They halted on a knoll. Below them lay the farm, with the *vua* rows straight and green in the red soil of the fields.

'You can make it from here,' the Cytha said. 'I am wearing thin. It is an awful effort to keep on being smart. I want to go back to ignorance and comfort.'

'It was nice knowing you,' Duncan told it politely. 'And thanks for sticking with me.'

He started down the hill, leaning heavily on the rifle-crutch. Then he frowned troubledly and turned back.

'Look,' he said, 'you'll go back to animal again. Then you will forget. One of these days, you'll see all that nice, tender *vua* and – '

'Very simple,' said the Cytha. 'If you find me in the *vua*, just begin hunting me. With you after me, I will quickly get smart and remember once again and it will be all right.'

'Sure,' agreed Duncan. 'I guess that will work.'

The Cytha watched him go stumping down the hill.

Admirable, it thought. Next time I have a brood, I think I'll raise a dozen like him.

It turned around and headed for the deeper brush.

It felt intelligence slipping from it, felt the old, uncaring comfort coming back again. But it glowed with anticipation, seethed with happiness at the big surprise it had in store for its new-found friend.

Won't he be happy and surprised when I drop them at his door, it thought.

Will he be ever pleased!

SHADOW WORLD

I rolled out early to put in an hour or so of work on my sector model before Greasy got breakfast slopped together. When I came out of my tent, Benny, my Shadow, was waiting for me. Some of the other Shadows were also standing around, waiting for their humans, and the whole thing, if one stopped to think of it, was absolutely crazy. Except that no one ever stopped to think of it; we were used to it by now.

Greasy had the cookshack stove fired up and smoke was curling from the chimney. I could hear him singing lustily amid the clatter of his pans. This was his noisy time. During the entire morning, he was noisy and obnoxious, but towards the middle of the afternoon, he turned mousy quiet. That was when he began to take a really dangerous chance and hit the peeper.

There were laws which made it very rough on anyone who had a peeper. Mack Baldwin, the project superintendent, would have raised merry hell if he had known that Greasy had one. But I was the only one who knew it. I had found out by accident and not even Greasy knew I knew and I had kept my mouth shut.

I said hello to Benny, but he didn't answer me. He never answered me; he had no mouth to answer with. I don't suppose he even heard me, for he had no ears. Those Shadows were a screwy lot. They had no mouths and they had no ears and they hadn't any noses.

But they did have an eye, placed in the middle of the face, about where the nose would have been if they'd had noses.

163

And that eye made up for the lack of ears and mouth and nose.

It was about three inches in diameter, and, strictly speaking, it wasn't built exactly like an eye; it had no iris or no pupil, but was a pool of light and shadow that kept shifting all round so it never looked the same. Sometimes it looked like a bowl of goop that was slightly on the spoiled side, and at other times it was hard and shining like a camera lens, and there were other times when it looked sad and lonely, like a mournful hound dog's eyes.

They were a weird lot for sure, those Shadows. They looked mostly like a rag doll before anyone had gotten around to painting on the features. They were humanoid and they were strong and active and I had suspected from the very first that they weren't stupid. There was some division of opinion on that latter point and a lot of the boys still thought of them as howling savages. Except they didn't howl — they had no mouths to howl with. No mouths to howl or eat with, no nose to smell or breathe with, and no ears to hear with.

Just on bare statistics, one would have put them down as plain impossible, but they got along all right. They got along just fine.

They wore no clothes. On the point of modesty, there was no need of any. They were as bare of sexual characteristics as they were of facial features. They were just a gang of rag dolls with massive eyes in the middle of their faces.

But they did wear what might have been a decoration or a simple piece of jewellery or a badge of Shadowhood. They wore a narrow belt, from which was hung a bag or sack in which they carried a collection of trinkets that jingled when they walked. No one had ever seen what was in those sacks. Cross straps from the belt ran over the shoulders, making the whole business into a simple harness, and at the juncture of the straps upon their chest was mounted a huge jewel. Intricately carved, the jewel sparkled like a diamond, but no one knew if it was or not. No one ever got close enough to see. Make a motion towards that jewel and the Shadow disappeared.

That's right. Disappeared.

I said hello to Benny and he naturally didn't answer and I
164

walked around the table and began working on the model. Benny stood close behind me and watched me as I worked. He seemed to have a lot of interest in that model. He had a lot of interest in everything I did. He went everywhere I went. He was, after all, my Shadow,

There was a poem that started out: *I have a little shadow* . . . I had thought about it often, but couldn't recall who the poet was or how the rest of it went. It was an old, old poem and I remembered I had read it when I was a kid. I could close my eyes and see the picture that went with the words, the brightly coloured picture of a kid in his pyjamas, going up a stairway with a candle in his hand and the shadow of him on the wall beyond the stairs.

I took some satisfaction in Benny's interest in the sector model, although I was aware his interest probably didn't mean a thing. He might have been just as interested if I'd been counting beans.

I was proud of that model and I spent more time on it than I had any right to. It had my name, Robert Emmett Blake, spelled out in full on the plaster base and the whole thing was a bit more ambitious than I originally had intended.

I had let my enthusiasm run away with me and that was not too hard to understand. It wasn't every day that a conservationist got a chance to engineer from scratch an absolutely virgin Earth-type planet. The layout was only one small sector of the initial project, but it included almost all the factors involved in the entire tract and I had put in the works – the dams and roads, the power sites and the mill sites, the timber management and the water conservation features and all the rest of it.

I had just settled down to work when a commotion broke out down at the cookshack. I could hear Greasy cussing and the sound of thudding whacks. The door of the shack burst open and a Shadow came bounding out with Greasy just a leap behind him. Greasy had a frying pan and he was using it effectively, with a nifty backhand technique that was beautiful to see. He was laying it on the Shadow with every leap he took and he was yelling maledictions that were enough to curl one's hair.

The Shadow legged it across the camp with Greasy close

behind. Watching them, I thought how it was a funny thing that a Shadow would up and disappear if you made a motion towards its jewel, but would stay and take the kind of treatment Greasy was handing out with that frying pan.

When they came abreast of my model table, Greasy gave up the chase. He was not in the best condition.

He stood beside the table and put both fists belligerently on his hips, so that the frying pan, which he still clutched, stood out at a right angle from his body.

'I won't allow that stinker in the shack,' he told me, wheezing and gasping. 'It's bad enough to have him hanging around outside and looking in the windows. It's bad enough falling over him every time I turn around. I will not have him snooping in the kitchen; he's got his fingers into everything he sees. If I was Mack, I'd put the lug on all of them. I'd run them so fast, so far, that it would take them – '

'Mack's got other things to worry about,' I told him rather sharply. 'The project is way behind schedule, with all the breakdowns we've been having.'

'Sabotage,' Greasy corrected me. 'That's what it is. You can bet your bottom dollar on that. It's them Shadows, I tell you, sabotaging the machines. If it was left to me, I'd run them clear out of the country.'

'It's their country,' I protested. 'They were here before we came.'

'It's a big planet,' Greasy said. 'There are other parts of it they could live in.'

'But they have got a right here. This planet is their home.'

'They ain't got no homes,' said Greasy.

He turned around abruptly and walked back towards the shack. His Shadow, which had been standing off to one side all the time, hurried to catch up with him. It didn't look as if it had minded the pounding he had given it. But you could never tell what a Shadow was thinking. Their thoughts don't show on them.

What Greasy had said about their not having any homes was a bit unfair. What he meant, of course, was that they were just a sort of carefree bunch of gypsies, but to me the planet was their home and they had a right to go any place they wanted on it and use any part of it they wished. It should

166

make no difference that they settled down on no particular spot, that they had no villages and possibly no shelters or that they raised no crops.

Come to think of it, there was no reason why they should raise crops, for they had no mouths to eat with, and if they didn't eat, how could they keep on living and if . . .

You see how it went. That was the reason it didn't pay to think too much about the Shadows. Once you started trying to get them figured out, you got all tangled up.

I sneaked a quick look sideways to see how Benny might be taking this business of Greasy beating up his pal, but Benny was just the same as ever. He was all rag doll.

Men began to drift out of the tents and the Shadows galloped over to rejoin their humans, and everywhere a man might go, his Shadow tagged behind him.

The project centre lay there on its hilltop, and from where I stood beside my sector table, I could see it laid out like a blueprint come to life.

Over there, the beginning of the excavation for the administration building, and there the gleaming stakes for the shopping centre, and beyond the shopping centre, the ragged, first-turned furrows that in time would become a street flanked by neat rows of houses.

It didn't look much like a brave beginning on a brand-new world, but in a little while it would. It would even now, if we'd not run into so much hard luck. And whether that hard luck could be traced to the Shadows or to something else, it was a thing that must be faced and somehow straightened out.

For this was important. Here was a world on which Man would not repeat the ancient, sad mistakes that he had made on Earth. On this, one of the few Earth-like planets found so far, Man would not waste the valuable resources which he had let go down the drain on the old home planet. He'd make planned use of the water and the soil, of the timber and the minerals, and he'd be careful to put back as much as he took out. This planet would not be robbed and gutted as Earth had been. It would be used intelligently and operated like a well-run business.

I felt good, just standing there, looking out across the valley

167

and the plains towards the distant mountains, thinking what a fine home this would be for mankind.

The camp was becoming lively now. Out in front of the tents, the men were washing up for breakfast and there was a lot of friendly shouting and a fair amount of horseplay. I heard considerable cussing down in the equipment pool and I knew exactly what was going on. The machines, or at least a part of them, had gone daffy again and half the morning would be wasted getting them repaired. It certainly was a funny deal, I thought, how those machines got out of kilter every blessed night.

After a while, Greasy rang the breakfast bell and everyone dropped everything and made a dash for it and their Shadows hustled along behind them.

I was closer to the cookshack than most of them and I am no slouch at sprinting, so I got one of the better seats at the big outdoor table. My place was just outside the cookshack door, where I'd get first whack at seconds when Greasy lugged them out. I went past Greasy on the run and he was grumbling and muttering the way he always was at chow, although sometimes I thought that was just a pose to hide his satisfaction at knowing his cooking still was fit to eat.

I got a seat next to Mack, and a second later Rick Thorne, one of the equipment operators, grabbed the place on the other side of me. Across from me was Stan Carr, a biologist, and just down the table, on the other side, was Judson Knight, our ecologist.

We wasted no time in small talk; we dived into the wheat cakes and the side pork and the fried potatoes. There is nothing in all the Universe like the morning air of Stella IV to hone an edge on the appetite.

Finally we had enough of the edge off so we would waste time being civil.

'It's the same old story again this morning,' Thorne said bitterly to Mack. 'More than half the equipment is all gummed up. It'll take hours to get it moving.'

He morosely shovelled food into his mouth and chewed with unnecessary savagery. He shot an angry glance at Carr across the table. 'Why don't you get it figured out?' he asked.

'Me?' said Carr, in some astonishment. 'Why should I be
168

the one to get it figured out? I don't know anything about machines and I don't want to know. They're stupid contraptions at best.'

'You know what I mean,' said Thorne. 'The machines are not to blame. They don't gum up themselves. It's the Shadows and you're a biologist and them Shadows are your business and – '

'I have other things to do,' said Carr. 'I have this earthworm problem to work out, and as soon as that is done, Bob here wants me to run some habit-patterns on a dozen different rodents.'

'I wish you would,' I said. 'I have a hunch some of those little rascals may cause us a lot of trouble once we try our hand at crops. I'd like to know ahead of time what makes the critters tick.'

That was the way it went, I thought. No matter how many factors you might consider, there were always more of them popping up from under rocks and bushes. It seemed somehow that a man never quite got through the list.

'It wouldn't be so bad,' Thorne complained, 'if the Shadows would leave us alone and let us fix the damage after they've done their dirty work. But not them. They breathe down our necks while we're making the repairs, and they've got their faces buried in those engines clear up to their shoulders, and every time you move, you bump into one of them. Someday,' he said fiercely, 'I'm going to take a monkey wrench and clear some space around me.'

'They're worried about what you're doing to their machines,' said Carr. 'The Shadows have taken over those machines just like they've adopted us.'

'That's what you think,' Thorne said.

'Maybe they're trying to find out about the machines,' Carr declared. 'Maybe they gum them up so that, when you go to fix them, they can look things over. They haven't missed a single part of any machine so far. You were telling me the other day it's a different thing wrong every time.'

Knight said, solemn as an owl: 'I've been doing a lot of thinking about this situation.'

'Oh, you have?' said Thorne, and the way he said it, you could see he figured that what Knight might think would cut no ice.

169

'I've been seeking out some motive,' Knight told him. 'Because if the Shadows are the ones who are doing it, they'd have to have a motive. Don't you think so, Mack?'

'Yeah, I guess so,' said Mack.

'For some reason,' Knight went on, 'those Shadows seem to like us. They showed up as soon as we set down and they've stayed with us ever since. The way they act, they'd like us to stay on and maybe they're wrecking the machines so we'll have to stay.'

'Or drive us away,' Thorne answered.

'That's all right,' said Carr, 'but why should they want us to stay? What exactly is it they like about us? If we could only get that one on the line, we might be able to do some bargaining with them.'

'Well, I wouldn't know,' Knight admitted. 'There might be a lot of different reasons.'

'Name just three of them,' Thorne challenged him nastily.

'Gladly,' said Knight, and he said it as if he were slipping a knife into the left side of Thorne's gizzard. 'They may be getting something from us, only don't ask me what it is. Or they may be building us up to put the bite on us for something that's important. Or they may be figuring on reforming us, although just what's in us they object to, I can't faintly imagine. Or they may worship us. Or maybe it's just love.

'Is that all?' asked Thorne.

'Just a start,' said Knight. 'They may be studying us and they may need more time to get us puzzled out. They may be prodding us to get some reactions from us – '

'Studying us!' yelled Thorne, outraged. 'They're just lousy savages!'

'I don't think they are,' Knight replied.

'They don't wear any clothes,' Thorne thundered, slamming the table with his fist. 'They don't have any tools. They don't have a village. They don't know how to build a hut. They don't have any government. They can't even talk or hear.'

I was disgusted with Thorne.

'Well, we got that settled,' I said. 'Let's go back to work.'

I got up off the bench, but I hadn't gone more than a step or two before a man came pounding down from the radio hut, waving a piece of paper in his hand. It was Jack Pollard, our

170

communications man, who also doubled in brass as an electronics expert.

'Mack!' he was hollering. 'Hey, Mack!'

Mack lumbered to his feet.

Pollard handed him the paper. 'It was coming in when Greasy blew the horn,' he gasped. 'I was having trouble getting it. Relayed a long way out.'

Mack read the paper and his face turned hard and red.

'What's the matter, Mack?' I wanted to know.

'There's an inspector coming out,' he said, and he choked on each and every word. He was all burned up. And maybe scared as well.

'Is it likely to be bad?'

'He'll probably can the lot of us,' said Mack.

'But he can't do that!'

'That's what you think. We're six weeks behind schedule and this project is hotter than a pile. Earth's politicians have made a lot of promises, and if those promises don't pay off, there'll be hell to pay. Unless we can do something and do it fast, they'll bounce us out of here and send a new gang in.'

'But considering everything, we haven't done so badly,' Carr said mildly.

'Don't get me wrong,' Mack told him. 'The new gang will do no better, but there has to be some action for the record and we're the ones who'll get it in the neck. If we could lick this breakdown business, we might have a chance: If we could say to that inspector: "Sure, we've had a spot of trouble, but we have it licked and now we're doing fine – " if we could say that to him, then we might save our hides.'

'You think it's the Shadows, Mack?' asked Knight.

Mack reached up and scratched his head. 'Must be them. Can't think of anything else.'

Somebody shouted from another table: 'Of course it's them damned Shadows!'

The men were getting up from their seats and crowding around.

Mack held up his hands. 'You guys get back to work. If any of you got some good ideas, come up to the tent and we'll talk them over.'

They started jabbering at him.

171

'Ideas!' Mack roared. 'I said *ideas!* Anyone that comes up without a good idea, I'll dock him for being off the job.'

They quieted down a little.

'And another thing,' said Mack. 'No rough stuff on the Shadows. Just go along the way we always have. I'll fire the man who strongarms them.'

He said to me: 'Let's go.'

I followed him, and Knight and Carr fell in beside me. Thorne didn't come. I had expected that he would.

Inside Mack's tent, we sat down at a table littered with blueprints and spec sheets and papers scribbled with figures and offhand diagrams.

'I suppose,' said Carr, 'that it has to be the Shadows.'

'Some gravitational peculiarity?' suggested Knight. 'Some strange atmospheric condition? Some space-warping quality?'

'Maybe,' said Mack. 'It all sounds a bit far-fetched, but I'm ready to grab any straw you shove at me.'

'One thing that puzzles me,' I put in, 'is that the survey crew didn't mention Shadows. Survey believed the planet was uninhabited by any sort of intelligence. It found no signs of culture. And that was good, because it meant the project wouldn't get all tangled up with legalities over primal rights. And yet the minute we landed, the Shadows came galloping to meet us, almost as if they'd spotted us a long way off and were waiting for us to touch down.'

'Another funny thing,' said Carr, 'is how they paired off with us – one Shadow to every man. Like they had it all planned out. Like they'd married us or something.'

'What are you getting at?' growled Mack.

I said: 'Where were the Shadows, Mack, when the survey gang was here? Can we be absolutely sure they're native to this planet?'

'If they aren't native,' demanded Mack, 'how did they get here? They have no machines. They haven't even got tools.'

'There's another thing about that survey report,' said Knight, 'that I've been wondering about. The rest of you have read it – '

We nodded. We had not only read it, we had studied and digested it. We'd lived with it day and night on the long trip out to Stella IV.

172

'The survey report told about some cone-shaped things,' said Knight. 'All sitting in a row, as if they might be boundary markers. But they never saw them except from a long way off. They had no idea what they were. They just wrote them off as something that had no real significance.'

'They wrote off a lot of things as having no significance,' said Carr.

'We aren't getting anywhere,' Mack complained. 'All we do is talk.'

'If we could talk to the Shadows,' said Knight, 'we might be getting somewhere.'

'But we can't!' argued Mack. 'We tried to talk to them and we couldn't raise a ripple. We tried sign language and we tried pantomime and we filled reams of paper with diagrams and drawings and we got exactly nowhere. Jack rigged up that electronic communicator and he tried it on them and they just sat and looked at us, all bright and sympathetic, with that one big eye of theirs, and that was all there was. We even tried telepathy – '

'You're wrong there, Mack,' said Carr. 'We didn't try telepathy, because we don't know a thing about it. All we did was sit in a circle, holding hands with them and thinking hard at them. And of course it was no good. They probably thought it was just a game.'

'Look,' pleaded Mack, 'that inspector will be here in ten days or so. We have to think of something. Let's get down to cases.'

'If we could run the Shadows off somehow,' said Knight. 'If we could scare them away – '

'You know how to scare a Shadow?' Mack asked. 'You got any idea what they might be afraid of?'

Knight shook his head.

'Our first job,' said Carr, 'is to find out what a Shadow is like. We have to learn what kind of animal he is. He's a funny kind, we know. He doesn't have a mouth or nose or ears . . .'

'He's impossible,' Mack said. 'There ain't no such animal.'

'He's alive,' said Carr, 'and doing very well. We have to find out how he gets his food, how he communicates, what tolerances he may have, what his responses are to various kinds of stimuli. We can't do a thing about the Shadows until we have some idea of what we're dealing with.'

Knight agreed with him. 'We should have started weeks ago. We made a stab at it, of course, but our hearts were never in it. We were too anxious to get started on the project.'

Mack said bitterly: 'Fat lot of good it did us.'

'Before you can examine one, you have to have a subject,' I answered Knight. 'Seems to me we should try to figure out how to catch a Shadow. Make a sudden move towards one and he disappears.'

But even as I said it, I knew that was not entirely right. I remembered how Greasy had chased his Shadow from the cookshack, lamming him with the frying pan.

And I remembered something else and I had a hunch and got a big idea, but I was scared to say anything about it. I didn't even, for the moment, dare to let on to myself I had it.

'We'd have to take one by surprise somehow and knock him out before he had a chance to disappear,' Carr said. 'And it has to be a sure way, for if we try it once and fail we've put the Shadows on their guard and we'll never have another chance.'

Mack warned, 'No rough stuff. You can't go using violence until you know your critter. You don't do any killing until you have some idea how efficiently the thing you are killing can up and kill you back.'

'No rough stuff,' Carr agreed. 'If a Shadow can bollix up the innards of some of those big earthmovers, I wouldn't like to see what he could do to a human body.'

'It's got to be fast and sure,' said Knight, 'and we can't even start until we know it is. If you hit one on the head with a baseball bat, would the bat bounce or would you crush the Shadow's skull? That's about the way it would be with everything we could think of at the moment.'

Carr nodded. 'That's right. We can't use gas, because a Shadow doesn't breathe.'

'He might breathe through his pores,' said Knight.

'Sure, but we'd have to know before we tried using gas. We might jab a hypo into one, but what would you use in the hypo? First you'd have to find something that would knock a Shadow out. You might try hypnotism – '

174

'I'd doubt hypnotism,' said Knight.

'How about Doc?' I asked. 'If we could knock out a Shadow, would Doc give him a going over? If I know Doc, he'd raise a lot of hell. Claim the Shadow was an intelligent being and that it would be in violation of medical ethics to examine one without first getting its consent.'

'You get one,' Mack promised grimly, 'and I'll handle Doc.'

'He'll do a lot of screaming.'

'I'll handle Doc,' repeated Mack. 'This inspector is going to be here in a week or so – '

'We wouldn't have to have it *all* cleared up,' said Knight. 'If we could show the inspector that we had a good lead, that we were progressing, he might play ball with us.'

I was seated with my back to the entrance of the tent and I heard someone fumbling with the canvas.

Mack said: 'Come in, Greasy. Got something on your mind?'

Greasy walked in and came up to the table. He had the bottom of his apron tucked into his trouser band, the way he always did when he wasn't working, and he held something in his hand. He tossed it on the table.

It was one of the bags that the Shadows carried at their belts!

We all sucked in our breath and Mack's hair fairly stood on end.

'Where did you get this?' he demanded.

'Off my Shadow, when he wasn't looking.'

'When he wasn't looking!'

'Well, you see, it was this way, Mack. That Shadow is always into things. I stumble over him everywhere I go. And this morning he had his head halfway into the dishwasher and that bag was hanging on his belt, so I grabbed up a butcher knife and just whacked it off.'

As Mack got up and pulled himself to his full height, you could see it was hard for him to keep his hands off Greasy.

'So that was all you did,' he said in a low, dangerous voice.

'Sure,' said Greasy. 'There was nothing hard about it.'

'All you've done is spill the beans to them! All you've done is made it almost impossible – '

'Maybe not,' Knight interrupted in a hurry.

175

'Now that the damage has been done,' said Carr, 'we might as well have a look. Maybe there's a clue inside that bag.'

'I can't open it,' grumbled Greasy. 'I tried every way I know. There's no way to open it.'

'And while you were trying to open it,' asked Mack, 'what was the Shadow doing?'

'He didn't even notice. He had his head inside that washer. He's as stupid as – '

'Don't say that! I don't want anyone thinking a Shadow's stupid. Maybe they are, but there's no sense believing it until we're sure.'

Knight had picked up the bag and was turning it around and around in his hand. Whatever was inside was jingling as he turned and twisted it.

'Greasy's right,' he said. 'I don't see any way to get it open.'

'You get out of here!' Mack roared at Greasy. 'Get back to your work. Don't you ever make another move towards any of the Shadows.'

Greasy turned around and left, but he was no more than out of the tent when he gave a yelp that was enough to raise your scalp.

I almost knocked the table over getting out of there to see what was going on.

What was happening was no more than plain solemn justice.

Greasy was running for all he was worth, and behind him was the Shadow with a frying pan, and every jump that Greasy took, the Shadow let him have it, and was every bit as good with that frying pan as Greasy was.

Greasy was weaving and circling, trying to head back for the cookshack, but each time the Shadow got him headed off and went on chasing him.

Everyone had stopped work to watch. Some of them were yelling advice to Greasy and some of the others were cheering on the Shadow. I'd have liked to stay and watch, but I knew that if I was going to put my hunch into execution, I'd never have a better chance to do it.

So I turned and walked swiftly down the street to my own tent and ducked inside and got a specimen bag and came out again.

I saw that Greasy was heading for the equipment pool and

that the Shadow still was one long stride behind. Its arm was holding up well, for the frying pan never missed a lick.

I ran down to the cookshack and, at the door, I stopped and looked back. Greasy was shinnying up the derrick of a shovel and the Shadow was standing at the bottom, waving the frying pan as though daring him to come down and take it like a man. Everyone else was running towards the scene of action and there was no one, I was sure, who had noticed me.

So I opened the cookshack door and stepped inside.

The dishwasher was chugging away and everything was peaceable and quiet.

I was afraid I might have trouble finding what I was looking for, but I found it in the third place I looked – underneath the mattress on Greasy's bunk.

I pulled the peeper out and slipped it in the bag and got out of there as fast as I could go.

Stopping at my tent, I tossed the bag into a corner and threw some old clothes over it and then went out again.

The commotion had ended. The Shadow was walking back towards the cookshack, with the pan tucked underneath its arm, and Greasy was climbing down off the shovel. The men were all gathered around the shovel, making a lot of noise, and I figured that it would take a long, long time for Greasy to live down what had happened. Although, I realized, he had it coming to him.

I went back into Mack's tent and found the others there. All three of them were standing beside the table, looking down at what lay upon the surface.

The bag had disappeared and had left behind a little pile of trinkets. Looking at the pile, I could see that they were miniatures of frying pans and kettles and all the other utensils that Greasy worked with. And there, half protruding out of the pile, was a little statuette of Greasy.

I reached out a hand and picked up the statuette. There was no mistaking it – it was Greasy to a T. It was made of some sort of stone, as if it might have been a carving, and was delicate beyond all belief. Squinting closely, I could even see the lines on Greasy's face.

'The bag just went away,' said Knight. 'It was lying here

when we dashed out, and when we came back, it was gone and all this junk was lying on the table.'

'I don't understand,' Carr said.

And he was right. None of us did.

'I don't like it,' Mack said slowly.

I didn't like it, either. It raised too many questions in my head and some of them were resolving into some miserable suspicions.

'They're making models of our stuff,' said Knight. 'Even down to the cups and spoons.'

'I wouldn't mind that so much,' Carr said. 'It's the model of Greasy that gives me the jitters.'

'Now let's sit down,' Mack told us, 'and not go off on any tangents. This is exactly the sort of thing we could have expected.'

'What do you mean?' I prompted.

'What do we do when we find an alien culture? We do just what the Shadows are doing. Different way, but the same objective. We try to find out all we can about this alien culture. And don't you ever forget that, to the Shadows we're not only an alien culture, but an *invading* alien culture. So if they had any sense at all, they'd make it their business to find out as much about us as they could in the shortest time.'

That made sense, of course. But this making of models seemed to be carrying it beyond what was necessary.

And if they had made models of Greasy's cups and spoons, of the dishwasher and the coffee pot, then they had other models, too. They had models of the earthmovers and the shovels and the dozers and all the rest of it. And if they had a model of Greasy, they had models of Mack and Thorne and Carr and all the rest of the crew, including me.

Just how faithful would those models be? How much deeper would they go than mere external appearances?

I tried to stop thinking of it, for I was doing little more than scaring myself stiff.

But I couldn't stop. I went right on thinking.

They had been gumming up equipment so that the mechanics had to rip the machines all apart to get them going once again. There seemed no reason in the world why the Shadows should be doing that, except to find out what the innards of

178

those machines were like. I wondered if the models of the equipment might not be faithful not only so far as the outward appearance might go, but faithful as well on the most intricate construction of the entire machine.

And if that was true, was that faithfulness also carried out in the Greasy statuette? Did it have a heart and lungs, blood vessels and brain and nerve? Might it not also have the very essence of Greasy's character. The kind of animal he was, what his thoughts and ethics might be?

I don't know if, at that very moment, the others were thinking the same thing, but the looks on their faces argued that they might have been.

Mack put out a finger and stirred the contents of the pile, scattering the miniatures all about the tabletop.

Then his hand darted out and picked up something and his face went red with anger.

Knight asked: 'What is it, Mack?'

'A peeper!' said Mack, his words rasping in his throat. 'There's a model of a peeper!'

All of us sat and stared and I could feel the cold sweat breaking out on me.

'If Greasy has a peeper,' Mack said woodenly. 'I'll break his scrawny neck.'

'Take it easy, Mack,' said Carr.

'You know what a peeper is?'

'Sure I know what a peeper is.'

'You ever see what a peeper does to a man who used one?'

'No, I never did.'

'I have.' Mack threw the peeper model back on the table and turned and went out of the tent. The rest of us followed him.

Greasy was coming down the street, with some of the men following along behind, kidding him about the Shadow treeing him.

Mack put his hands on his hips and waited.

Greasy got almost to us.

'Greasy!' said Mack.

'Yes, Mack.'

'You hiding out a peeper?'

Greasy blinked, but he never hesitated. 'No, sir,' he said,

179

lying like a trooper. 'I wouldn't rightly know one if somebody should point it out to me. I've heard of them, of course.'

'I'll make a bargain with you,' said Mack. 'If you have one, just hand it over to me and I'll bust it up and fine you a full month's wages and that's the last that we'll say about it. But if you lie to me and we find you have one hidden out, I'll can you off the job.'

I held my breath. I didn't like what was going on and I thought what a lousy break it was that something like this should happen just when I had swiped the peeper. Although I was fairly sure that no one had seen me sneak into the cookshack – at least I didn't think they had.

Greasy was stubborn. He shook his head. 'I haven't got one, Mack.'

Mack's face got hard. 'All right. We'll go down and see.'

He headed for the cookshack and Knight and Carr went along with him, but I headed for my tent.

It would be just like Mack, when he didn't find the peeper in the cookshack, to search the entire camp. If I wanted to stay out of trouble, I knew, I'd better be zipping out of camp and take the peeper with me.

Benny was squatted outside the tent, waiting for me. He helped me get the roller out and then I took the specimen bag with the peeper in it and stuffed it in the roller's carrying bag.

I got on the roller and Benny jumped on the carrier behind me and sat there showing off, balancing himself – like a kid riding a bicycle with no hands.

'You hang on,' I told him sharply. 'If you fall off this time, I won't stop to pick you up.'

I am sure he didn't hear me, but however that may be, he put his arms around my waist and we were off in a cloud of dust.

Until you've ridden on a roller, you haven't really lived. It's like a roller coaster running on the level. But it is fairly safe and it gets you there. It's just two big rubber doughnuts with an engine and a seat and it could climb a barn if you gave it half a chance. It's too rambunctious for civilized driving, but it is just the ticket for an alien planet.

We set off across the plain towards the distant foothills. It was a fine day, but for that matter, every day was fine on

180

Stella IV. It was an ideal planet, Earthlike, with good weather nearly all the time, crammed with natural resources, free of vicious animal life or deadly virus – a planet that virtually pleaded for someone to come and live on it.

And in time there'd be people here. Once the administration centre was erected, the neat rows of houses had been built, once the shopping centre had been installed, the dams built, the power plant completed – then there would be people. And in the years to come, sector by sector, project community by community, the human race would spread across the planet's face. But it would spread in an orderly progression.

Here there would be no ornery misfits slamming out on their own, willy-nilly, into the frontier land of wild dream and sudden death; no speculators, no strike-it-rich, no go-for-broke. Here there would be no frontier, but a systematic taking over. And here, for once, a planet would be treated right.

But there was more to it than that, I told myself.

If man was to keep going into space, he would have to accept the responsibility of making proper use of the natural resources that he found there. Just because there might be a lot of them was no excuse for wasting them. We were no longer children and we couldn't gut every world as we had gutted Earth.

By the time an intelligence advances to a point where it can conquer space, it must have grown up. And now it was time for the human race to prove that it was adult. We couldn't go ravaging out into the Galaxy like a horde of greedy children.

Here on this planet, it seemed to me, was one of the many proving grounds on which the race of Man must stand and show its worth.

Yet if we were to get the job done, if we were to prove anything at all, there was another problem that first must be met and solved. If it was the Shadows that were causing all our trouble, then somehow we must put a stop to it. And not merely put a stop to it, but understand the Shadows and their motives. For how can anybody fight a thing, I asked myself, that he doesn't understand?

And to understand the Shadows, we'd agreed back in the tent, we had to know what kind of critters they might be. And

181

before we could find that out, we had to grab off one for examination. And that first grab had to be perfect, for if we tried and failed, if we put them on their guard, there'd be no second chance.

But the peeper, I told myself, might give us at least one free try. If I tried the peeper and it didn't work, no one would be the wiser. It would be a failure that would go unnoticed.

Benny and I crossed the plain on the roller and headed into the foothills. I made for a place that I called the Orchard, not because it was a formal orchard, but because there were a lot of fruit-bearing trees in the areas. As soon as I got around to it, I was planning to run tests to see if any of the fruit might be fit for human food.

We reached the Orchard and I parked the roller and looked around. I saw immediately that something had happened. When I had been there just a week or so before, the trees had been loaded with fruit, and it seemed to be nearly ripe, but now it all was gone.

I peered underneath the trees to see if the fruit had fallen off and it hadn't. It looked for all the world as if someone had come in and picked it.

I wondered if the Shadows had done the picking, but even as I thought it, I knew it couldn't be. The Shadows didn't eat.

I didn't get the peeper out right away, but sat down beneath a tree and sort of caught my breath and did a little thinking.

From where I sat, I could see the camp and I wondered what Mack had done when he hadn't found the peeper. I could imagine he'd be in a towering rage. And I could imagine Greasy, considerably relieved, but wondering just the same what had happened to the peeper and perhaps rubbing it into Mack a little how he had been wrong.

I got the feeling that maybe it would be just as well if I stayed away a while. At least until mid-afternoon. By that time, perhaps, Mack would have cooled off a little.

And I thought about the Shadows.

Lousy savages, Thorne had said. Yet they were far from savages. They were perfect gentlemen (or ladies, God knows which they were, if either) and your genuine savage is no gentleman on a number of very fundamental points. The Shadows were clean in body, healthy and well-mannered. They had a certain cultural poise. They were, more than

182

anything else, like a group of civilized campers, but unencumbered by the usual camp equipment.

They were giving us a going over – there could be no doubt of that. They were learning all they could of us and why did they want to know? What use could they make of pots and pans and earthmovers and all the other things?

Or were they merely taking our measure before they clobbered us?

And there were all the other questions, too.

Where did they hang out?

How did they disappear, where did they go?

How did they eat and breathe?

How did they communicate?

Come right down to it, I admitted to myself, the Shadows undoubtedly knew a great deal more about us than we knew about them. Because when you tried to chalk up what we knew about them, it came out to almost exactly nothing.

I sat under the tree for a while longer, with the thoughts spinning in my head and not adding up. Then I got to my feet and went over to the roller and got out the peeper.

It was the first time I'd ever had one in my hands and I was interested and slightly apprehensive. For a peeper was nothing one should monkey with.

It was a simple thing to look at – like a lopsided pair of binoculars, with a lot of selector knobs on each side and on the top of it.

You looked into it and you twisted the knobs until you had what you wanted and then there was a picture. You stepped into the picture and you lived the life you found there – the sort of life you picked by the setting of the knobs. And there were many lives to pick from, for there were millions of combinations that could be set up on the knobs and the factors ranged from the lightest kind of frippery to the most abysmal horror.

The peeper was outlawed, naturally – it was worse than alcoholism, worse than dope, the most insidious vice that had ever hit mankind. It threw psychic hooks deep into the soul and tugged forever more. When a man acquired the habit, and it was easy to acquire, there was no getting over it. He'd spend the rest of his life trying to sort out his life from all the fantasied ones, getting further and further from reality all the while, till nothing was real any more.

I squatted down beside the roller and tried to make some sense out of the knobs. There were thirty-nine of them, each numbered from one to thirty-nine, and I wondered what the numbering meant.

Benny came over and hunkered down beside me, with one shoulder touching mine, and watched what I was doing.

I pondered over the numbering, but pondering did no good. There was only one way to find out what I was looking for. So I set all the knobs back to zero on the graduated scales, then twisted No. 1 up a notch or two.

I knew that was not the way to work a peeper. In actual operation, one would set a number of the knobs at different settings, mixing in the factors in different proportions to make up the kind of life that one might want to sample. But I wasn't after a life. What I wanted to find out was what factor each of the knobs controlled.

So I set No. 1 up a notch or two and lifted the peeper and fitted it to my face and I was back again in the meadow of my boyhood – a meadow that was green as no meadow ever was before, with a sky as blue as old-time watered silk and with a brook and butterflies.

And more than that – a meadow that lay in a day that would never end, a place that knew no time, and a sunlight that was the bright glow of boyish happiness.

I knew exactly how the grass would feel beneath bare feet and I could remember how the sunlight would bounce off the wind-ripples of the brook. It was the hardest thing I ever did in my entire life, but I snatched the peeper from my eyes.

I squatted there, with the peeper cradled in my lap. My hands were unsteady, longing to lift the peeper so I could look once again at that scene out of a long-lost boyhood, but I made myself not do it.

No. 1 was not the knob I wanted, so I turned it back to zero and, since No. 1 was about as far away as one could imagine from what I was looking for, I turned knob 39 up a notch or two.

I lifted the peeper halfway to my face and then I turned plain scared. I put it down again until I could get a good grip
184

on my courage. Then I lifted it once more and stuck my face straight into a horror that reached out and tried to drag me in.

I can't describe it. Even now, I cannot recall one isolated fragment of what I really saw. Rather than seeing, it was pure impression and raw emotion – a sort of surrealistic representation of all that is loathsome and repellent, and yet somehow retaining a hypnotic fascination that forbade retreat.

Shaken, I snatched the peeper from my face and sat frozen. For a moment, my mind was an utter blank, with stray wisps of horror streaming through it.

Then the wisps gradually cleared away and I was squatting once again on the hillside with the Shadow hunkered down beside me, his shoulder touching mine.

It was a terrible thing, I thought, an act no human could bring himself to do, even to a Shadow. Just turned up a notch or two, it was terrifying; turned on full power, it would twist one's brain.

Benny reached out a hand to take the peeper from me. I jerked it away from him. But he kept on pawing for it and that gave me time to think.

This, I told myself, was exactly the way I had wanted it to be. All that was different was that Benny, by his nosiness, was making it easy for me to do the very thing I'd planned.

I thought of all that depended on our getting us a Shadow to examine. And I thought about my job and how it would bust my heart if the inspector should come out and fire us and send in another crew. There just weren't planets lying around every day in the week to be engineered. I might never get another chance.

So I put out my thumb and shoved 39 to its final notch and let Benny have the peeper.

And even as I gave it to him, I wondered if it would really work or if I'd just had a pipe-dream. It might not work, I thought, for it was a human mechanism, designed for human use, keyed to the human nervous system and response.

Then I knew that I was wrong, that the peeper did not operate by virtue of its machinery alone, but by the reaction of the brain and the body of its user – that it was no more than a trigger mechanism to set loose the greatness and the beauty and the horror that lay within the user's brain. And

185

horror, while it might take a different shape and form, appear in a different guise, was horror for a Shadow as well as for a human.

Benny lifted the peeper to that great single eye of his and thrust his head forward to fit into the viewer. Then I saw his body jerk and stiffen and I caught him as he toppled and eased him to the ground.

I stood there above him and felt the triumph and the pride – and perhaps a little pity, too – that it should be necessary to do a thing like this to a guy like Benny. To play a trick like this on my Shadow who had sat, just moments ago, with his shoulder touching mine.

I knelt down and turned him over. He didn't seem so heavy and I was glad of that, because I'd have to get him on the roller and then make a dash for camp, going as fast as I could gun the roller, because there was no telling how long Benny would stay knocked out.

I picked up the peeper and stuck it back into the roller's bag, then hunted for some rope or wire to tie Benny on so he would not fall off.

I don't know if I heard a noise or not. I'm half inclined to think that there wasn't any noise – that it was some sort of built-in alarm system that made me turn around.

Benny was sagging in upon himself and I had a moment of wild panic, thinking that he might be dead, that the shock of the horror that leaped out of the peeper at him had been too much for him to stand.

And I remembered what Mack had said: 'Never kill a thing until you have figured out just how efficiently it may up and kill you back.'

If Benny was dead, then we might have all hell exploding in our laps.

If he was dead, though, he sure was acting funny. He was sinking in and splitting at a lot of different places, and he was turning to what looked like dust, but wasn't dust, and then there wasn't any Benny. There was just the harness with the bag and the jewel and then there wasn't any bag, but a handful of trinkets lying on the ground where the bag had been.

And there was something else.

186

There still was Benny's eye. The eye was a part of a cone that had been in Benny's head.

I recalled how the survey party had seen other cones like that, but had not been able to get close to them.

I was too scared to move. I stood and looked and there were a lot of goose pimples rising on my hide.

For Benny was no alien. Benny was no more than the proxy of some other alien that we had never seen and could not even guess at.

All sorts of conjectures went tumbling through my brain, but they were no more than panic-pictures, and they flipped off and on so fast, I couldn't settle on any one of them.

But one thing was clear as day – the cleverness of this alien for which the Shadows were the front.

Too clever to confront us with anything that was more than remotely human in its shape – a thing for which we could feel pity or contempt or perhaps exasperation, but something that would never rouse a fear within us. A pitiful little figure that was a caricature of our shape and one that was so stupid that it couldn't even talk. And one that was sufficiently alien to keep us puzzled and stump us on so many basic points that we would, at last, give up in sheer bewilderment any attempts that we might make to get it puzzled out.

I threw a quick glance over my shoulder and kept my shoulders hunched, and if anything had moved, I'd have run like a frightened rabbit. But nothing moved. Nothing even rustled. There was nothing to be afraid of except the thoughts within my head.

But I felt a frantic urge to get out of there and I went down on my hands and knees and began to gather what was left of Benny.

I scooped up the pile of trinkets and the jewel and dumped them in the bag along with the peeper. Then I went back and picked up the cone, with the one eye looking at me, but I could see that the eye was dead. The cone was slippery and it didn't feel like metal, but it was heavy and hard to get a good grip on and I had quite a time with it. But I finally got it in the bag and started out for camp.

I went like a bat winging out of hell. Fear was roosting on one shoulder and I kept that roller wheeling.

*

I swung into camp and headed for Mack's tent, but before I got there, I found what looked like the entire project crew working at the craziest sort of contraption one would ever hope to see. It was a mass of gears and cams and wheels and chains and whatnot, and it sprawled over what, back home, would have been a good-sized lot, and there was no reason I could figure for building anything like that.

I saw Thorne standing off to one side and superintending the work, yelling first at this one and then at someone else, and I could see that he was enjoying himself. Thorne was that kind of bossy jerk.

I stopped the roller beside him and balanced it with one leg.

'What's going on?' I asked him.

'We're giving them something to get doped out,' he said. 'We're going to drive them crazy.'

'Them? You mean the Shadows?'

'They want information, don't they?' Thorne demanded. 'They've been underfoot day and night, always in the way, so now we give them something to keep them occupied.'

'But what does it do?'

Thorne spat derisively. 'Nothing. That's the beauty of it.'

'Well,' I said, 'I suppose you know what you're doing. Does Mack know what's going on?'

'Mack and Carr and Knight are the big brains that thought it up,' said Thorne. 'I'm just carrying out orders.'

I went on to Mack's tent and parked the roller there and I knew that Mack was inside, for I heard a lot of arguing.

I took the carrier bag and marched inside the tent and pushed my way up to the table and, up-ending the sack, emptied the whole thing on the tabletop.

And I plumb forgot about the peeper being in there with all the other stuff.

There was nothing I could do about it. The peeper lay naked on the table and there was a terrible silence and I could see that in another second Mack would blow his jets.

He sucked in his breath to roar, but I beat him to it.

'Shut up, Mack!' I snapped. 'I don't want to hear a word from you!'

I must have caught him by surprise, for he let his breath out slowly, looking at me funny while he did it, and Carr and

188

Knight were just slightly frozen in position. The tent was deathly quiet.

'That was Benny,' I said, motioning at the tabletop. 'That is all that's left of him. A look in the peeper did it.'

Carr came a bit unfrozen. 'But the peeper! We looked every-where – '

'I knew Greasy had it and I stole it when I got a hunch. Remember, we were talking about how to catch a Shadow – '

'I'm going to bring charges against you!' howled Mack. 'I'm going to make an example out of you! I'm going to – '

'You're going to shut up.' I said at him. 'You're going to stay quiet and listen or I'll heave you out of here tin cup over appetite.'

'Please!' begged Knight. 'Please, gentlemen, let's act civilized.'

And that was a hot one – him calling us gentlemen.

'It seems to me,' said Carr, 'that the matter of the peeper is somewhat immaterial if Bob has turned it to some useful purpose.'

'Let's all sit down,' Knight urged, 'and maybe count to ten. Then Bob can tell us what is on his mind.'

It was a good suggestion. We all sat down and I told them what had happened. They sat there listening, looking at all that junk on the table and especially at the cone, for it was lying on its side at one end of the table, where it had rolled, and it was looking at us with that dead and fishy eye.

'Those Shadows,' I finished up, 'aren't alive at all. They're just some sort of spy rig that something else is sending out. All we need to do is lure the Shadows off, one by one, and let them look into the peeper with knob 39 set full and – '

'It's no permanent solution,' said Knight. 'Fast as we destroyed them, there'd be other ones sent out.'

I shook my head. 'I don't think so. No matter how good that alien race may be, they can't control those Shadows just by mental contact. My bet is that there are machines involved, and when we destroy a Shadow, it would be my hunch that we knock out a machine. And if we knock out enough of them, we'll give those other people so much headache that they may come out in the open and we can dicker with them.'

'I'm afraid you're wrong,' Knight answered. 'This other race

189

keeps hidden, I'd say, for some compelling reason. Maybe they have developed an underground civilization and never venture on the surface because it's a hostile environment to them. But maybe they keep track of what is doing on the surface by means of these cones of theirs. And when we showed up, they rigged the cones to look like something slightly human, something they felt sure we would accept, and sent them out to get a good close look.'

Mack put up his hands and rubbed them back and forth across his head. 'I don't like this hiding business. I like things out in the open where I can take a swipe at them and they can take a swipe at me. I'd have liked it a whole lot better if the Shadows had really been the aliens.'

'I don't go for your underground race,' Carr said to Knight. 'It doesn't seem to me you could produce such a civilization if you lived underground. You'd be shut away from all the phenomena of nature. You wouldn't – '

'All right,' snapped Knight, 'what's *your* idea?'

'They might have matter transmission – in fact, we know they do – whether by machine or mind, and that would mean that they'd never have to travel on the surface of the planet, but could transfer from place to place in the matter of a second. But they still would need to know what was going on, so they'd have their eyes and ears like a TV radar system – '

'You jokers are just talking round in circles,' objected Mack. 'You don't know what the score is.'

'I suppose you do,' Knight retorted.

'No, I don't,' said Mack. 'But I'm honest enough to say straight out I don't.'

'I think Carr and Knight are too involved,' I said. 'These aliens might be hiding only until they find out what we're like – whether they can trust us or if it would be better to run us off the planet.'

'Well,' said Knight, 'no matter how you figure it, you've got to admit that they probably know practically all there is to know about us – our technology and our purpose and what kind of animals we are and they probably have picked up our language.'

'They know too much,' said Mack. 'I'm getting scared.'

190

There was a scrabbling at the flap and Thorne stuck in his head.

'Say, Mack,' he said, 'I got a good idea. How about setting up some guns in that contraption out there?. When the Shadows crowd around – '

'No guns,' Knight said firmly. 'No rockets. No electrical traps. You do just what we told you. Produce all the useless motion you can. Get it as involved and as flashy as possible. But let it go at that.'

Thorne withdrew sulkily.

Knight explained to me: 'We don't expect it to last too long, but it may keep them occupied for a week or so while we get some work done. When it begins to wear off, we'll fix up something else.'

It was all right, I suppose, but it didn't sound too hot to me. At the best, it bought a little time and nothing more. It bought a little time, that is, if we could fool the Shadows. Somehow I wasn't sure that we could fool them much. Ten to one, they'd spot the contraption as a phoney the minute it was set in motion.

Mack got up and walked around the table. He lifted the cone and tucked it beneath one arm.

'I'll take this down to the shop,' he said. 'Maybe the boys can find out what it is.'

'I can tell you now,' said Carr. 'It's what the aliens use to control the Shadows. Remember the cones the survey people saw? This is one of them. My guess is that it's some kind of a signal device that can transmit data back to base, wherever that might be.'

'No matter,' Mack said. 'We'll cut into it and see what we can find.'

'And the peeper?' I asked.

'I'll take care of that.'

I reached out a hand and picked it up. 'No, you won't. You're just the kind of bigot who would take it out and smash it.'

'It's illegal,' Mack declared.

Carr sided with me. 'Not any more. It's a tool now – a weapon that we can use.'

I handed it to Carr. 'You take care of it. Put it in a good safe place. We may need it again before all this is over.'

I gathered the junk that had been in Benny's bag and picked up the jewel and dropped it into a pocket of my coat.

Mack went out with the cone underneath his arm. The rest of us drifted outside the tent and stood there, just a little footloose now that the excitement was all over.

'He'll have Greasy's hide,' worried Knight.

'I'll talk to him,' Carr said. 'I'll make him see that Greasy may have done us a service by sneaking the thing out here.'

'I suppose,' I said, 'I should tell Greasy what happened to the peeper.'

Knight shook his head. 'Let him sweat a while. It will do him good.'

Back in my tent, I tried to do some paper work, but I couldn't get my mind to settle down on it. I guess I was excited and I'm afraid that I missed Benny and I was tangled up with wondering just what the situation was, so far as the Shadows were concerned.

We had named them well, all right, for they were little more than shadows – meant to shadow us. But even knowing they were just camouflaged spy rigs, I still found it hard not to think of them as something that was alive.

They were no more than cones, of course, and the cones probably were no more than observation units for those hidden people who hung out somewhere on the planet. For thousands of years, perhaps, the cones had been watching while this race stayed in hiding somewhere. But maybe more than watching. Maybe the cones were harvesters and planters – perhaps hunters and trappers – bringing back the plunder of the wilds to their hidden masters. More than likely, it had been the cones that had picked all the Orchard fruit.

And if there was a culture here, if another race had primal rights upon the planet, then what did that do to the claims that Earth might make? Did it mean we might be forced to relinquish this planet, after all – one of the few Earthlike planets found in years of exploration.

I sat at my desk and thought about the planning and the work and the money that had gone into this project, which, even so, was no more than a driblet compared to what eventually would be spent to make this into another Earth.

Even on this project centre, we'd made no more than an initial start. In a few more weeks, the ships would begin bringing in the steel mill and that in itself was a tremendous task – to bring it in, assemble it, mine the ore to get it going and finally to put it into operation. But simpler and easier, infinitely so, than freighting out from Earth all the steel that would be needed to build this project alone.

We couldn't let it go down the drain. After all the years, after all the planning and the work, in face of Earth's great need for more living space, we could not give up Stella IV. And yet we could not deny primal rights. If these beings, when they finally showed themselves, would say that they didn't want us here, then there would be no choice. We would simply have to clear out.

But before they threw us out, of course, they would steal us blind. Much of what we had would undoubtedly be of little value to them, but there would be some of it that they could use. No race can fail to enrich itself and its culture by contact with another. And the contact was a completely one-sided bargain – the exchange flowed only in their direction.

They were, I told myself, just a bunch of cosmic sharpers.

I took the junk that had been in Benny's bag out of my pocket and spread it on the desk and began to sort it out. There was the sector model and the roller and the desk and my little row of books and the pocket chess set and all the other stuff that belonged to me.

There was all the stuff but me.

Greasy's Shadow had carried a statuette of Greasy, but I found none of me and I was a little sore at Benny. He could have gone to the extra effort to have made a statuette of me.

I rolled the things around on the desk top with a finger and wondered once again just how deeply they went. Might they not be patterns rather than just models? Perhaps, I told myself, letting my imagination run away with me, perhaps each of these little models carried in some sort of code a complete analysis and description of whatever the article might be. A human, making a survey or an analysis, would write a sheaf of notes, would capture the subject matter in a page or two of symbols. Maybe these little models were the equivalent of a human notebook, the aliens' way of writing.

And I wondered how they wrote, how they made the models, but there wasn't any answer.

I gave up trying to work and went out of the tent and climbed up the little rise to where Thorne and the men were building their flytrap for the Shadows.

They had put a lot of work and ingenuity into it and it made no sense at all — which, after all, was exactly what it was meant to do.

If we could get the Shadows busy enough trying to figure out what this new contraption was, maybe they'd leave us alone long enough to get some work done.

Thorne and his crew had gotten half a dozen replacement motors out of the shop and had installed those to be used as power. Apparently they had used almost all the spare equipment parts they could find, for there were shafts and gears and cams and all sorts of other things all linked together in a mindless pattern. And here and there they had set up what looked like control boards, except, of course, that they controlled absolutely nothing, but were jammed with flashers and all sorts of other gimmicks until they looked like Christmas trees.

I stood around and watched until Greasy rang the dinner bell, then ran a foot race with all the others to get to the tables.

There was a lot of loud talk and joking, but no one wasted too much time eating. They bolted their food and hurried back to the flytrap.

Just before sunset, they set it going and it was the screwiest mass of meaningless motion that anyone had ever seen. Shafts were spinning madly and a million gears, it seemed, were meshing, and cams were wobbling with their smooth, irregular strokes, and pistons were going up and down and up and down.

It was all polished bright and it worked slicker than a whistle and it was producing nothing except motion, but it had a lot of fascination — even for a human. I found myself standing rooted in one spot, marvelling at the smoothness and

194

precision and the remorseless non-purpose of the weird contraption.

And all the time the fake control boards were sparkling and flashing with the lamps popping on and off, in little jagged runs and series, and you got dizzy watching them, trying to make some pattern out of them.

The Shadows had been standing around and gaping ever since work had started on the trap, but now they crowded closer and stood in a tight and solemn ring around the thing and they never moved.

I turned around and Mack was just behind me. He was rubbing his hands in satisfaction and his face was all lit up with smiles.

'Pretty slick,' he said.

I agreed with him, but I had some doubts that I could not quite express.

'We'll string up some lights,' said Mack, 'so they can see it day and night and then we'll have them pegged for good.'

'You think they'll stay with it?' I asked. 'They won't catch on?'

'Not a chance.'

I went down to my tent and poured myself a good stiff drink, then sat down in a chair in front of the tent.

Some of the men were stringing cable and others were rigging up some batteries of lights and down in the cookshack I could hear Greasy singing, but the song was sad. I felt sorry for Greasy.

Mack might be right, I admitted to myself. We might have built a trap that would cook the Shadows' goose. If nothing else the sheer fascination of all that motion might keep them stuck there. It had a hypnotic effect even for a human and one could never gauge what effect it might have on the alien mind. Despite the evident technology of the aliens, it was entirely possible that their machine technology might have developed along some divergent line, so that the spinning wheel and the plunging piston and the smooth fluid gleam of metal was new to them.

I tried to imagine a machine technology that would require no motion, but such a thing was entirely inconceivable to me. And for that very reason, I thought, the idea of all this motion might be just as inconceivable to an alien intellect.

*

The stars came out while I sat there and no one wandered over to gab and that was fine. I was just as satisfied to be left alone.

After a time, I went into the tent, had another drink and decided to go to bed.

I took off my coat and slung it on the desk. When it hit, there was a thump, and as soon as I heard that thump, I knew what it was. I had dropped Benny's jewel into the pocket of the coat and had then forgotten it.

I fished into the pocket and got out the jewel, fearing all the while that I had broken it. And there was something wrong with it – it had somehow come apart. The jewel face had come loose from the rest of it and I saw that the jewel was no more than a cover for a box-shaped receptacle.

I put it on the desk and swung the jewel face open and there, inside the receptacle, I found myself.

The statuette was nestled inside a weird piece of mechanism and it was as fine a piece of work as Greasy's statuette.

It give me a flush of pride and satisfaction. Benny, after all, had not forgotten me!

I sat for a long time looking at the statuette, trying to puzzle out the mechanism. I had a good look at the jewel and I finally figured out what it was all about.

The jewel was no jewel at all; it was a camera. Except that instead of taking two-dimensional pictures, it worked in three dimensions. And that, of course, was how the Shadows made the models. Or maybe they were patterns rather than just models.

I finished undressing, and got into bed and lay on the cot, staring at the canvas, and the pieces all began to fall together and it was beautiful. Beautiful, that is, for the aliens. It made us look like a bunch of saps.

The cones had gone out and watched the survey party and had not let it get close to them, but they had been ready for us when we came. They'd disguised the cones to look like something that we wouldn't be afraid of, something perhaps that we could even laugh at. And that was the safest kind of disguise that anyone could assume – something that the victim might think was mildly funny. For no one gets too upset about what a clown might do.

But the Shadows had been loaded and they'd let us have it

and apparently, by the time we woke up, they had us pegged and labelled.

And what would they do now? Still stay behind their log, still keep watching us, suck us dry of everything that we had to offer?

And when they were ready, when they'd gotten all they wanted or all they felt that they could get, they'd come out and finish us.

I was somewhat scared and angry and felt considerably like a fool and it was frustrating just to think about.

Mack might kid himself that he had solved the problem with his flytrap out there, but there was still a job to do. Somehow or other we had to track down these hiding aliens and break up their little game.

Somewhere along the way, I went to sleep, and suddenly someone was shaking me and yelling for me to get out.

I came half upright and saw that it was Carr who had been shaking me. He was practically gibbering. He kept pointing outside and babbling something about a funny cloud and I couldn't get much more out of him.

So I shucked into my trousers and my shoes and went out with him and headed for the hilltop at a run. Dawn was just breaking and the Shadows still were clustered around the flytrap and a crowd of men had gathered just beyond the flytrap and were looking towards the east.

We pushed our way through the crowd up to the front and there was the cloud that Carr had been jabbering about, but it was a good deal closer now and was sailing across the plains, slowly and majestically, and flying above it was a little silver sphere that flashed and glittered in the first rays of the sun.

The cloud looked, more than anything, like a mass of junk. I could see what looked like a derrick sticking out of it and here and there what seemed to be a wheel. I tried to figure out what it might be, but I couldn't, and all the time it was moving closer to us.

Mack was at my left and I spoke to him, but he didn't answer me. He was just like Benny – he couldn't answer me. He looked hypnotized.

The closer that cloud came, the more fantastic it was and the more unbelievable. For there was no question now that it

197

was a mass of machinery, just like the equipment we had. There were tractors and earthmovers and shovels and dozers and all the other stuff, and in between these bigger pieces was all sorts of little stuff.

In another five minutes, it was hovering almost over us and then slowly it began to lower. While we watched, it came down to the ground, gently, almost without a bump, even though there were a couple or three acres of it. Besides the big equipment, there were tents and cups and spoons and tables and chairs and benches and a case or two of whisky and some surveying equipment – there was, it seemed to me, almost exactly all the items there were in the camp.

When it had all sat down, the little silver sphere came down, too, and floated slowly towards us. It stopped a little way away from us and Mack walked out towards it and I followed Mack. Out of the corner of my eye, I saw that Carr and Knight were walking forward, too.

We stopped four or five feet from it and now we saw that the sphere was some sort of protective suit. Inside it sat a pale little humanoid. Not human, but at least with two legs and arms and a single head. He had antennae sprouting from his forehead and his ears were long and pointed and he had no hair at all.

He let the sphere set down on the ground and we got a little closer and squatted down so we would be on a level with him.

He jerked a thumb backward over his shoulder, pointing at the mass of equipment he'd brought.

'Is pay,' he announced in a shrill, high, piping voice.

We didn't answer right away. We did some gulping first.

'Is pay for what?' Knight finally managed to ask him.

'For fun,' the creature said.

'I don't understand,' said Mack.

'We make one of everything. We not know what you want, so we make one of all. Unfortunate, two lots are missing. Accident, perhaps.'

'The models,' I said to the others. 'That's what he's talking about. The models were patterns and the models from Greasy's Shadow and from Benny – '

'Not all,' the creature said. 'The rest be right along.'

'Now wait a minute,' said Carr. 'Let us get this straight. You
198

are paying us. Paying us for what? Exactly what did we do for you?'

Mack blurted out: 'How did you make this stuff?'

'One question at a time,' I pleaded.

'Machines can make,' the creature said. 'Knowing how, machines can make anything. Very good machines.'

'But why?' asked Carr again. 'Why did you make it for us?'

'For fun,' the creature explained patiently. 'For laugh. For watch. Is a big word I cannot – '

'Entertainment?' I offered.

'That is right,' the creature said. 'Entertainment is the word. We have a lot of time for entertainment. We stay home, watch our entertainment screen. We get tired of it. We seek for something new. You something new. Give us much interesting. We try to pay you for it.'

'Good Lord!' exclaimed Knight. 'I begin to get it now. We were a big news event and so they sent out all those cones to cover us. Mack, did you saw into that cone last night?'

'We did,' said Mack. 'As near as we could figure, it was a TV sender. Not like ours, of course – there would be differences. But we figured it for a data-sending rig.'

I turned back to the alien in his shiny sphere. 'Listen carefully,' I said. 'Let's get down to business. You are willing to keep on paying if we provide you entertainment?'

'Gladly,' said the creature. 'You keep us entertained, we give you what you want.'

'Instead of one of everything, you will make us many of one thing?'

'You show it to us,' the creature said. 'You let us know how many.'

'Steel?' asked Mack. 'You can make us steel?'

'No recognize this steel. Show us. How made, how big, how shaped. We make.'

'If we keep you entertained?'

'That right,' the creature said.

'Deal?' I asked.

'Deal,' the creature said.

'From now on? No stopping?'

'Long as you keep us happy.'

'That may take some doing,' Mack told me.

'No, it won't,' I said.

'You're crazy!' Mack yelped. 'They'll never let us have them!'

'Yes, they will,' I answered. 'Earth will do anything to cinch this planet. And don't you see, with this sort of swap, we'll beat the cost. All Earth has to do is send out one sample of everything we need. One sample will do the trick. One I-beam and they'll make a million of them. It's the best deal Earth has ever made.'

'We do our part,' the creature assured us happily. 'Long as you do yours.'

'I'll get that order right off now,' I said to Mack. 'I'll write it up and have Jack send it out.'

I stood up and headed back towards the camp.

'Rest of it,' the creature said, motioning over his shoulder.

I swung around and looked.

There was another mass of stuff coming in, keeping fairly low. And this time it was men – a solid press of men.

'Hey!' cried Mack. 'You can't do that! That just isn't right!'

I didn't need to look. I knew exactly what had happened. The aliens had duplicated not only our equipment, but the men as well. In that crowd of men were the duplicates of every one of us – everyone, that is, except myself and Greasy.

Horrified as I might have been, outraged as any human would be, I couldn't help but think of some of the situations that might arise. Imagine two Macks insisting on bossing the operation! Picture two Thornes trying to get along together!

I didn't hang around. I left Mack and the rest of them to explain why men should not be duplicated. In my tent, I sat down and wrote an imperative, high-priority, *must-deliver* order for five hundred peepers.

MIRAGE

They came out of the Martian night, six pitiful little creatures looking for a seventh.

They stopped at the edge of the campfire's lighted circle and stood there, staring with their owlish eyes at the three Earthmen.

The Earthmen froze at whatever they were doing.

'Quiet,' said Wampus Smith, talking out of the corner of his bearded lips. 'They'll come in if we don't make a move.'

From far away came a faint, low moaning, floating in across the wilderness of sand and jagged pinnacles of rock and the great stone buttes.

The six stood just at the firelight's edge. The reflection of the flames touched their fur with highlights of red and blue and their bodies seemed to shimmer against the backdrop of the darkness on the desert.

'Venerables,' Lars Nelson said to Richard Webb across the fire.

Webb's breath caught in his throat. Here was a thing he had never hoped to see. A thing that no human being could ever hope to see – six of the Venerables of Mars walking in out of the desert and the darkness, standing in the firelight. There were many men, he knew, who would claim that the race was now extinct, hunted down, trapped out, hounded to extinction by the greed of the human sand men.

The six had seemed the same at first, six beings without a difference; but now, as Webb looked at them, he saw those minor points of bodily variation which marked each one of them as a separate individual. Six of them, Webb thought, and there should be seven.

Slowly they came forward, walking deeper into the camp-fire's circle. One by one they sat down on the sand facing the three men. No one said a word and the tension built up in the circle of the fire, while far towards the north the thing kept up its keening, like a sharp, thin knife blade cutting through the night.

'Human glad,' Wampus Smith said, finally, talking in the patois of the desert. 'He waited long.'

One of the creatures spoke, its words half English, half Martian, all of it pure gibberish to the ear that did not know.

'We die,' it said. 'Human hurt for long. Human help some now. Now we die, human help?'

'Human sad,' said Wampus and even while he tried to make his voice sad, there was elation in it, a trembling eagerness, a quivering as a hound will quiver when the scent is hot.

'We are six,' the creature said. 'Six not enough. We need another one. We do not find the Seven, we die. Race die forever now.'

'Not forever,' Smith told them.

The Venerable insisted. 'Forever. There other Sixes. No other Seven.'

'How can human help?'

'Human know. Human have Seven somewhere!'

Wampus shook his head. 'Where we have Seven?'

'In cage. On Earth. For human to see.'

Wampus shook his head again. 'No Seven on Earth.'

'There was one,' Webb said softly. 'In a zoo.'

'Zoo,' said the creature, tonguing the unfamiliar word. 'We mean that. In cage.'

'It died,' said Webb. 'Many years ago.'

'Human have one,' the creature insisted. 'Here on planet. Hid out. To trade.'

'No understand,' said Wampus but Webb knew from the way he said it that he understood.

'Find Seven. Do not kill it. Hide it. Knowing we come. Knowing we pay.'

'Pay? What pay?'

'City,' said the creature. 'Old city.'

202

'That's your city,' Nelson said to Webb. 'The ruins you are hunting.'

'Too bad we haven't got a Seven,' Wampus said. 'We could hand it over and they'd lead us to the ruins.'

'Human hurt for long,' the creature said. 'Human kill all Sevens. Have good fur. Women human wear it. High pay for Seven fur.'

'Lord, yes,' said Nelson. 'Fifty thousand for one at the trading post. A cool half million for a four-skin cape made up in New York.'

Webb sickened at the thought of it, at the casual way in which Nelson mentioned it. It was illegal now, of course, but the law had come too late to save the Venerables. Although a law, come to think of it, should not have been necessary. A human being, in all rightness – an intelligent form of life, in all rightness, should not hunt down and kill another intelligent being to strip off its pelt and sell it for fifty thousand dollars.

'No Seven hid,' Wampus was saying. 'Law says friends. No dare hurt Seven. No dare hide Seven.'

'Law far off,' said the creature. 'Human his own law.'

'Not us,' said Wampus. 'We don't monkey with the law.'

And that's a laugh, thought Webb.

'You help?' asked the creature.

'Try, maybe,' Wampus told them cagily. 'No good, though. You can't find. Human can't find.'

'You find. We show city.'

'We watch,' said Wampus. 'Close watch. See Seven, bring it. Where you be?'

'Canyon mouth.'

'Good,' said Wampus. 'Deal?'

'Deal,' said the creature.

Slowly the six of them got to their feet and turned back to the night again. At the edge of the firelit circle they stopped. The spokesman turned back to the three men.

'Bye,' he said.

'Goodbye,' said Wampus.

Then they were gone, back into the desert.

The three men sat and listened for a long time, not knowing what they listened for, but with ears taut to hear the slightest sound, trying to read out of sound some of the movement of life that surged all around the fire.

On Mars, thought Webb, one always listens. That is the survival price. To watch and listen and be still and quiet. And ruthless, too. To strike before another thing can strike. To see or hear a danger and be ready for it, to be half a second quicker than it is quick. And to recognize that danger once you see or hear it.

Finally Nelson took up again the thing he had been doing when the six arrived, whetting his belt knife to a razor sharpness on a pocket whetstone.

The soft, sleek whirr of metal travelling over stone sounded like a heartbeat, a pulse that did not originate within the firelight circle, but something that came out of the darkness, the pulse and beat of the wilderness itself.

Wampus said: 'It's too bad, Lars, that we don't know where to pick up a Seven.'

'Yeah,' said Lars.

'Might turn a good deal,' Wampus said. 'Likely to be treasure in that old city. All the stories say so.'

Nelson grunted. 'Just stories.'

'Stones,' said Wampus. 'Stones so bright and polished they could put your eyes out. Sacks of them. Tire a man out just packing them away.'

'Wouldn't need more than one load,' Nelson declared. 'Just one load would set you up for life.'

Webb saw that both of them were looking at him, squinting their eyes against the firelight.

He said, almost angrily, 'I don't know about the treasure.'

'You heard the stories,' Wampus said.

Webb nodded. 'Let's say it this way. I'm not interested in the treasure. I don't expect to find any.'

'Wouldn't mind if you did, would you?' Lars asked.

'It doesn't matter,' Webb told them. 'One way or the other.'

'What do you know about this city?' Wampus demanded, and it wasn't just conversation, it was a question asked with an answer expected, for a special purpose. 'You been muttering around and dropping hints here and there but you never came cold out and told us.'

For a moment, Webb stared at the man. Then he spoke slowly. 'Just this. I figured out where it might be. From a

204

knowledge of geography and geology and some understanding of the rise of cultures. I figured where the grass and wood and water would have been when Mars was new and young. I tried to locate, theoretically, the likeliest place for a civilization to arise. That's all there's to it.'

'And you never thought of treasure?'

'I thought of finding out something about the Martian culture,' Webb said. 'How it rose and why it fell and what it might be like.'

Wampus spat. 'You aren't even sure there is a city,' he said disgustedly.

'Not until just now,' said Webb. 'Now I know there is.'

'From what them little critters said?'

Webb nodded. 'From what they said. That's right.'

Wampus grunted and was silent.

Webb watched the two across the campfire from him.

They think I'm soft, he thought. They despise me because I'm soft. They would leave me in a minute if it served their purpose or they'd put a knife into me without a second thought if that should serve their purpose, if there was something I had that they wanted.

There had been no choice, he realized. He could not have gone alone into this wilderness, for if he'd tried he probably wouldn't have lived beyond the second day. It took special knowledge to live here and a special technique and a certain kind of mind. A man had to develop a high survival factor to walk into Mars beyond the settlements.

And the settlements were now very far away. Somewhere to the east.

'Tomorrow,' Wampus said, 'we change directions. We go north instead of west.'

Webb said nothing. His hand slid around cautiously and touched the gun at his belt, to make sure that it was there.

It had been a mistake to hire these two, he knew. But probably none of the others would have been better. They were all of a breed, a toughened, vicious band of men who roamed the wilderness, hunting, trapping, mining, taking what they found. Wampus and Nelson had been the only two at the post when he had arrived. All the other men had gone a week before, back to their hunting grounds.

At first they had been respectful, almost fawning. But as the days went on they felt surer of their ground and had grown insolent. Now Webb knew that he'd been taken for a sucker. The two stayed at the post, he knew now, for no other reason than that they were without a grubstake. He was that grubstake. He supplied them with the trappings they needed to get back into the wilderness. Once he had been a grubstake, now he was a burden.

'I said,' declared Wampus, 'that tomorrow we go north.'

Webb still said nothing.

'You heard me, didn't you?' asked Wampus.

'The first time,' Webb said.

'We go north,' said Wampus, 'and we travel fast.'

'You got a Seven staked out somewhere?'

Lars snickered. 'Ain't that the damnedest thing you ever heard of? Takes seven of them. Now with us, it just takes a man and a woman.'

'I asked you,' said Webb to Wampus, 'if you have a Seven caged up somewhere?'

'No,' said Wampus. 'We just go north, that's all.'

'I hired you to take me west.'

Wampus snarled at him. 'I thought you'd say that, Webb. I just wanted to know exactly how you felt about it.'

'You want to leave me stranded here,' said Webb. 'You took my money and agreed to guide me. Now you have something else to do. You either have a Seven or you think you know where you can find one. And if I knew and talked, you would be in danger. So there's only one of two things that you can do with me. You can kill me or you can leave me and let something else do the job for you.'

Lars said: 'We're giving you a choice, ain't we?'

Webb looked at Wampus and the man nodded. 'You got your choice, Webb.'

He could go for his gun, of course. He could get one of them, most likely, before the other got him. But there would be nothing gained. He would be just as dead as if they shot him out of hand. As far as that went he was as good as dead anyhow, for hundreds of miles stretched between him and the settlements, and even if he were able to cross those many miles there was no guarantee that he could find the settlements.

206

'We're moving out right now,' said Wampus. 'Ain't smart to travel in the dark, but ain't the first time that we had to do it. We'll be up north in a day or two.'

Lars nodded. 'Once we get back to the settlements, Webb, we'll h'ist a drink to you.'

Wampus joined in the spirit of the moment. 'Good likker, Webb. We can afford good likker then.'

Webb said nothing, did not move. He sat on the ground, relaxed.

And that, he told himself, was the thing that scared him. That he could sit and know what was about to happen and be so unconcerned about it.

Perhaps it had been the miles of wilderness that made it possible, the harsh, raw land and the vicious life that moved across the land — the ever-hungering, ever-hunting life that prowled and stalked and killed. Here life was stripped to its essentials and one learned that the line between life and death was a thin line at best.

'Well,' said Wampus finally, 'what will it be, Webb?'

'I think,' said Webb gravely, 'I think I'll take my chances on living.'

Lars clucked his tongue against his teeth. 'Too bad,' he said. 'We was hoping it'd be the other way around. Then we could take all the stuff. As it is, we got to leave you some.'

'You can always sneak back,' said Webb, 'and shoot me as I sit here. It would be an easy thing.'

'That,' said Wampus, 'is not a bad idea.'

Lars said. 'Give me your gun, Webb. I'll throw it back to you when we leave. But we ain't taking a chance of you plugging us while we're getting ready.'

Webb lifted his gun out of his holster and handed it over. Still sitting where he was, he watched them pack and stow the supplies into the wilderness wagon.

Finally it was done.

'We're leaving you plenty to last,' Wampus told him. 'More than enough.'

'Probably,' said Webb. 'You figure I can't last very long.'

'If it was me,' said Wampus, 'I'd take it quick and easy.'

Webb sat for a long time, listening to the motor of the wagon until it was out of hearing, then waiting for the gun blast that would send him toppling face forward into the flaming campfire.

But finally he knew that it would not come. He piled more fuel on the fire and crawled into his sleeping bag.

In the morning he headed east, following backward along the tracks of the wilderness wagon. They'd guide him, he knew, for a week or so, but finally they would disappear, brushed out by drifting sand and by the action of the weak and whining wind that sometimes blew across the bleakness of the wilderness.

At least while he followed them he would know he was going in the right direction. Although more than likely he would be dead before they faded out, for the wilderness crawled with too much sudden death for him to be sure of living from one moment to the next.

He walked with the gun hanging in his hand, watching every side, stopping at the top of ridges to study the terrain in front of him before he moved down into it.

The unaccustomed pack which he had fashioned inexpertly out of his sleeping bag grew heavier as the day progressed and chafed his shoulders raw. The sun was warm. As warm as the night would be cold, and thirst mounted in his throat to choke him. Carefully he doled out sips of water from the scanty supply the two had left him.

He knew he would not get back. Somewhere between where he stood and the settlements he would die of lack of water, or of an insect bite, or beneath the jaws and fangs of some charging beast or from sheer exhaustion.

There was, once you thought it out, no reason why a man should try to get back, since there was utterly no chance that he would get back. But Webb didn't stop to reason it out; he set his face towards the east and followed the wagon tracks.

For there was a *humanness* in him that said he must try at least – that he must go as far as he could go, that he must avoid death as long as he could. So on he went, going as far as he could go and avoiding death.

He spotted the ant colony in time to circle it, but he circled it too closely and the insects, catching scent of food within their grasp, streamed out after him. It took a mile of running before he outdistanced them.

He saw the crouching beast camouflaged against the sand,
208

where it was waiting for him, and shot it where it lay. Later in the day, when another monstrosity came tearing out from behind a rock outcropping, his bullet caught it between the eyes before it had covered half the distance.

For an hour he squatted, unmoving, on the sand, while a huge insect that looked like a bumble-bee, but wasn't, hunted for the thing that it had sighted only a moment before. But since it could recognize a thing through motion only, it finally gave up and went away. Webb remained squatting for another half hour against the chance that it had not gone away but lurked somewhere watching for the motion it had sighted, to take up the hunt again.

These times he avoided death, but he knew that the hour would come when he would not see a danger or, having seen it, would not move fast enough to stop it.

The mirages came to haunt him, to steal his eyes from the things that he should be watching. Mirages that flickered in the sky, with their feet upon the ground. Tantalizing pictures of things that could not be on Mars, of places that might have been there at one time – but that very long ago.

Mirages of broad, slow rivers with the slant of sail upon them. Mirages of green forests that stretched across the hills, so clear, so close, that one could see the little clumps of wild flowers that grew among the trees. And in some of them the hint of snow-capped mountains, in a world that knew no mountains.

He kept a watch for fuel as he went along, hoping to find a cache of 'embalmed' wood cropping out of the sand – wood left over from that dim age when these hills and valleys had been forest-covered, wood that had escaped the ravages of time and now lay like the dried mummies of trees in the aridness of the desert.

But there was none to be found and he knew that more than likely he would have to spend a fireless night. He could not spend a night in the open without fire. If he tried it, he would be gobbled up an hour after twilight had set in.

He must somehow find shelter in one of the many caves of the weird rock formations that sprang out of the desert. Find a cave and clean out whatever might be in it, block its entrance with stones and boulders and sleep with gun in hand.

It had sounded easy enough when he thought of it, but

209

while there were many caves, he was forced to reject them one by one since each of them had too large an opening to be closed against attack. A cave, he knew, with an unclosed mouth, would be no better than a trap.

The sun was less than an hour high when he finally spotted a cave that would serve the purpose, located on a ledge of stone jutting out of a steep hill.

From the bottom he stood long minutes surveying the hill. Nothing moved. There were no telltale flecks of colour.

Slowly he started up, digging his feet into the shifting talus of the slope, fighting his way up foot by foot, stopping for long minutes to regain his breath and to survey the slope ahead.

Gaining the ledge, he moved cautiously towards the cave, gun levelled, for there was no telling what might come out of it.

He debated on his next move. Flash his light inside to see what was there? Or simply thrust his gun into the opening and spray the inside with its lethal charge?

There could be no squeamishness, he told himself. Better to kill a harmless thing than to run the chance of passing up a danger.

He heard no sound until the claws of the thing were scrabbling on the ledge behind him. He shot one quick glance over his shoulder and saw the beast almost on top of him, got the impression of gaping mouth and murderous fangs and tiny eyes that glinted with a stony cruelty.

There was no time to turn and fire. There was time for just one thing.

His legs moved like driving pistons, hurling his body at the cave. The stone lip caught his shoulder and ripped through his clothing, gashing his arm, but he was through, through and rolling free. Something brushed his face and he rolled over something that protested in a squeaking voice. Off in one corner there was a thing that mewed quietly to itself.

On his knees, Webb swung his gun around to face the opening of the cave, saw the great bulk of the beast that had charged him trying to squeeze its way inside.

It backed away and then a great paw came in, feeling this way and that, hunting for the food that crouched inside the cave.

210

Mouths jabbered at Webb, a dozen voices speaking in the lingo of the desert, and he heard them say:

'Human, human, kill, kill, kill.'

Webb's gun spat and the paw went limp and was pulled slowly from the cave. The great grey body toppled and they heard it strike the slope below the ledge and go slithering away down the talus slope.

'Thanks, human,' said the voices. 'Thanks, human.'

Slowly Webb sat down, cradling the gun in his lap.

All around him he heard the stir of life.

Sweat broke out on his forehead and he felt moisture running from his armpits down his sides.

What was in the cave? What was in here with him?

That they had talked to him didn't mean a thing. Half the so-called animals of Mars could talk the desert lingo — a vocabulary of a few hundred words, part of them Earthian, part of them Martian, part of them God-knew-what.

For here on Mars many of the animals were not animals at all, but simply degenerating forms of life that at one time must have formed a complex civilization. The Venerables, who still retained some of the shape of bipeds, would have reached the highest culture, but there must have been many varying degrees of culture, living by compromise or by tolerance.

'Safe,' a voice told him. 'Trust. Cave law.'

'Cave law?'

'Kill in cave, no. Kill outside cave, yes. Safe in cave.'

'I no kill,' said Webb. 'Cave law good.'

'Human knows cave law?'

Webb said: 'Human keep cave law.'

'Good,' the voice told him. 'All safe now.'

Webb relaxed. He slipped his gun into his holster and took off his pack, laid it down alongside and rubbed his raw and blistered shoulders.

He could believe these things, he told himself. A thing so elemental and so simple as cave law was a thing that could be understood and trusted. It arose from a basic need, the need of the weaker life forms to forget their mutual differences and their mutual preying upon one another at the full of night, the need to find a common sanctuary against the bigger and the more vicious creatures and the lonely killers who took over with the going of the sun.

211

A voice said, 'Come light. Human kill.'

Another voice said, 'Human keep cave law in dark. No cave law in light. Human kill come light.'

'Human no kill come light,' said Webb.

'All human kill,' said one of the things. 'Human kill for fur. Human kill for food. We fur. We food.'

'This human never kill,' said Webb. 'This human friend.'

'Friend?' one of them asked. 'We not know friend. Explain friend.'

Webb didn't try. There was no use, he knew. They could not understand the word. It was foreign to this wilderness.

At last he asked, 'Rocks here?'

One of the voices answered, 'Rocks in cave. Human want rocks?'

'Pile in cave mouth,' said Webb. 'No killer get in.'

They digested that for a while. Finally one of them spoke up. 'Rock good.'

They brought rocks and stones and, with Webb helping them, wedged the cave mouth tight.

It was too dark to see the things, but they brushed against him as they worked and some of them were soft and furry and others had hides like crocodiles that tore his skin as he brushed against them. And there was one that was soft and pulpy and gave him the creeps.

He settled down in one corner of the cave, with his sleeping bag between his body and the wall. He would have liked to crawl into it, but that would have meant unpacking, and if he unpacked his supplies, he knew, there'd be none come morning.

Perhaps, he reasoned, the body heat of all the things in here would keep the cave from getting too cold. Cold yes, but not too cold for human life. It was, he knew, a gamble at best.

Sleep at night in friendship, kill one another and flee from one another with the coming of the dawn. Law, they called it. Cave law. Here was one for the books, here was something that was not even hinted at in all the archaeological tomes that he had ever read.

And he had read them all. There was something here on Mars that fascinated him. A mystery and a loneliness, an emptiness and a retrogression that haunted him and finally sent him out to try to pierce some of that mystery, to try to

212

hunt for the reason for that retrogression, to essay to measure the greatness of the culture that in some far dim period had come tumbling down.

There had been some great work done along that line. Axelson with his scholarly investigation of the symbolic water jugs and Mason's sometimes fumbling attempt to trace the great migrations. Then there was Smith, who had travelled the barren world for years jotting down the wind-blown stories whispered by the little degenerating things about an ancient greatness and a golden past. Myths, most of them, of course, but some place, somewhere, lay the answer to the origin of the myths. Folklore does not leap full blown from the mind; it starts with a fact, and that fact is added to, and the two facts are distorted and you have a myth. But at the bottom, back of all of it, is the starting point of fact.

So it was, so it must be with the myth that told about the great and glowing city that had stood above all other things of Mars – a city that was known to the far ends of the planet.

A place of culture, Webb told himself, a place where all the achievements and all the dreams and every aspiration of the once-great planet would have come together.

And yet in more than a hundred years of hunting and digging Earth's archaeologists had found no trace of any city, let alone that city of all cities. Kitchen middens and burial places and wretched huddling places where broken remnants of the great people had lived for a time – there were plenty of these. But no great city.

It must be somewhere, Webb was convinced. That myth could not lie, for it was told too often at too many different places by too many different animals that had once been people.

Mars fascinated me, he thought, and it still fascinates me, but now it will be the death of me, for there's death in its fascination. Death in the lonely stretches and death waiting on the buttes. Death in this cave, too, for they may kill me come the morning to prevent my killing them; they may keep their truce of the night just long enough to make an end of me.

The law of the cave? Some holdover from the ancient day,

213

some memory of a now forgotten brotherhood? Or a device necessitated by the evil days that had come when the brotherhood had broken?

He laid his head back against the rock and closed his eyes and thought, if they kill me, they kill me, but I will not kill them. For there has been too much human killing on the planet Mars. I will repay part of the debt at least. I will not kill the ones who took me in.

He remembered himself creeping along the ledge outside the cave, debating whether he should have a look first or stick in the muzzle of his gun and sweep the cave as a simple way of being sure there would be nothing there to harm him.

I did not know, he said, I did not know.

A soft furry body brushed against him and a voice spoke to him. 'Friend means no hurt? Friend means no kill?'

'No hurt,' said Webb. 'No kill.'

'You saw six?' the voice asked.

Webb jerked from the wall and sat very still.

'You saw six?' the voice was insistent.

'I saw six,' said Webb.

'When?'

'One sun.'

'Where six?'

'Canyon mouth,' said Webb. 'Wait at canyon mouth.'

'You hunt Seven?'

'No,' said Webb. 'I go home.'

'Other humans?'

'They north,' said Webb. 'They hunt Seven north.'

'They kill Seven?'

'Catch Seven,' said Webb. 'Take Seven to six. See city.'

'Six promise?'

'Six promise,' said Webb.

'You good human. You friend human. You no kill Seven.'

'No kill,' insisted Webb.

'All humans kill. Kill Seven sure. Seven good fur. Much pay. Many Sevens die for human.'

'Law says no kill,' declared Webb. 'Human law says Seven friend. No kill friend.'

'Law? Like cave law?'

'Like cave law,' said Webb.

'You good friend of Seven?'

214

'Good friend of all,' said Webb.

'I Seven,' said the voice.

Webb sat quietly and let the numbness clear out of his brain.

'Seven,' he finally said. 'You go canyon mouth. Find six. They wait. Human friend glad.'

'Human friend want city,' said the creature. 'Seven friend to human. Human find Seven. Human see city. Six promise.'

Webb almost laughed aloud in bitterness. Here at last, the chance that he had hoped might come. Here at last, the thing that he had wanted, the thing he had come to Mars to do. And he couldn't do it.

'Human no go,' he said. 'Human die. No food. No water. Human die.'

'We care for human,' Seven told him. 'No friend human before. All kill humans. Friend human come. We care for it.'

Webb was silent for a while, thinking.

Then he asked: 'You give human food? You find human water?'

'Take care,' said Seven.

'How Seven know I saw six?'

'Human tell. Human think. Seven know.'

So that was it – telepathy. Some vestige of a former power, some attribute of a magnificent culture, not quite forgotten yet. How many of the other creatures in this cave would have it, too?

'Human go with Seven?' Seven asked.

'Human go,' said Webb.

He might as well, he told himself. Going east, back towards the settlements, was no solution to his problem. He knew he'd never reach the settlements. His food would run out. His water would run out. Some beast would catch him and make a meal of him. He didn't have a chance.

Going with the little creature that stood beside him in the darkness of the cave, he might have a chance. Not too good a chance, perhaps, but at least a chance. There would be food and water, or at least a chance of food and water. There would be another to help him watch for the sudden death that roamed the wilderness, to warn him, to help him recognize the danger.

215

'Human cold,' said Seven.

'Cold,' admitted Webb.

'One cold,' said Seven. 'Two warm.'

The furry thing crawled into his arms, put its arms around his body. After a moment, he put his arms around it.

'Sleep,' said Seven. 'Warm. Sleep.'

Webb ate the last of his food, and the seven Venerables told him, 'We care.'

'Human die, Webb insisted. 'No food. Human die.'

'We take care,' the seven little creatures told him, standing in a row. 'Later we take care.'

He took it to mean that there was no food for him now, but later there would be.

They took up the march again.

It was an interminable thing, that march. A thing to make a man cry out in his sleep. A thing to shiver over when they had been lucky enough to find wood and sat hunched around the fire. Day after endless day of sand and rock, of crawling up to a high ridge and plunging down the other side, of slogging through the heat across the level land that had been sea bottom in the days long gone.

It became a song, a drum beat, a three-note marching cadence that rang through the human's head, an endless thing that hammered in his brain through the day and stayed with him hours after they had stopped for night. Until he was dizzy with it, until his brain was drugged with the hammer of it, so that his eyes refused to focus and the gun bead was a fuzzy globe when he had to use the weapon against the crawling things and charging things and flying things that came at them out of nowhere.

Always there were the mirages, the everlasting mirages of Mars that seemed to lie just beneath the surface of reality. Flickering pictures painted in the sky the water and the trees and the long green sweep of grass that Mars had not known for countless centuries. As if, Webb told himself, the past were very close behind him, as if the past might still exist and were trying to catch up, reluctant to be left behind in the march of time.

He lost count of the days and steeled himself against the speculation of how much longer it might be, until it seemed

216

that it would go on forever, that they would never stop, that they would face each morning the barren wilderness they must stagger through until the fall of night.

He drank the last of the water and reminded them he could not live without it.

'Later,' they told him. 'Water later.'

That was the day they came to the city, and there, deep in a tunnel far beneath the topmost ruins there was water, water dripping, drop by slow and tantalizing drop, from a broken pipe. Dripping water, and that was a wondrous thing on Mars.

The seven drank sparingly, as they had been steeled for century upon century to get along with little water, had adapted themselves to this and it was no hardship for them. But Webb lay for hours beside the broken pipe, holding cupped hands to collect a little before he lapped it down, lying there in the coolness that was a blessed thing.

He slept and awoke and drank again, and he was rested and no longer thirsty, but his body cried for food. And there was no food nor anyone to get him food. For the little ones were gone.

They will come back, he said. They are gone for just a little while and will be back again. They have gone to get me food and they will bring it to me. And he thought very kindly of them.

He picked his way upward through the tunnel down which they'd come and at last came to the ruins that lay on the hill that thrust upward from the surrounding country so that when one stood on the hill's top there were miles of distance, dropping away on every side.

There wasn't much that one could see of the ruined city. It would have been entirely possible to walk past the hill and not know the city was there. During thousands of years it had crumbled and fallen in upon itself and some of it had dissolved to dust, and the sand had crept in and covered it and sifted among its fragments until it was simply a part of the hill.

Here and there Webb found broken fragments of chiselled masonry and here and there a shard of pottery, but a man could have walked past these, if he had not been looking, and taken them for no more than another rock scattered among the trillions of fragmentary rocks littered on the surface of the planet.

The tunnel, he found, led down into the bowels of the fallen city, into the burial mound of the fallen greatness and the vanished glory of a proud people whose descendants now scuttled animal-like in the ancient deserts and talked in an idiom that was no more than a memory of the literacy that must have flourished once in the city on the hill.

In the tunnel Webb found evidence of solid blocks of carven stone, broken columns, paving blocks and something that seemed at one time to have been a beautifully executed statue.

At the end of the tunnel he cupped his hands at the pipe and drank again, then went back to the surface and sat on the ground beside the tunnel mouth and stared out across the emptiness of Mars.

It would take power and tools and many men to uncover and sift the evidence of the city. It would take years of painstaking, scholarly work – and he didn't even have a shovel. And worst of all, he had no time. For if the seven did not show up with food he would one day go down into the darkness of the tunnel and there eventually join his human dust with the ancient dust of this alien world.

There had been a shovel, he remembered, and Wampus and Lars, when they deserted him, had left it for him. A rare consideration, surely, he told himself. But of the supplies which he had carried away from the campfire that long gone morning there were just two things left, his sleeping bag and the pistol at his belt. All else he could get along without, those two were things that he had to have.

An archaeologist, he thought. An archaeologist sitting on top of the greatest find that any archaeologist had ever made and not able to do a single thing about it.

Wampus and Lars had thought that there would be treasure here. And there was no certain treasure, no treasure revealed and waiting for the hands of men to take. He had thought of glory, and there was no glory. He had thought of knowledge, and without a shovel and some time, there simply was no knowledge. No knowledge beyond the bare knowing that he had been right, that the city did exist.

And yet there was certain other knowledge gained along the way. The knowledge that the seven types of the Venerables did in fact still exist, that from this existence the race might still continue despite the guns and snares and the greed and

218

guile of Earthmen who had hunted Seven for its fifty-thousand-dollar pelt.

Seven little creatures, seven different sexes. All of them essential to the continuance of the race. Six little creatures looking for the seventh, and he had found the seventh. Because he had found the seventh, because he had been the messenger, there would be at least one new generation of the Venerables to carry on the race.

What use, he thought, to carry on a race that had failed its purpose?

He shook his head.

You can't play God, he said. You can't presume to judge. Either there is a purpose in all things or there's no purpose in anything, and who is there to know?

Either there is purpose that I reached this city or there is no purpose. There is a purpose that I may die here or it is possible that my dying here will be no more than another random factor in the great machination of pure chance that moves the planets through their courses and brings a man homeward at the end of day.

And there was another knowledge – the knowledge of the endless reaches and the savage loneliness that was the Martian wilderness. The knowledge of that and the queer, almost non-human detachment that it fused into the human soul.

Lessons, he thought.

The lesson that one man is an insignificant flyspeck crawling across the face of eternity. The lesson that one life is a relatively unimportant thing when it stands face to face with the overriding reality of the miracle of all creation.

He got up and stood at his full height and knew his insignificance and his humility in the empty sweep of land that fell away on every side and in the arching sky that vaulted overhead from horizon to horizon and in the utter silence that lay upon the land and sky.

Starving was a lonely and awful business.

Some deaths are swift and clean. But starving is not one of these.

The seven did not come. Webb waited for them, and because he still felt kindly towards them he found excuses for them. They did not realize, he told himself, how short a time a man

219

can go without nourishment. The strange mating, he told himself, involving seven personalities, probably was a complicated procedure and might take a great deal more time than one usually associated with such phenomena. Or something might have happened to them, they might be having trouble of their own. As soon as they had worked it out they would come, and they would bring him food.

So he starved with kindly thoughts and with a great deal more patience than a man in dissimilar circumstances might be expected to do.

And he found, even when he felt the lassitude of under-nourishment creeping along his muscles and his bones, even when the sharp pangs of hunger had settled to a gnawing horror that never left him, even when he slept, that his mind was not affected by the ravages that his body was undergoing; that his brain, apparently, was sharpened by the lack of food, that it seemed to step aside from his tortured body and become a separate entity that drew in upon itself and knotted all its faculties into a hard-bound bundle that was scarcely aware of external factors.

He sat for long hours upon a polished rock, perhaps part of that once-proud city, which he found just a few yards from the tunnel mouth, and stared out across the sun-washed wilderness that stretched for miles towards a horizon that it never seemed to reach. He sought for purpose with a sharp-edged mind that probed at the roots of existence and of happenstance and sought to evolve out of the random factors that moved beneath the surface of the universe's orderliness some evidence of a pattern that would be understandable to the human mind. Often he thought he had it, but it always slid away from him like quicksilver escaping from a clutching hand.

If Man was ever to find the answer, he knew, it must be in a place like this, where there was no distraction, where there was a distance and a barrenness that built up to a vast impersonality which emphasized and underscored the inconsequence of the thinker. For if the thinker introduced himself as a factor out of proportion to the fact, then the whole problem was distorted and the equation, if equation there be, could never be solved.

At first he had tried to hunt animals for food, but strangely, while the rest of the wilderness swarmed with vicious life that hunted timid life, the area around the city was virtually deserted, as if someone had drawn a sacred chalk mark around it. On his second day of hunting he killed a small thing that on Earth could have been a mouse. He built a fire and cooked it and later hunted up the sundried skin and sucked and chewed at it for the small nourishment that it might contain. But after that he did not kill a thing, for there was nothing to be killed.

Finally he came to know the seven would not come, that they never had intended to come, that they had deserted him exactly as his two human companions had deserted him before. He had been made a fool, he knew, not once, but twice.

He should have kept on going east after he had started. He should not have come back with Seven to find the other six who waited at the canyon's mouth.

You might have made it to the settlements, he told himself. You just might have made it. Just possibly have made it.

East. East towards the settlements.

Human history is a trying – a trying for the impossible – and attaining it. There is no logic, for if humanity had waited upon logic it would still be a cave-living and an earth-bound race.

Try, said Webb, not knowing exactly what he said.

He walked down the hill again and started out across the wilderness, heading towards the east. For there was no hope upon the hill and there was hope towards the east.

A mile from the base of the hill, he fell. He staggered, falling and rising, for another mile. He crawled a hundred yards. It was there the seven found him.

'Food!' he cried at them and he had a feeling that although he cried it in his mind there was no sound in his mouth. 'Food! Water!'

'We take care,' they said, and lifted him, holding him in a sitting position.

'Life,' Seven told him, 'is in many husks. Like nested boxes that fit inside each other. You live one and peel it off and there's another life.'

'Wrong,' said Webb. 'You do not talk like that. Your thought does not flow like that. There is something wrong.'

221

'There is an inner man,' said Seven. 'There are many inner men.'

'The subconscious,' said Webb and while he said it in his mind, he knew that no word, no sound came out of his mouth. And he knew now, too, that no words were coming out of Seven's mouth, that here were words that could not be expressed in the patois of the desert, that here were thoughts and knowledge that could not belong to a thing that scuttled, fearsome, through the Martian wilderness.

'You peel an old life off and you step forth in a new and shining life,' said Seven, 'but you must know the way. There is a certain technique and a certain preparation. If there is no preparation and no technique, the job is often bungled.'

'Preparation,' said Webb. 'I have no preparation. I do not know about this.'

'You are prepared,' said Seven. 'You were not before, but now you are.'

'I thought,' said Webb.

'You thought,' said Seven, 'and you found a partial answer. Well-fed, earth-bound, arrogant, there would have been no answer. You found humility.'

'I do not know the technique,' said Webb. 'I do not . . .'

'We know the technique,' Seven said. 'We take care.'

The hilltop where the dead city lay shimmered, and there was a mirage on it. Out of the dead mound of its dust rose the pinnacles and spires, the buttresses and the flying bridges of a city that shone with colour and with light; out of the sand came the blaze of garden beds of flowers and the tall avenues of trees and a music that came from the slender bell towers.

There was grass beneath his feet instead of sand blazing with the heat of the Martian noon. There was a path that led up the terraces of the hill towards the wonder city that reared upon its heights. There was the distant sound of laughter and there were flecks of colour moving on the distant streets and along the walls and through the garden paths.

Webb swung around and the seven were not there. Nor was the wilderness. The land stretched away on every hand and it was not wilderness, but a breath-taking place with groves of trees and roads and flowing water courses.

He turned back to the city again and watched the movement of the flecks of colour.

222

'People,' he said.

And Seven's voice, coming to him from somewhere, from elsewhere, said: 'People from many planets. And from beyond the planets. And some of your own people you will find among them. For you are not the first!'

Filled with wonder, a wonder that was fading, that would be entirely faded before he reached the city, Webb started walking up the path.

Wampus Smith and Lars Nelson came to the hill many days later. They came on foot because the wilderness wagon had broken down. They came without food except the little food they could kill along the way; and they came with no more than a few drops of water sloshing in their canteens – and there was no water to be found.

There, a short distance from the foot of the hill, they found the sun-dried mummy of a man face downward on the sand, and when they turned him over they saw who he was.

Wampus stared across the body at Lars. 'How did he get here?' he croaked.

'I don't know,' said Lars. 'He never could have made it, not knowing the country and on foot. And he wouldn't have travelled this way anyhow. He would have headed east, back to the settlements.'

They pawed through his clothing and found nothing. But they took his gun, for the charges in their own were running very low.

'What's the use?' said Lars. 'We can't make it, Wampus.'

'We can try,' said Wampus.

Above the hill a mirage flickered – a city with shining turrets and dizzy pinnacles and rows of trees and fountains that flashed with leaping water. To their ears came, or seemed to come, the sound of many bells.

Wampus spat with lips that were cracked and dried, spat with no saliva in his mouth.

'Them damn mirages,' he said. 'They drive a man half crazy.'

'They seem so close,' said Lars. 'So close and real. As if they were someplace else and were trying to break through.'

Wampus spat again. 'Let's get going,' he said.

The two men turned towards the east and, as they moved, they left staggering, uneven tracks through the sand of Mars.

223